"What I need is for you [illegible] stay in Montana. You wi[ll] [illegible] morning, including a plane ticket to a [illegible] called Braden."

Everything went through Jack's mind, from militia-based groups to terrorists.

"Yes, sir. What am I facing?"

"Two days ago, a set of prints from a recent murder victim came through NCIC that didn't match up with any we had on file. The body was discovered in Brighton Beach."

"Isn't that the place they call Little Russia?"

"Some do, I believe. The thing is...the prints rang a bell at Interpol. A really big bell."

Suddenly the hair stood on the back of Jack's neck.

"How big?"

"The prints belong to a Russian scientist named Vaclav Waller."

"And?"

"Vaclav Waller died in a plane crash off the coast of Florida over thirty years ago."

**"Intense, fast-paced, and cleverly crafted."**
                    —*Library Journal* on *Storm Warning*

*Also available from MIRA Books and*
*DINAH McCALL*

STORM WARNING
THE RETURN

*Watch for the newest novel of romantic suspense from*
*DINAH McCALL*
*April 2003*

*MIRA Books is also proud to publish*
*Dinah McCall under her real name*
SHARON SALA

*Watch for Sharon Sala's newest release*
DARK WATER
*November 2002*

# DINAH McCALL
# WHITE MOUNTAIN

MIRA

ISBN 1-55166-894-7

WHITE MOUNTAIN

Visit us at www.mirabooks.com

**Printed in U.S.A.**

The miracle of life is just that—a miracle. From the hour of our birth to the moment we draw our last breath, we are living. Some of us are better at it than others, but it's the only chance we are given.

Each life is unique only to that person. All the thoughts, all the emotions, all the failures and successes, can be shared to a degree, but it is impossible to share a soul. When it is gone, the shell that it inhabited is cast aside, as worthless as the box in which a jewel is carried.

Because I believe that we are given only one life, one time, I choose to dedicate this book to my loved ones who have already left this earth for a better place, and especially to my sister, Diane, whose passing cost me so many tears.

Save me a place beside you, honey.

I miss you more than words can say.

# 1

Frank Walton was dying. He had suspected it for some time, but only last month his suspicions had been confirmed. And while he would have preferred to stay on this earth longer, he had accepted his fate just as he'd faced and dealt with every other adversity that had been thrust at him.

Deal with it, then get past it. That was his motto.

Or at least it had been until now. He would deal with his upcoming demise later. For now, uppermost in his mind had been the need to go home— to go back to the place of his birth and see the people and hear the language and the music. Just once. Before it was too late.

Only he couldn't. To them, he was already dead.

Still, he'd had to know if what he'd done had been worth it. He'd needed to look at it again with a fresh view. Maybe then he would know if it had all been worthwhile.

But to do that, he'd had to leave Montana for the state of New York, then head to Brooklyn and Brighton Beach. It was as close as he could possibly come to his homeland—to eat the food of his childhood and hear the language of the place he'd called home. Now, after two weeks in Brighton Beach, he'd come to a grudging acceptance that it was too late to turn back time.

He exited the small café with a smile on his lips. The warm, dark-red borscht and savory bread he'd just had for his lunch had reminded him of the meals his mother had served during the short winter days and long cold nights in his Russian homeland. The food had been sparse but the love within his household overflowing.

Even though the September day was almost balmy, he knew if he would but close his eyes, he could recall every nuance of that time: his father sitting near the fireplace with his musette, smoking cigarettes that he'd rolled on his own and sipping vodka between songs, he and his brothers and sisters dancing wildly, mimicking the high kicks of a Cossack dance while his mother's laughter rang out above the din.

Ah, God. He'd given it up—all of it—and for a higher cause. At least that was what he'd told himself for the past thirty-odd years. But now that he'd come to the end of his days, he was starting to question whether the sacrifices had been worth it. What had he accomplished? What had *any* of them accomplished?

A trio of gulls squawked noisily as they circled overhead, breaking Frank's concentration. Squinting against the afternoon sun, he tilted his head, anxious not to miss their feats of derring-do as they dive-bombed the beach beyond the boardwalk. One did not see seagulls in Montana.

The sun was warm against his balding head. He inhaled briefly, then exhaled on a sigh, for the first time in his life, wishing he believed in a power higher than that of mortal man. Sunshine could not reach where he was bound.

A woman leaned out from a third-story window and yelled down into the street. A man just coming out of the building paused and looked up, then called back to her, their voices mingling with the sounds of traffic and people and the noise of the day. Steam from beneath the streets rose upward from the sidewalk grates, blending with the guttural mingling of vowels and consonants that made up the Russian language. It was all music to Frank Walton's ears. He wanted to shout back—to sing the songs of his youth and dance until there was no more breath in his body. But he'd given up that part of his life too long ago. Not even now—when he was so close to his deathbed—could he take the chance and reveal his true self.

So he thrust his hands in his pockets and moved on down the street, satisfied for the moment just to be in this place.

Vasili Rostov cursed the ache in his knee as he stepped into an alcove away from the wind to light a cigarette. When the end caught and the tobacco began to burn, he took a deep drag and then held it, waiting for the nicotine to kick in. It came quickly, wrapping around his senses and easing the tension in his mind. He exhaled slowly, letting the smoke out through his nose as he turned. The old man he'd been trailing was still in sight. So he took another drag from the cigarette before he began to move, always staying at least a block behind. As he walked, his gaze moved from window to window, eying the opulence and abundance of that which was America. Not for the first time, he thought of staying. After the job was finished, of course. He loved his homeland, but the constant chaos in the government was disgusting to him—not like the old days. Then he'd been one of the youngest and best of Russia's finest agents, revered in higher circles, and proud of his KGB status and the strength in his body. Women had fawned over him. Other agents had envied him. His superiors had depended on him.

Now he did nothing. They called it retirement. For Rostov, it was like being sent to an early grave. Even though he was in his mid-sixties, he was still strong. His belly was hard and flat, and the years had added character to his face rather than age.

Ironically, it wasn't age that had sidelined him. It was his inability to keep up with the ever-changing modes of technology. These days, a good portion of the spy game depended upon understanding everything from lasers to computer chips, which left him out of the running. So his days were spent in taverns, reliving the past with others of his ilk, and the nights in his one-room flat, watching government-run television programs on a twelve-inch black-and-white set with the scent of a neighbor's boiling cabbage and potatoes drifting in from the crack beneath his front door. Communism had been good to him and his family. It had made his country strong. With the coming of democracy, his world had crumbled as surely as the Berlin Wall. For several years afterward, people had stood in the streets selling personal belongings just to keep from starving. Homelessness had become rampant, and the long lines at bread bakeries and supermarkets were made even more tragic by the fact that there had been little food available to buy for those who still had money.

Now things were better, but they would never be the same. Democracy was as obscene to him as a four-letter word, and now the Russian Mafia had more power than the government. He'd learned to adjust, because it was what he did best. He'd settled into a routine that, while less than stimulating, was more luxurious than what he'd known as a child.

And then a week ago there had come a knock at his door. He'd opened it to find four dour-looking men who'd told him to pack a suitcase. Within hours, he'd been briefed, given American money and a cell phone, and put on a plane bound for New York City. The reason was almost comical to Rostov. He was back in action for the simple reason that he *was* part of the past. He'd come to America for one reason only. To find a ghost.

Now, here he was, tailing a stoop-shouldered old man with a fondness for borscht. He didn't look like a ghost to Rostov, but from the color of his complexion, he wasn't far from becoming one.

When the old man stopped at a crosswalk, Rostov paused, too, turning toward the windows of the jewelry shop by which he was standing. To the passersby, it would appear that his interest was on the display of rubies and pearls, but in truth, the window was his mirror to the sidewalk across the street.

He stood until the light turned green and the Walk sign began to flash, then he pivoted quickly. Dodging traffic, he bolted across the street, losing himself in the stream of pedestrians through which the old man was moving.

He knew the man's name was Frank Walton. Supposedly a retired botanist from Braden, Montana, who had come to Brighton Beach for a holiday. But there was a particular reason why Vasili Rostov had been yanked out of retirement and sent on this mission, and the picture in his pocket was part of the mystery. Tonight he would meet this old man face-to-face. If what Rostov suspected was true, his name would once again be spoken with respect.

Frank laid his safety razor by the sink and then peered at his face in the foggy mirror before pronouncing himself shaved. His belly hurt—part of the growing cancer eating away at his inner parts—yet he was determined not to let it ruin the upcoming evening. The hotel concierge had told him about a wonderful restaurant only a few blocks from the hotel that offered a floor show with dinner. The chance to hear more music from his homeland was too enticing to miss. Ignoring the gnawing pain, he swiped a towel across his face, splashed on some pine-scented aftershave and went to finish dressing.

Tomorrow he would be going back to Montana—back to his friends and to Isabella. He smiled as he thought of her—dark, laughing eyes and a heart-shaped face—the daughter he'd never had. She called him Uncle, just as she did all of Samuel's friends.

Samuel Abbott was Isabella's father. He'd been their leader from the beginning. A frown turned his smile upside down as he glanced at the phone. They hadn't wanted him to leave Braden, and yet he hadn't been able to bring himself to tell them why. They didn't know about the cancer. He would tell them later—when he could no longer conceal the pain.

He glanced again at the phone. He should really call and let them know he was coming home tomorrow, but then he looked at the clock and changed his mind. It was getting late, and if he didn't hurry, he would be late for his reservation. He didn't want to miss the start of the show.

Shrugging off the thought, he told himself it wouldn't really matter. He would be home by this time tomorrow, and then he could talk to his heart's content.

A few minutes later he was in the hotel lobby, then out on the street. More than a dozen people were curbside, waiting for cabs. He frowned, realizing he should have called ahead for a cab, and then looked at his watch to check the time. If he waited much longer he would be late. The restaurant was about twenty blocks away, which, in his weakened state, might as well have been miles, yet he opted to walk.

It was a fine September evening. Traffic was brisk. The air had cooled since sunset, making the walk more pleasant. Obviously he wasn't the only one who thought so. The sidewalk traffic was as busy as that in the well-lit streets. He walked with his head up and his shoulders back, and for a time he let himself believe he was young and strong—and home.

About five blocks from his destination, he heard someone call out a name. At first, it didn't register, and he kept on walking. But then he heard it again.

Vaclav Waller. Someone had yelled the name Vaclav Waller.

He stumbled, then froze—afraid to turn around, afraid not to. Before he could move, a man stepped out of the alley to his right. The man spoke again, and only then did Frank realize the man was speaking to him in Russian.

"I'm sorry," he said, pretending ignorance. "Were you speaking to me?"

This time the answer came back in perfect English.

"What do you think, old man?"

When Vasili Rostov stepped into the light, Frank Walton shuddered. He didn't know him, but he knew his kind. He'd seen that cold, passionless gaze far too many times in his youth not to know the kind of man he was facing. And with recognition came the knowledge that they'd found him—after all these years, when he was almost at the end of his life.

"I think you've made a mistake," Frank muttered, and began to walk away. He'd taken only three steps when the man grabbed his arm.

"No mistake," Rostov said, speaking Russian again. "We talk."

Before Frank could call out for help, the man stuck a knife to his throat and forcibly pulled him into the darkened alley. Still speaking in Russian, the man lowered his voice and told Frank to keep quiet, then increased the pressure of the blade against Frank's throat.

A sudden stinging sensation was all Frank needed to know that the man had drawn blood. Fear momentarily stilled his voice, but it was followed by sudden anger. He might be old and dying, but he would not be threatened—not now, and not by the likes of a man such as this.

"I know who you are," the man said.

Frank answered in English. "I don't know what you're saying."

The sting against his throat became pain.

"Don't lie to me, old man. I knew you in Minsk. I was assigned to guard you at a medical symposium. You were born and raised in Georgia and educated in Moscow. You are Vaclav Waller. You were nominated for a Nobel Prize in 1969 and reported to have died in a plane crash off the southern coast of the United States in 1970."

Frank stifled a groan. He didn't know how this had happened, but he could only blame himself. Someone here must have recognized him. He had come to Brighton Beach to pay homage to his roots and instead had brought down the fragile house of cards that he'd built for himself.

"What do you want?" Frank asked. "I have money. Take my wallet. It's in my coat pocket."

Rostov cursed. "I do not want your money, old man. I want the truth."

Frank blinked. This time the man had spoken in English again. Was he starting to buy his story, or was he just playing along?

"I do not know the truth of which you speak," Frank said. "Just take my money and let me go. I don't want trouble."

At that moment a car sped by outside the alley.

Behind it the sound of approaching sirens could be heard, and Rostov's hold tightened.

Frank saw how the sirens made the big man antsy. The police were obviously after someone else, but maybe he could make this work to his advantage.

"The police are coming," he said. "Someone saw you drag me into this alley. Just let me go and I won't tell. I am an old man. I don't want any trouble."

"Your trouble is just beginning," Rostov said. "You don't have to talk to me. You can talk to my superiors…when we get back to Moscow."

Frank saw him reach toward his pocket with one hand. He knew the drill. Inside there would be a hypodermic syringe filled with some sort of drug that would render him unconscious. It only took a moment for the decision to be made. Yes, he'd wanted to go home once more before he died, but not like this. He was going to die anyway. Now was as good a time as any.

Before Rostov knew what was happening, Frank grabbed his hand and lunged forward, plunging the knife blade into his own chest.

Rostov grunted in surprise and took a sudden step backward, but it was too late. The damage was already done.

"What have you done?" he cried, as Frank Walton slumped to the ground.

The taste of blood was in Frank's mouth. "Killed

the messenger,'' he mumbled, then exhaled slowly. *So this is dying*. Thought ceased. He'd cheated cancer after all.

Two police cars sped quickly past the entrance to the alley, in obvious pursuit of the car that had just passed, but Rostov was in a panic. He'd misjudged the old fool. Who would have thought he still had it in him?

Kneeling by the dead man's side, he quickly removed all the identification from the body, then used Walton's handkerchief to remove his fingerprints from the knife. Nervous now, and not wanting to be seen in the alley where a dead man was lying, he tossed the knife into a nearby Dumpster, then slipped over the fence at the back of the alley.

Ten blocks away, he stripped the cash and identification papers from the wallet, dropped Frank's hotel key into his pocket and then tossed the empty wallet into a trash can by a bus stop. The body wouldn't be found until morning. It would take even longer for it to be identified. Confident that the death would appear to have been a robbery, he headed for Frank's hotel. That crazy old man had upset his plans completely. Now he was torn between having to lie to his superiors and admitting that he was too old for this job after all.

It wasn't until he was standing at a street corner and waiting for the light to change that he realized the old man's last words had been spoken in fluent and perfect Russian.

He cursed beneath his breath as he started across the street. All he could do was hope he would find a clue in Walton's hotel room that would keep him in good standing with the powers that be.

A few minutes later, he entered the hotel and headed straight for the elevator, confident that he would not be noticed. He'd followed the old man more than once, so he already knew the floor and room number. There was no one in the hallway when he exited the elevator, so he headed straight for room 617 without hesitation.

Once inside, he began a thorough sweep of the room, hoping to find something that would give answers as to why Vaclav Waller had faked his own death, as well as what he had been doing for the past thirty years. All he found were some out-of-style clothes and a plane ticket to Braden, Montana. The flight was due out at 9:45 a.m. tomorrow.

He stood for a moment, contemplating the wisdom of what he was thinking, and then a slight smile broke the somberness of his face. He had Walton's ID. It would be a simple matter to substitute his picture for Walton's and fly back to Braden on Walton's ticket.

He nodded to himself, slipped the plane ticket into his jacket pocket and began methodically packing Walton's clothes into his suitcase. It wouldn't do to have the hotel put out an alarm when the old man went missing. All he had to do was leave the room key on the bed and walk away with Frank

Walton's things. The hotel would assume the man was gone, bill the room to the credit card he would have had to show when checking in, and no one would be the wiser. Less than an hour later, room 617 was empty and Rostov was gone, taking the last vestiges of Frank Walton's presence in Brighton Beach with him.

Detective Mike Butoli was nursing a hangover and a broken toe when he came in to work. The coffee he'd purchased from the coffee shop on the corner was too weak for the condition he was in. He needed some of his father's recipe this morning, with a healthy shot of the ''hair of the dog,'' and then he just might be able to make it through the day. However, his father had been dead for years, and thanks to a weak moment last night, he was going to have to start all over on a new sobriety day.

He'd made it almost six months this time and was pissed at himself for giving in to temptation. When he drank, he had blackouts, so he had no idea which had come first, the broken toe or the first drink, and from the way he was feeling, it didn't really matter. His goddamn foot hurt almost as much as his head.

''Hey, Butoli. You look like hell.''

Butoli glared at Larry Marshall and thought about tossing the sorry-assed coffee on the prick's clean white shirt, then decided against it. He had yet to figure out how the man had ever made detective.

"You should know," he muttered, as he set his coffee down on the desk and started to remove his suit coat.

"Don't get too comfy," Marshall said. "Flanagan is looking for you."

Butoli pivoted without stopping and headed for the lieutenant's office, limping with every step.

"Hey, Lieutenant, you wanted to see me?"

Barney Flanagan looked up, then frowned. Butoli was a damned good cop when he laid off the sauce, but something told him Butoli had suffered a "weak moment" last night.

"Are you drunk?" Flanagan growled.

"No, sir. Not now, sir."

"Then why in hell are you leaning against my door? Stand up straight, damn it."

"I broke my toe. This is as straight as I can stand."

Flanagan muttered beneath his breath as he laid a file on the opposite edge of his desk.

"Sanitation found a stiff in the alley behind Ivana's Bar and Grill. Go do your thing."

Butoli took the file without comment and started out the door.

"Butoli!"

He stopped and turned. "Yes, sir?"

"I don't give a damn what you do on your own time, but you better not drink on mine or I'll have your ass."

Butoli's stomach rolled. God, but he needed something stronger than the coffee.

"Lieutenant, right now, my ass is the only thing on my body that doesn't hurt, and I'd really hate to part with it."

Flanagan smirked. "Life's a bitch. Go find me a killer, and take Marshall with you."

"But Evans is my partner."

"Not since last night. His old man died. He's gone to Tennessee. Won't be back for at least a week."

Butoli groaned. "Damn it, Lieutenant, not Marshall. He's a prick."

"Yes, but he's a sober one. Now go do your job, and play nice while you're at it."

Butoli stifled a curse and limped back to his desk.

"Hey, Marshall, we got a new stiff, so get your pocketbook, you're coming with me."

Larry Marshall glared as he got up from his desk.

"That's sexual harassment," Marshall muttered as he took his handgun from his desk and slipped it into a shoulder holster.

"Are you gay?" Butoli asked.

Marshall's nostrils flared angrily. "No."

"Then it's not sexual harassment, it's only a joke. And while we're at it, you're driving."

Marshall smirked as they headed for the elevator.

"Why? Too drunk to drive?"

"Not yet," Butoli said, and then pointed to the

hole he'd cut in the end of his best pair of loafers. "I broke my toe last night."

"Shame it wasn't your head," Marshall muttered, as they exited the building toward the parking lot.

"I heard that," Butoli said.

"Good. At least there's nothing wrong with your ears," Marshall said, as he got behind the wheel. "Where are we going?"

"Alley behind Ivana's Bar and Grill."

Larry Marshall floored the accelerator, taking small pleasure in the fact that Mike Butoli's skin looked like it was turning green.

*White Mountain Cemetery, Braden, Montana—The Same Day*

A stiff wind lifted the hem of Margaret Watson's dress, then tugged at the black wide-brimmed hat she'd been determined to wear. She grabbed at her skirttail with one hand and her hat with the other as she leaned toward her best friend, Harriet Tyler. Lowering her voice, she glanced toward the young woman in black sitting near the open grave.

"Poor thing. With her father dead and all, she's all alone now. No husband. No kids. Just that big old hotel outside of town."

Harriet stared at the woman in question as she whispered back.

"She's not exactly alone. Her uncles are still there."

Margaret sniffed. "They're not really her uncles, you know."

Harriet shrugged. "Well, yes, I suppose, but I don't hold with blood being the only tie to family. They were Sam Abbott's friends and colleagues. They've lived at Abbott House for as long as I can remember. When Sam's wife, Isabella, died, they all did their part in raising that little girl. If she wants to call them her uncles, then who are we to argue?"

Margaret sniffed again, disapproval evident in her posture.

"It just doesn't seem right," she muttered. "All those men. You would have thought at least one of them would have married again."

Harriet grinned. "You're just peeved because Samuel Abbott didn't return your affections."

This time Margaret's disapproval was directed at Harriet.

"You don't know what you're talking about," she muttered. "Now do be quiet. The preacher is about to say a prayer."

Isabella Abbott was numb. If it hadn't been for the firm grip of her Uncle David's arm around her shoulders, she might have thought she was dreaming. For the past fifteen minutes she'd been looking at a clump of dirt on the toe of the pastor's shoe, trying to ignore the shiny bronze casket suspended over the open grave beside him.

Her father was dead. It had been so sudden. One minute he was laughing and talking, and the next he'd been clutching his chest. With two doctors beside him, he'd still died before the ambulance had arrived. For the past three days he'd been lying in state at the Jewel Funeral Home, and now they'd come to lay him to rest.

Her gaze slid from the toe of the pastor's shoe to the mound of white roses covering the casket. Her vision blurred as she drew a deep, shuddering breath.

*Oh, Daddy…how am I going to face life without you?*

David Schultz felt every one of his seventy-eight years as he stared at the long bronze casket. One of these days he would meet a similar fate. They all would. And when that happened, Isabella would be alone. Worry deepened as he pulled Isabella a little closer within his embrace. Samuel's death had caught them all unaware. Changes were inevitable, and he hated change.

Suddenly the preacher was saying Amen and people were starting to move. Isabella stood abruptly. He stood with her, looking around for the other uncles, but he need not have bothered. Like him, they were there—beside her, behind her—as always, sheltering her since the day she'd been born.

"Are you all right, darling?"

Isabella looked up into the dear, familiar face of her Uncle David and nodded.

"I will be," she said, trying to smile through tears. "I'm just sick about Uncle Frank, though. He will be so upset when he comes home and learns that Daddy died."

"It's his own fault for not giving us a way to contact him," David said, still a bit miffed that his old friend had been so secretive about the trip he'd taken.

"I know, but it's still too bad. He's going to be riddled with guilt," Isabella said.

"As he should be," Thomas Mowry said, adding his own opinion to the conversation as he gave Isabella a hug.

Isabella let Uncle Thomas's warmth enfold her, but the moment was brief, as well-wishers began gathering around her, anxious to pay their condolences. She glanced at her Uncle David, giving him a nod.

David quickly stepped forward and raised his hand as he made a brief announcement.

"Please," he said. "We thank you so much for coming. Samuel loved this community and the people in it. Isabella is exhausted, so we are taking her home, but she has asked me to invite all of those who care to come to Abbott House. There is food and drink. Please make yourselves welcome."

Isabella tried to smile, but the faces around her had become a blur. She drew a deep, shuddering breath and let herself be led to a waiting car. Moments later they were driving away from the cemetery toward White Mountain, the place that she called home.

She closed her eyes, mentally preparing herself for the hours ahead. It would be nightfall before she would be able to shed the duties of hostess. Then she would grieve.

# 2

The grandfather clock in the hotel lobby was striking the hour as Isabella came out of her room. It was already midnight, and she still had not been able to sleep. Luckily the hotel was almost empty, although two guests had arrived to check in during the wake following her father's funeral and she hadn't had the heart to turn them away.

Her head ached. Her eyes were swollen from crying. Every time she closed them, she saw her father's casket being lowered into the grave. Unable to lie still in her comfortable bed when she knew her father was in a box six feet under the ground, she'd crawled out of bed.

But it wasn't sorrow that had pulled her out of her room. It was hunger. She felt guilty—almost ashamed of the fact—but it was the first time in three days that she'd felt like eating.

The family quarters were on the lower floor of the house, behind the main staircase, and as she came around the corner, she stopped at the foot of the stairs beneath the painting on the opposite wall. It was a massive canvas, almost life-size, and the first thing to be seen upon entering the hotel. Isabella paused in the shadows, looking intently at the first Isabella. The woman who'd been her mother, and who had died giving birth to her, was little more than a face with a name.

She stared at the painting, accepting the fact that, except for the different hairstyle and clothing, it could very well have been a portrait of herself. She sighed, the sound little more than a soft shifting of air in the silent room.

But for a vague longing for something she'd never known, she had no emotional ties to the woman, although her father had never been able to look at that painting without coming close to tears. At the thought of her father, she wrapped her arms around herself and tried not to cry. At least one positive thing had come out of this nightmare. Her parents were now together.

When her stomach rumbled again, she dropped her gaze and headed for the kitchen. The large commercial-sized refrigerators were full of leftovers from the wake, so she had a wide variety of foods from which to choose. Getting a plate from the cabinet, she settled on a piece of cold chicken and a small helping of pasta salad. The silverware drawer squeaked as she opened it to get a fork, and when it did, she winced. The uncles' rooms were on the top floor, which was two flights up from where she was, yet it wouldn't be the first time in her life she'd gotten caught during a midnight snack attack.

She stood for a moment, listening for the sound of footsteps coming down the staircase, and when she heard nothing but the ticking of the grandfather clock out in the lobby, she breathed a sigh of relief. She didn't want to talk any more today—not even to them.

She went onto the back stoop and sat down on the steps, balancing her plate on her lap as she took her first bite. The pasta in the salad was perfectly al dente and coated with a tangy vinaigrette. When the first bite of food hit her stomach, she inhaled slowly, allowing herself to get past the guilt of self-satisfaction and admit that it was good. As she ate, her gaze moved beyond the backyard of the hotel to the mountain looming on the horizon.

White Mountain.

For as long as she could remember, it had been the backdrop for her life. Somewhere in the ancient past of this land, a massive shift in the tectonic plates below the earth's surface had created heat and pressure beyond man's imagination, resulting in the birth of the mountain range of which White Mountain was a part.

She had often wondered why it was called White Mountain, because it was black as a witch's heart, with a thick stand of trees halfway up its steep slopes. Her father had suggested that it must have been named during the winter months, because then it was usually covered with snow.

It was some time later before Isabella noticed

she'd eaten all her food. As she stood, she also realized that part of her melancholy had eased. She wanted to smile, but her heart was too sore to allow herself the notion, although her father would have been pleased. He'd always said that the world looked far too grim on an empty stomach.

With one last look at the overpowering peak, she went back in the house, quietly locking the door behind her. She set her plate in the sink and then started back to her room. It wasn't going to be easy without her father, but she accepted his death as an inevitable part of life. The uncles were all of the same generation as her father, and she didn't want to think of the days when she would eventually have to give them up, too. The saddest thing was knowing that Uncle Frank had yet to learn of her father's death. He was going to be devastated that he hadn't known, and guilt-ridden at not being here to help her through the ordeal. Isabella just wished he would come back, or at least call. He'd never been away this long before.

A few moments later she entered her room and went back to bed. It wasn't long before exhaustion claimed her and she finally fell asleep.

Detective Mike Butoli swung his sore foot over the curb and stepped up with a hop as he headed into the crime lab. The coroner's office had yet to perform the autopsy on his latest case, and he was chafing under the delay.

An unidentified stiff in a Brighton Beach alley was not high priority, nor was it the only unidentified victim awaiting dissection, but for some reason the case was weighing heavily on Butoli's mind. They'd put the stiff's fingerprints into the system, hoping for a match, and at Lieutenant Flanagan's suggestion had sent them to Interpol, as well. With the high concentration of Russian immigrants in Brighton Beach, it stood to reason that one or the other would result in an identification.

He had been a cop for almost twenty years, the last twelve as a detective. He'd seen far more of the evil and depravity of the human condition than anyone should be exposed to and couldn't remember the last time he had taken a case personally.

Until now.

Maybe it was because his headache was competing with the pain in his foot to see which could rack up the most misery. Maybe it was the guilt he was feeling for having fallen off the wagon after six long months of sobriety. But whatever the reason, yesterday, as he stood in that alley looking down into the old man's face, he kept wondering what journey the man's life had been on would cause it to end in an alley in Brighton Beach.

Today he had a dead man with no identification, no witnesses to the crime, and he wanted answers to both. Information from the coroner's office would have to wait, but he was coming to the crime lab with more optimism. If he got lucky, the analysis of the crime scene evidence would give him something to go on.

Since he was expected, he walked into the lab without knocking and headed toward the small middle-aged man who was feeding information into a computer.

"Hey, Yoda, what have you got for me?"

Malcolm Wise had long ago accepted his nickname, but not without some disgust. It wasn't his fault that nature had doomed him to look more like the famous character from the *Star Wars* series than he did his own parents. He turned to see Detective Butoli coming toward him and hit Save on the keyboard before giving him his full attention.

"Why are you limping?" Wise asked.

"Broke my toe."

Wise smirked. "I won't ask how."

"Well hell, now I am disappointed. I thought Yoda had all the answers."

"Can the crap," Wise said. "Short and balding is sexy to some women."

"Then thank God I was born a man," Butoli countered. "About my stiff…got anything that will help?"

Wise moved toward his desk. "The knife in his chest that was found in a Dumpster was Russian-made."

Butoli rolled his eyes. "Damn, Yoda. This is Brighton Beach. It's full of Russian immigrants. Give me something I can use."

"The skin under his fingernails isn't his own."

Butoli stifled a curse and popped a couple of breath mints in his mouth.

"Anything that might help me put a name to the man?"

Wise grinned as he lifted a plastic bag from a box and slid it across the table.

Butoli caught it before it slipped off onto the floor.

"What's this?" he asked.

"The victim's shirt."

"What's so special about a shirt?"

"Maybe the name underneath the tag might help you."

Butoli's eyes lit up.

"His name? As in a laundry mark?"

"At least part of it," Wise said. "F. Walton. Now all you have to do is find someone missing a man named Walton and your mystery is solved."

"Only part of it," Butoli said, thinking of who had put the knife in the old man's chest. "Anything else that might help?"

Wise shrugged. "You're the detective. I just got through faxing a preliminary report to your office. It should be on your desk when you get back. Some of the tests will take longer. I'll let you know when the lab work is done."

Butoli slapped the little man on the back.

"Thanks, Yoda. This is the first good news I've had in two days."

Wise smirked. "May the force be with you. Now go away. I have work to do."

Butoli left the crime lab with a bounce in his step that had little to do with his sore toe. Finally a name to go with the face—at least most of a name. He was going to swing by the office, pick up Marshall and a picture of the victim, and then take a ride back down to Brighton Beach. Maybe someone would remember a man named Walton. Hell. Maybe he was kin to John Boy. Wouldn't that be a kick in the pants?

Five hours later, Butoli slid into the passenger seat as Larry Marshall got in behind the wheel. They'd been in and out of every place of business within a fifteen block radius of the area where the old man's body had been found, with no response. It wasn't until they'd gone into a small Russian restaurant adjacent to a thrift store that they'd gotten lucky.

The manager had frowned at their badges as he stubbed out a roll-your-own cigarette, glanced at the picture, then shook his head without looking up.

But Butoli had persisted.

"Come on, buddy. Look again. Somebody stuck a knife in his heart and left him to die in an alley alone. Somewhere he's probably got family who are worried sick. I'm not asking you to ID a killer, just the man. It's the least he deserves. Now look again. Have you seen him before?"

The manager looked up with a distrustful glare. His experience with public authority had begun at the age of seventeen, half a world away in a Soviet prison. He felt no need to cooperate. But the look on the cop's face seemed less threatening than most, so when Butoli shoved the picture back toward him, he shrugged, then looked down.

"Yeah...maybe I see him before...two...three times. He liked my borscht."

"Is he a local?"

*"Nyet,"* the manager answered, then qualified the Russian "no" with a negative shake of his head.

"How do you know?" Butoli asked.

"One time I think he pay with what you call traveler's check."

"Did you see anyone with him?"

The manager shook his head again.

Larry Marshall leaned against the counter, putting himself in the man's personal space with only a small bit of wood and glass between them. The manager took a defensive step back as Larry fired his first question.

"Any idea where he was staying?"

The manager shook his head again. "But maybe not too far away."

"What makes you say that?" Marshall asked.

"He was old...sick, too, I think."

"How do you know?"

The manager shrugged again, then glanced nervously around. It wasn't good business to be friendly with the police.

"His skin...it was not a good color. But he did not ask for cab, so maybe he had room not too far away."

"Good deduction," Butoli said, and slipped the picture in his pocket. "Sir, I thank you for your help. If you think of anything else...anything at all...give me a call."

He handed the manager his card, and then they left.

"Next on the list, hotels and rooming houses," Marshall said, as he started the car and pulled away from the curb.

"Maybe we'll get lucky again," Butoli said. "But in the meantime, don't get pushy with these people. Few of them have any reason to trust authority."

Marshall patted the part in his hair without heeding Butoli's caution.

"They're in America now. If they don't like the way we do things here, they can go back where they came from."

Butoli's toe was killing him, and his patience was gone. He had the strongest urge to slap the back of Larry Marshall's head just to see the look on his face. Instead, he popped a couple of painkillers and leaned back against the seat.

Less than half an hour later, Butoli's prediction was proven right. The desk clerk at the Georgian

Hotel identified the picture before Larry Marshall could get out his notebook.

"Oh my...he is dead?" the clerk asked.

Butoli nodded.

"Poor man, but glad it didn't happen here."

Marshall smirked. "Yeah, I see your point. Not good for business, huh?"

The clerk flushed. "Sorry. I didn't say that right. I'm sorry Mr. Walton is dead. He seemed like nice man, but you know what I mean...right?"

Butoli frowned. No luggage had been found with the body. Maybe they'd just found their motive for the old man's death. People had been killed for far less than a suitcase of clothes.

"What name did he register under?" he asked.

"Walton... Frank Walton. I remember I teased him and asked if he was related to John Boy. You know...from TV show."

"Exactly when did he check out?" Butoli asked.

The clerk turned to the computer and typed in the name.

"Here it is. Yesterday morning."

Butoli's frown deepened. The coroner had told them that the old man had probably died between 7:00 and 9:00 p.m. the night before his body was discovered. So if Walton was already dead, then he couldn't have checked himself out. His pulse skipped a beat.

"You're sure? Did he check out at the desk?"

The clerk scanned the screen and then looked up.

''I was not on duty. All I know is room key was turned in and his bill put on credit card he gave on arrival.''

''We'll need that credit card number,'' Marshall said.

The clerk frowned. ''I am not supposed to give—''

''It's to confirm identification and to make sure it wasn't a stolen card, understand?''

The clerk hesitated and then copied it from the screen to a piece of paper and handed it to Marshall.

''Had his room been slept in?'' Butoli asked.

The clerk shook his head. ''I don't know. You have to check with housekeeping.''

''Then get somebody up here,'' Butoli said. ''We'll wait.''

''Can you speak Russian?'' the clerk asked.

''No,'' Butoli said.

''Then I need to call manager, too, or you get nowhere with the help.''

''You don't speak Russian?'' Marshall asked.

''I am not Russian. I am Slovak.''

''Whatever,'' Marshall muttered.

A short while later they were in the manager's office, conducting a half-assed interrogation through a man who quite obviously wished them to be anywhere else but here. The reluctant hotel manager was standing beside a cowering housemaid, who obviously thought she was in some kind of trouble. Despite the fact that they'd assured her otherwise, she hadn't stopped crying since she'd entered the room.

"What the hell did you say to her?" Butoli growled.

The manager, who was also of Russian descent, glared back at Butoli.

"I said nothing," he snapped. "She makes her own conclusion."

"Fine," Butoli said. "So ask her this. Did she clean Mr. Walton's room every day?"

The manager translated the question, and the housemaid quickly nodded.

"Ask her if he ever had any visitors."

The little maid shrank even smaller against the chair, muttering beneath her breath as she shrugged.

"She says she saw no one but him in the room."

Butoli nodded and smiled at the woman, hoping she would take that as a sign he meant her no harm. It didn't seem to work. She covered her face with her hands and refused to look him in the eye.

"God almighty," Butoli mumbled, then took a deep breath and started over. "Did she clean that same room on the morning Walton checked out?"

"She says yes, but that there was not much to do. He had not slept in his bed."

Butoli's attention sharpened. "What about his clothing…his luggage? Was it still in the room?"

The manager relayed the questions, then translated her answer again.

"She says everything was gone. She turn in room

key she found on bed later, when she finish her shift.'' Then the manager added, ''It is the way we do it here. Sometimes guests use speedy checkout system. Checkout on room TV. It is very up-to-date process. Georgian Hotel is finest in Brighton Beach.''

Butoli looked at his partner. It was obvious from Marshall's expression that he was thinking the same thing Butoli was. Someone had come back to Frank Walton's room and removed every trace of the man's presence. But why?

He sighed. This case was turning out to be more complicated than he'd first believed. They could no longer assume it was a run-of-the-mill mugging gone bad. Someone had gone to a great deal of trouble to delay the identification of a dead man by removing all his personal ID, then gone to his hotel and taken everything he had with him, making it appear as if he'd checked out.

But why?

He put his notebook in his pocket and gave the manager a card.

''Please tell your employee that we appreciate her help, and that if she remembers anything else that might help us catch the man who killed Mr. Walton, to please call us.''

The manager relayed the message.

The housemaid stood, gave the men a nervous glance and bolted out the door.

Butoli shook his head. "What's she so scared about?"

The manager didn't bother to hide a sneer. "Being sent back, of course."

Larry Marshall looked up from his notepad.

"Back to where?" he asked

"Russia."

Marshall's gaze sharpened. "What? Are you hiring illegals? You can't do that. You have to report them to—"

"Thank you for your cooperation," Butoli said, then grabbed his partner by the arm and all but dragged him out of the hotel.

"What do you think you're doing?" Marshall yelped.

Butoli took a deep breath, mentally counting from one to ten before he trusted himself to answer.

"Marshall, for once in your life, just shut the fuck up."

Larry Marshall's face turned a dark, angry red. "It's people like you who screw up the systems we have in place."

"Maybe," Butoli muttered. "But it was people like you who put the cockamamie systems in place to begin with. For God's sake! We're trying to get them to help us find a killer, and you're threatening to call INS? What the hell were you thinking?"

Then he threw up his hands and headed for the car, leaving Marshall with no option but to follow.

Marshall got in and started the engine.

"Where to?" he asked.

Butoli glared. "Back to the precinct. We've got a name to go with the body, and a credit card number that should give us enough background information to find his next of kin."

"But don't you think we should—"

The look on Butoli's face was enough to stifle what he'd been going to say. Instead, he pulled into the traffic and took a right turn at the next block.

Isabella handed a room key to the couple who'd just checked in. In the years since her father and Uncle David had opened White Mountain Fertility Clinic, she'd seen hundreds like them—people desperate for a child of their own and willing to try anything to make it happen.

"There is an elevator just to the right of the staircase," she said.

"We'll take the stairs," the woman said. "Exercise is good for me."

Isabella smiled. "Do you need help with your luggage?"

The man shook his head. "No. We only have the two bags. We can manage just fine. Oh…what time does the kitchen open? We have an appointment in town in the morning, and we don't want to be late."

"We start serving breakfast at six o'clock and if you need a taxi into Braden, you'll need to call ahead and expect about a fifteen to twenty minute wait."

The couple nodded their understanding and started up the stairs, their heads tilted slightly toward each other as they spoke in undertones.

Isabella hurt for their sadness. It was evident in every aspect of their expressions and posture. How sad to want a child so desperately and yet be unable to make it happen. Even sadder were the children who were born to people who didn't care. It didn't make sense. Why didn't God just give babies to people who wanted them and let the people who were unfit to be parents be the ones who were barren? But she knew her thoughts were fanciful. Nothing in life was fair. She thought of her father dying so suddenly and leaving not only family, but waiting patients, behind.

The staff at White Mountain Fertility Clinic was well-trained and able to continue without her father's presence. In the past few years he'd even talked about the time when he would retire and leave the creation of life to those younger than himself. Besides her father, Uncle David and Uncle Jasper still held active roles in the clinic, even though they took fewer and fewer new patients with each passing year.

Without thinking, her gaze automatically slid to the portrait above the staircase, unaware that the gentleness in the woman's dark brown eyes mirrored her own. Her wandering thoughts stopped abruptly when the phone rang. Making herself concentrate on the present, she lifted her chin and picked up the phone.

"Abbott House."

"This is Detective Mike Butoli with the Brighton Beach police. I need to speak to Samuel Abbott."

Isabella's breath caught as a quick film of tears blurred her vision. It was the first time this had happened since her father's death, but she knew it wouldn't be the last. She cleared her throat and made herself answer.

"I'm sorry, Detective, but Samuel Abbott recently passed away. I'm his daughter, Isabella Abbott. Maybe I can help."

Mike Butoli frowned. He hated this part of his job more than spinach—and only God and his mother knew how much he hated spinach.

"Did you know a man named Franklin Walton?"

His use of the past tense made Isabella's heart drop.

"Uncle Frank? What's happened to him? Has he been injured? Is he all right?"

Butoli sighed. Damn. As many times as he'd done this, it never got easier.

"I'm very sorry to tell you, Miss Abbott, but Mr. Walton was found murdered in an alley a few days ago."

The wail that came out of her mouth was a mixture of disbelief and despair.

"Nooo," she cried, and staggered backward onto a chair.

John Michaels and Rufus Toombs, two of the
men she called uncles, were just coming off the elevator from their third-floor apartments when they
heard her cry. Without hesitation, they rushed forward.

"Isabella...darling, what's wrong?"

She recognized the voices but couldn't focus on
the faces. Everything around her was fast going
black. Before she could answer, she slid out of the
chair onto the floor in a faint.

Rufus quickly knelt at her side, while John went
for the phone dangling from her hand.

"Hello? Hello? Who's there, please?"

Butoli knew the woman had not received the
news well.

"This is Detective Butoli with the Brighton
Beach P.D."

"What did you say to Isabella? What has happened?" John cried.

"Are you her family?" Butoli asked.

"Yes, yes," John muttered. "What has happened?"

"We just identified a murder victim as Franklin
Walton, of Braden, Montana. The address on his
credit card listed Abbott House as his home. Is this
correct?"

John Michaels's heart sank. Now it made sense.
Now they knew why Frank had never called home.

"Yes," he whispered. "Yes, that is correct."

"I'm sorry to ask, but someone must come and

identify the body. Just to make sure. You understand.''

John's fingers were trembling and he wanted to
cry, but he made himself focus as he picked up a
pen.

"Yes, I understand. Just tell me where we must
go."

As he wrote, Rufus was running for the house
phone. Within seconds, he had David Schultz on the
phone.

"Get down here," he cried. "Isabella has
fainted."

John hung up the phone as Rufus made his way
back around the desk.

"David is on his way," Rufus said.

"He can't help," John said, and covered his face
in his hands.

"What are you talking about?" Rufus muttered,
as he dropped to Isabella's side again. "She's just
fainted. She's going to be okay. Isn't she?"

"It isn't Isabella. It's Frank."

Rufus's eyes widened, rearranging the pond of
wrinkles that age had settled on his face.

"What about Frank?"

"He's dead. Murdered."

Rufus blanched and sat down hard on the floor
beside Isabella. Unconsciously, he grabbed her
hand, clutching it tightly in his own.

"Dear Lord," Rufus mumbled. "Do you
think—''

"Don't say it," John muttered. "Don't even think it."

"What are we going to do?"

"Go get him and bring him home to bury."

"But—"

Isabella moaned.

"Hush," John said sternly.

Rufus swallowed what he'd been about to say. Seconds later, David and Jasper came flying down the stairs, their speed belying their ages.

"What happened?" David asked, as he set his medical bag at Isabella's side and pulled out a stethoscope.

"You won't need that," John said. "She fainted. Just pop some smelling salts and get her to her room. We've got bigger trouble."

David rocked back on his heels.

"What?"

"Frank's dead. Murdered."

David blanched.

"My God...where did it happen?"

"Brighton Beach."

David frowned. "I've heard of it, but I can't place the—"

"It's part of Brooklyn, I think. Due to the large population of Russian immigrants, some call it Little Russia."

Jasper Arnold's gasp was the only vocal sign of the four men's shock. Then Isabella began struggling to get up.

"What happened? Why did I—"

Suddenly she remembered, and her face crumpled as she was helped to her feet.

"Uncle Frank is dead," she said, and began to sob.

The four aging men encircled her.

"We know," they said. "Come with us, darling. You need to lie down."

"The desk," she mumbled.

"I'll call Delia from the office. She can take care of it for the rest of the day."

"What are we going to do?" Isabella asked, then covered her face in her hands.

The men looked at each other silently, but it was David who answered her.

"We're going to get him and bring him home. That's what we're going to do."

The sun was setting as Jack Dolan came out of his house and headed toward the deck surrounding his hot tub. Except for a bath towel wrapped loosely around his waist, he was completely nude. His house was on the outskirts of a Virginia suburb, only an hour or so's drive from Washington, D.C. The eight-foot-high privacy fence surrounding his backyard provided coveted privacy. Besides, his nearest neighbor was over a quarter of a mile away and traveled more than he did.

Exhaustion was evident in his stride as he reached the tub of bubbling water. Modesty was last on his list of social graces as he dropped the towel from around his waist and stepped down into the water. A few steps farther, he sank down onto a built-in seat and leaned back with a sigh as the jets sent a rush of warm, bubbling water against his skin.

He had two knife scars on his back, an old gunshot scar on his upper thigh, and ribs that were still healing from the last case he'd been on. His personal life was nonexistent, and his career as a Federal agent had been ongoing since his graduation from Boston University. He was thirty-eight years old and had nothing to show for it but a house he rarely slept in and some investments he might not live long enough to spend.

The water roiled around his limbs, easing the aches from old wounds and relaxing the tension in his muscles. He leaned his head against the back of the tub and closed his eyes. Something inside him was starting to give. He'd known it for almost six months. There was a restlessness to his behavior that had never been there before, and a longing for something he couldn't name. Although he couldn't name his frustration, one thing was blatantly clear. Something needed to give. Whether it would be him or his lifestyle was yet to be determined.

He swiped a wet hand across his face and rolled his head. The beginnings of a headache he'd had since noon were starting to ease. A small squirrel scolded from the pine tree at the corner of his yard, angry at the invasion into its territory.

"Back off, Chester. It's my yard, too," Jack said, and then smiled at himself.

Now he was talking to squirrels. He really needed a change.

He had not taken a vacation in over four years. Maybe what he was feeling was a simple case of burnout. But whatever the diagnosis, the cure would be the same—a much-needed change of pace.

He sat in the hot tub until his legs felt like gelatin and watched the moon come up. It wasn't until his phone began to ring that he dragged himself up and out of the tub. Wrapping the towel around his waist, he jogged into the house and picked up the phone.

"Dolan."

"Jack, how are your ribs?"

Unconsciously, Jack straightened to attention as he recognized the director's voice.

"They're fine, sir. What do you need?"

The director's chuckle rippled through the line.

"So you've taken up mind reading now, too?"

Jack grinned wryly. "Truthfully, sir, when was the last time you called just to chat?"

"Point taken," the director said. "What I need is for you to pack for an undetermined stay in Montana. You will receive a packet tomorrow morning, including a plane ticket to a small town called Braden."

Everything went through Jack's mind, from militia-based groups to terrorists.

"Yes, sir. What am I facing?"

"Oh… I'd say at least a week, maybe more, at a fine old hotel called Abbott House. The air is clean. There aren't any golf courses or rivers in which to fish, but I hear the scenery is great."

"Sir?"

The director chuckled again. "Not what you expected, is it?"

"No, sir, but I'm certain you're about to fill me in."

The director sighed. "Yes, well…as Paul Harvey always says… 'now for the rest of the story.' Two days ago, a set of prints from a dead man came through NCIC that didn't match up with any we had on file."

"I don't get it," Jack said. "Surely you aren't wanting me to establish an identity? That's a job for a homicide detective."

"Let me finish," the director said.

"Sorry," Jack said.

"Yes, well, this is where it gets weird. The body was discovered in Brighton Beach."

"Isn't that the place they call Little Russia?"

"Some do, I believe," the director said. "At any rate, I understand that because of the large number of immigrants in that area of Brooklyn, that from time to time when a situation warrants, the police also send prints through Interpol as a means of speeding up identification."

A puddle had formed on the floor where Jack was standing, so he dropped the towel from around his waist, put his foot in the middle of the towel and began swiping at the water while he continued to listen.

"Yes, sir, but I still don't—"

"I'm getting there," the director said. "The thing is...the prints rang a bell at Interpol. A really big bell."

Suddenly, the hair stood on the back of Jack's neck.

"How big?"

"The prints belong to a Russian scientist named Vaclav Waller."

"And?"

"Vaclav Waller died in a plane crash off the coast of Florida over thirty years ago."

Jack kicked aside the wet towel and headed for the back of the house to get some clothes.

"But he's dead now, right?"

"Oh yes, he's dead, all right. I sent a man directly to Brighton Beach as soon as the prints were flagged. Trouble is...they'd already identified the man as Frank Walton of Braden, Montana. Had a credit card number and everything from the hotel where he'd been staying."

Jack took a pair of sweats from the dresser and pulled them on with one hand as his boss continued.

"But..." the director added "...when my man ran a background check on the card owner, guess what he found?"

Jack dropped to the side of the bed.

"What?"

"The social security number the dead man was using belonged to a man named Frank Walton, only that Frank Walton died in 1955 at the age of twenty-four."

"So we've got a dead Russian pretending to be a dead American who's just died. Is that about it?"

The director's appreciation for the humor of the situation was suddenly missing.

"That's it, Jack, and I want to know what the hell is going on. The man who called himself Frank Walton has been living at a place called Abbott House for years. I want you in that hotel, and I want some answers to what the hell that man was up to. Considering Waller's background, there could have been a lot more to his disappearance than just defecting. However, I don't want you showing up there as FBI. For all intents and purposes, you are a man on vacation."

"Yes, sir."

"Keep me updated on what you learn."

"Yes, sir."

"Oh...and Jack."

"Sir?"

"You could send me a postcard."

Jack grinned as the line went dead.

# 3

It was fifteen minutes after two in the afternoon when Jack pulled his rental car into the parking lot of Abbott House. He parked and got out, stretching as he stood. A twinge of pain rippled across his belly from his still healing ribs, but the cool, rain-washed air felt good on his face. He got out his bag and headed for the door, noting absently that the place looked deserted, but when he walked inside, a short, middle-aged woman looked up from behind the desk and smiled.

"Welcome to Abbott House."

Jack nodded as he dropped his bag and pulled out his wallet.

"I'd like a room please."

"For two?" she asked, looking past him toward the door.

"No, just me," Jack answered and wondered why the woman looked surprised.

"Yes, sir, and how long will you be staying?"

"A week, maybe more," Jack said. "I'm doing some research in the area."

"Research?" the woman asked.

"For a book."

"Oooh, a writer, how interesting," she said. "Most of our guests are here because of the clinic, you know."

"What kind of clinic would that be?"

"White Mountain Clinic. It's a fertility clinic for women."

"I see." Then he gestured toward the parking lot. "Doesn't look like there's much business today. I thought the place was closed when I drove up."

The clerk's face fell. "Oh…that's because everyone is at the funeral. So sad."

Jack's interest kicked in. "Someone local, I assume."

She blinked back tears. "Yes, one of our residents, Franklin Walton. He'd lived here for many, many years, and his death was so unexpected." She leaned across the counter and lowered her voice. "He was murdered." Then she added, "But not here, of course. Braden is a quiet little town. Nothing like that ever happens here, thank God. The tragedy is that it's so soon after Dr. Abbott's passing. Isabella is distraught, as we all are."

Jack knew the name Franklin Walton. The man was the reason he was here. But he didn't know who Isabella was, and the Abbott name meant nothing to him other than the name of the hotel.

"Dr. Abbott? Was he the owner of this hotel?"

She nodded. "Yes, but he and Dr. Schultz and Dr. Arnold also founded White Mountain Fertility

Clinic. Most of the people who come to the clinic for help also stay here at Abbott House.''

''I see,'' Jack said.

''I'll need to see a credit card, sir.''

Jack pulled one out of his wallet and laid it on the counter. As she ran it through the system, he turned to survey the lobby. Like the house itself, it was quite grand to be in such an isolated location.

''This is quite a place,'' he said.

The clerk smiled.

''Yes, isn't it? It was built in the early nineteen hundreds by a well-to-do rancher who later went broke during the Depression. After that it went through a series of owners until Samuel Abbott bought it sometime during the seventies.''

''Interesting,'' Jack said. ''So am I to take it that Dr. Abbott and this Walton fellow were friends?''

The clerk looked up, a little curious as to the stranger's interest.

''Yes. Mr. Walton lived here, as do Isabella's other uncles.''

''Isabella?''

''Dr. Abbott's daughter.''

''Other uncles? Are you saying that the murdered man was her uncle?''

''No, none of them are related by blood, but Isabella called them her uncles just the same.''

Jack nodded. ''I know what you mean. Back home in Louisiana we sometimes call an elder mem-

ber of our community by such a title. It's our way
of giving them respect.''

''Yes, exactly,'' the clerk said, and then handed
him a key. ''You'll be on the second floor, room
200. That's the first one on your right at the top of
the stairs.''

''I noticed this house has three floors. Are any of
those available? I like heights.''

She shook her head. ''No, sir. I'm sorry, but the
third floor is the uncles' apartments.''

*One more bit of information to file away.* ''That's
fine,'' Jack said, and smiled openly, not wanting her
to question his curiosity. ''It never hurts to ask,
though, does it?''

Charmed by the big man's smile, the woman felt
herself blushing. He reminded her a bit of one of
those hot young actors, only he was a bit older and
had a much stronger jaw. Delia admired men with
strong jaws.

''If we can be of any further service, don't hesitate to ask. We begin serving breakfast at six
o'clock but the kitchen stays open until eleven
o'clock at night, so you can order à la carte any
time you choose.''

''Thanks,'' Jack said, and picked up his things
and started toward the stairs. As he did, he glanced
up, then froze, his gaze fixed on the painting above
the stairs.

The woman in the portrait was stunning. A thick
crown of black hair framed a heart-shaped face with

features as delicate as fine china. But she had the saddest eyes he'd ever seen.

"So beautiful."

"Yes, isn't she?" Delia said. "That's the late Isabella Abbott, Dr. Abbott's wife."

"She's dead?" The thought brought real pain.

"Yes, almost thirty years ago. She died in childbirth."

Jack took a step closer, locked into her enigmatic stare.

A phone rang behind him, and he jerked at the sound. Only after the clerk began to carry on a conversation with someone on the other end of the line did he manage to tear himself away from the portrait and move toward the stairs. Halfway up, he found himself at eye level with her face. She was looking straight at him, beseeching him for something he couldn't understand.

Breath caught in the back of his throat, and his mouth went dry. It was only with great effort that he tore himself away and continued up the stairs. Still rattled from the unexpected communion with a ghost, his hands were shaking as he stuck the key in the lock, then opened the door to his room. Without paying any attention to the fine old world furnishings, he walked inside, turned the lock as he dropped his bag, and sat down on the bed with a thump.

The room smelled like his grandmother's house—of lavender and roses, with a slightly musty air that had nothing to do with lack of cleanliness and more to do with age. A ripple of uneasiness made the skin crawl on his neck. He looked over his shoulder, half expecting to see Isabella Abbott looking back.

"I've got to get a grip," he muttered. "I'll unpack, scope out the place and make a preliminary report before dark."

But weariness overcame his good intentions as he lay back on the bed, telling himself he would rest for just a few minutes.

When he next opened his eyes, the room was in darkness. He rolled over and sat up with a start, confused for a moment as to where he was at. Then the scent of lavender drifted past and he remembered. He was in Abbott House.

His belly growled as he glanced at his watch. It was almost midnight. He'd missed dinner but was too hungry to wait until morning. Hopefully there would be a vending machine somewhere on the premises. All he had to do was find it.

As he slung his legs over the edge of the bed, he looked up and then out the window. The curtains had yet to be drawn against the night, and the silhouette of the mountain range behind the hotel was very visible. It loomed over the landscape—a dark and immovable force of nature against the blue-velvet texture of the sky.

Stretching tired muscles, Jack stood, then walked to the window. Below, the well-kept grounds of the hotel looked black outside the circle of illumination beneath the security lights. The place had a beauty of its own that was difficult to name. The grandeur of such a house seemed out of place in a land that still bore traces of wildness from its past. He thought of the man they had buried today. It was a good place in which to get lost.

But why he'd done it was the question of the day. Why had Vaclav Waller faked his own death? And why come here to Montana? There were any number of countries in which he could have chosen to hide.

He ran his fingers through his hair in quiet frustration and turned away from the window. Tomorrow was soon enough to worry about all that. Right now he wanted some food and the rest of a good night's sleep.

Isabella couldn't sleep. Every time she closed her eyes she kept seeing her Uncle Frank's face in the coffin. Even in death, she imagined she saw the horror he had experienced in knowing he was going to die.

They had laid Frank Walton to rest beside the man who'd been his best friend in life, but as the first shovel full of dirt had fallen onto his casket, Isabella had realized she had not known a thing about Frank Walton's family. He'd always spoken of his past in vague references and of his family in the past tense, so she'd just assumed that he had outlived them all. But what if he hadn't? What if there was the odd family member somewhere—a cousin, an in-law—someone who, if they had but known, would also have mourned his passing?

At the thought, she had looked up at the others and realized she knew little to nothing about them, as well. They had always been such constants in her life that she had taken them for granted, but she'd been jolted out of her complacency with the passing of her father and now her Uncle Frank. When this was over—when they could all think without wanting to cry, she was going to rectify her lack of knowledge. Family was everything, and now, except for five elderly men who were no blood kin at all, she had none.

The digital readout on her alarm clock read 12:10 a.m. She sat up with a sigh and swung her feet off the side of the bed. Maybe a glass of warm milk would help her sleep. It didn't sound appetizing, but it still beat the chemical hangover that a sleeping pill always gave her. Grabbing her long white robe from the closet, she stepped into her slippers and headed for the door, confident that she would be able to slip in and out of the kitchen without disturbing anyone else's sleep.

The soles of her slippers scooted silently along the polished hardwood floors as she moved down the hall. Seconds later, she circled the staircase and entered the lobby. Out of habit, she paused at the desk, checking the security of the hotel that was also her home. Satisfied that all was well, she started toward the kitchen. About halfway across the lobby, a hint of movement in the corner of the room caught her eye. Then, as the movement became mass and the mass became a man, her heart skipped a beat.

"Hello...who's there?" she called.

She heard a catch in his breath, and when he spoke, the husky timbre of his voice made her shiver.

Jack was still prowling about the premises in search of a vending machine when he heard a door open, then close. Instinctively he stepped back into the shadows, waiting to see who was coming, only to find himself face-to-face with a ghost. Not trusting what he thought he was seeing, he blinked, then rubbed his eyes. But the image didn't waver or fade away. For the first time in his life, he understood the life-altering fear of being unable to move.

It was the woman from the portrait, and she came out from behind the staircase and into the lobby, pausing at the desk as if in search of an unseen foe. The expression on her face was drawn, and although he knew it wasn't possible, he imagined that he heard her sigh. But that didn't make sense. Ghosts didn't breathe.

What was her name? Oh yes, Isabella. The clerk had called her Isabella.

Her beauty was evident, but it was the heartbreak in her expression that made his gut knot. What terrible tragedy had she endured in life that would carry over to the grave? She started across the lobby, then suddenly stopped and looked into the shadows where he was standing. When she called out, he nearly jumped out of his skin. From all he'd ever read, ghosts didn't carry on conversations, either. Hesitating briefly, he moved toward her without taking his gaze from her face and didn't stop until there was less than six feet between them.

"Isabella?"

The man's voice was barely above a whisper, yet her name on his lips echoed in Isabella's ears as if he'd shouted. She was used to strangers, but she'd never seen this man before. How had he known her name?

"How do you know me?" she asked.

Jack took a deep breath and reached for her hand. Isabella flinched at the unexpected intimacy.

The shock of solid flesh beneath Jack's hand was as surprising to him as his touch was to Isabella.

"You're real!"

Isabella frowned. "Sir...are you drunk?"

Jack combed a shaky hand through his hair.

"No, but I'm thinking I might like to be," he muttered.

"Are you a guest here?"

He nodded. "I checked in this afternoon."

"Ah," Isabella said. "That must have been when we were all at the funeral." Then she pulled her robe closer around her body and tightened the tie even more. "I'm Isabella Abbott. Is there something wrong with your room? Is there anything that you need?''

Jack couldn't stop staring at her. Even though he now knew his first impression of her had been nothing more than a midnight fancy, he turned to look over his shoulder to the portrait hanging over the stairs.

Suddenly Isabella understood.

She hid a smile. ''Did you think I was a ghost?''

Jack looked back at her and then shrugged, unwilling to admit where his thoughts had taken him. Government agents should believe in facts, not ghosts.

''Actually, I came down to look for some sort of vending machine. It seems I slept through dinner and everything else.'' When she smiled, Jack felt his stomach tilt, and was pretty sure it had nothing to do with hunger.

''I was on my way to the kitchen to heat some milk. I don't much like it, but it does help me sleep. If you don't mind a little potluck, I'm sure I can find something to make you a sandwich.''

''Thank you, ma'am. I would certainly appreciate it.''

This time her smile shot straight to his heart.

''I said I'd feed you, but not if you're going to call me, ma'am.'' She extended her hand. ''Please…call me Isabella.''

Jack hesitated, then clasped her hand. It felt soft and warm and fragile. He looked straight past her smile into her eyes and saw a wellspring of such sorrow that he was overwhelmed with contrition. He'd come here under false pretenses, and making friends with anyone, especially this woman, didn't set well with him. Then he took a deep breath and readjusted his thoughts. He wasn't making friends. He was simply getting himself some food.

"All right...Isabella, you have a deal."

"This way," she said, and led the way into the kitchen, flipping a switch as she entered.

Suddenly the room was bathed in light, and Jack was struck anew by her beauty. Her hair was thick and straight and black, and her eyes were the color of dark caramel. When she smiled, her eyebrows arched in an impish manner. But she was thin— almost too thin—and when she began to take food from the refrigerator to make his sandwich, he wanted to tell her to make one for herself, as well. Instead he made himself remember why he'd come and began a quiet but pointed questioning that would have made his supervisor proud.

"So, you said earlier that you were at a funeral. I hope it wasn't family."

Her posture stiffened, and then she paused in the act of putting mayonnaise onto the bread. When she answered, he had to strain to hear the words.

"Yes, actually, it was."

"I'm sorry for your loss," he said.

She reached back into the refrigerator, took out a

platter of meat and chose two of the leanest slices of ham, then laid them on the bread.

"Thank you. Do you like cheese?" she asked.

He knew she was trying to change the subject, but he was unwilling to let it go.

"Yes, please." His mind was racing, trying to think of a way to keep their conversation going. He remembered what the desk clerk had told him about the place. Maybe that would work. "So, have you always lived in Montana?"

She nodded.

"This is quite a place. Did you build it?"

She turned. "No, it's quite old, actually. My father bought it over thirty years ago. It's been in the family ever since. I was born here."

"Really?"

She nodded.

"So you are following your father's footsteps into the hotel business."

Her chin trembled, and at that moment he hated himself for continuing with the charade. To his intense relief, she answered without any more coercion.

"The hotel was only a sideline," she said softly. "My father was a doctor. He and Uncle David and Uncle Jasper founded the White Mountain Fertility Clinic in Braden."

Jack quickly picked up on her use of past tense.

"Your father is no longer living?"

Isabella bit the inside of her mouth to keep from

crying. She had to get used to talking about this. It was now a hard fact of her life.

"No. He died a little over a week ago."

"So it was his memorial service today?"

Isabella shook her head as her eyes filled with tears. "No, today was for my Uncle Frank. He was on vacation. Someone killed him." She took a quick breath and then turned around.

"I'm very sorry," Jack said. "That's got to be tough...losing two members of your family so close together."

"Yes. Thank you."

There was a long moment of silence as she completed the sandwich. He watched without comment, noting the methodical movements of her hands as she cut the sandwich at an angle, creating two triangular halves. Then she placed it on a plate, added pickles, olives and a handful of chips, and set it on a tray. Without wasted motion, she laid a white linen napkin beside the plate, then took a glass from the cabinet and turned to him, the glass held lightly in her hand. But there was nothing casual about the look she gave him. He felt pierced through by her stare.

"What would you like to drink?"

"What do you have?" he asked.

"This is a hotel. You can have pretty much anything you want."

"Any soft drink will do."

She took a can of cola from the refrigerator,

added some ice to his glass, and then put them on the tray before handing it to him.

"Here is your food. I hope it will hold you until morning. We begin serving breakfast at six o'clock."

Jack nodded and smiled. "It looks great. Thank you for going to so much trouble."

Isabella folded her hands in front of her and tilted her head to one side. For a moment Jack had a vision of a certain teacher who used to chastise him for being tardy when he was a child.

"You're welcome," she said. "Have a good night."

He'd been dismissed. Without a reason to linger longer, he picked up the tray and started out of the room. He was almost to the door when she spoke.

"Forgive my emotional outburst," she said softly. "The wound is still so fresh."

"There is nothing to forgive," he said, then looked at the tension on her face. "Will you be all right? I mean...I'd be happy to wait and walk you through the lobby."

The offer was unexpected, and because it was, it was that much more precious.

"No, but thank you just the same, Mr...."

"Dolan. Jack Dolan."

She tilted her head in the other direction, as if fitting the name to the man, then nodded, as if to herself.

"Good night, Jack Dolan."

He hesitated, then nodded.

"Good night, Miss Abbott."

She turned her back on him to pour a serving of milk in a pan and set it on a burner to heat. At that point he remembered that she'd told him she'd been unable to sleep.

As he started up the stairs with his tray, he glanced at the portrait. The resemblance between mother and daughter was uncanny. No wonder he'd thought she was a ghost. He glanced down at the tray full of food and grimaced. If he ate all of this, he would be sleepless, too. And even if he slept, he suspected his sleep would not be dreamless—not after the encounter he'd just had.

He shook his head and tore his gaze from the painting.

Ghosts indeed.

# 4

$V$asili Rostov stood with binoculars held close to his face, watching as the downstairs lights went out inside the hotel in the valley below. He watched until a light appeared at a second floor window before he dropped the binoculars onto his backpack and crawled into his sleeping bag. Whatever had been going on downstairs was obviously over.

He cursed softly in Russian, taking comfort in the familiar roll of the words on his tongue. Before they'd pulled him out of his anonymous existence, he had been able to convince himself that he was still as good as ever and that age had no bearing on his abilities. But now that he'd been on the move going on two weeks, he had to admit he was getting too old for this work. He missed his bed and his easy chair, where the cushions sank in all the right spots. And he missed his vodka. He always had a couple of shots before going to bed. Since he'd come to Montana, he'd been forced to endure cold camps and dried foods. The novelty of being back "on the job" was wearing thin. Couple that with a continuing urge to forget everything he'd been sent to do and get lost in America, as Vaclav Waller had done, and Vasili Rostov was an unhappy man.

He looked back down the mountain at the roof of the sprawling three-story hotel and grimaced. He needed to find a way to get inside without anyone knowing. It was the only place he knew to start looking for answers. But how to do that without arousing suspicion was, at the moment, beyond him.

The night sky was clear and cool, but despite the beauty of the stars, he would rather have been in a bed and under a roof. A pack of coyotes began to howl on a nearby hillside. He jerked in reflex and reached for his gun, cursing the fact that the only place to offer rooms on this forsaken bit of earth was the hotel below.

At the present time there was only one paying guest at Abbott House, a man who'd arrived earlier in the afternoon. Vasili had considered the wisdom of staying there himself and then discarded the notion. Since Frank Walton had known within seconds of their meeting who he was, Rostov couldn't afford a repeat of that debacle.

And he couldn't help thinking that if it hadn't been for Waller, all of this would be over. If only they had told him more about why they wanted Waller back, he might have foreseen Waller's drastic behavior and been able to prevent it. The very fact that the old man had been willing to die rather than let himself become Rostov's prisoner was highly suspicious. Then he tossed the thought aside. Maybe he had opted to die now rather than being tortured later for information he wasn't willing to give.

Rostov sighed and closed his eyes. If he'd learned one thing from living through the disintegration of the Soviet Republic, it was that there was no need for rehashing the past.

He shifted nervously within his sleeping bag and considered making a fire, then discarded the thought. The last thing he needed was for someone to get curious about a camper's fire and come snooping around.

Another series of yips told him that the coyotes were on the move now, running in the opposite direction to his camp. With a sigh of satisfaction, he crossed his hands across his chest, then patted the gun lying on his belly one last time before falling asleep.

*Southern Italy—3:00 a.m.*

Three men moved across the small town square, taking care to stay in the shadows. This wasn't the first time they'd set out to steal, but it was the first time they had agreed to rob God. Although the night was cool, a small man called Paulo was sweating profusely. He imagined the Devil's hand tightening around his throat with every step that took them closer to the small village church.

"We will die for this sin," he murmured.

Antonio, who was the eldest and the leader of the group, turned quickly and shoved Paulo roughly against the wall.

"Silence," he hissed.

Francesco, who was Paulo's cousin, tended to agree with his kin, but he was afraid of Antonio and rarely argued.

Hoping to soothe his cousin's fears, Francesco gave Paulo a wink.

"Think of the money we are going to make on this one job. It's more than we made all last year."

But Paulo would not be appeased.

"Dead men have no need for money," he said.

Antonio glared at the pair. "Then get out! I will do this job myself. *I* have no need for cowards."

Neither one of them had the gumption to anger a man who had killed his own father, and so Francesco smiled, trying to ease the tension.

"Paulo will be fine, my friend, have no fear."

"I'm not the one who's afraid," Antonio said. "So do we go?"

Reluctantly, the other two nodded, then followed him into the church. The massive double doors squeaked on ancient hinges as Antonio pushed them inward. Paulo flinched, then stopped just inside the doorway, again overwhelmed by the impact of what they were about to do.

"Quickly, quickly," Antonio muttered, and shoved them forward.

Paulo genuflected in the aisle and muttered a prayer for forgiveness before moving toward a faint glow of light above the altar at the front of the church.

"There it is," Antonio said. "Francesco, you've got the glass cutter. Paulo, you help him. I'll keep watch. And if you don't want a dead priest on your conscience, too, then get busy."

Paulo crossed himself one more time, muttering as he followed his cousin up a series of steps toward what appeared to be an oblong box made almost entirely of glass. The dimensions were about two feet wide, no more than four feet long and two feet deep. A niche had been chiseled out of the thick stone walls where the glass box now lay. Francesco leaned forward, peering intently at the brass plaque mounted beneath.

St. Bartholomew 1705–1735

A shiver of foreboding ran up Francesco's spine, but he shook it off, blaming it on Paulo's ridiculous predictions. They weren't going to be cursed for stealing a few old bones any more than they would be cursed for the sins they'd already committed.

"Help me," he ordered, and together they pulled the glass coffin from the niche, then set it on the floor.

"Hold this," Francesco said, and handed him a flashlight.

Paulo's hands were shaking as he took the light, but when it flashed on the ancient and yellowing skull within, his stomach lurched.

"Holy Mary, Mother of God, forgive me for this sin."

Seconds later, the faint sound of metal against glass could be heard as Francesco carefully cut out a panel on the backside of the coffin.

One minute passed, then another and another. Despite the coolness of the evening, sweat dripped from Francesco's forehead onto the glass. Paulo's hands were shaking so hard that he once almost dropped the flashlight. It had taken a sharp word from Antonio and a slap on the head before he had regained his equilibrium.

Suddenly Francesco rocked back on his heels, holding a long, slim panel of the old handmade glass.

"I'm in," he whispered.

Antonio spun, his eyes glittering eagerly as he took the glass from Francesco's hands and carefully laid it on the altar. Then he pulled a cloth sack from inside his jacket and thrust it in Francesco's face.

"Here. You know what we came for. Take it now."

Francesco stared down into the small casket, eyeing the fragile bones. He knew people who prayed to this saint for healing—and he knew people who had been healed. He couldn't bring himself to actually desecrate something that holy—not even for a whole lot of money.

"I can't," he whispered, and handed the sack back to Antonio.

Antonio cursed and shoved both men aside as he dropped to his knees.

''The light,'' he whispered. ''Hold the light so that I may see.''

Paulo angled the beam of the flashlight down into the casket, highlighting all that was left of the small man of God.

Antonio thrust his hand through the opening that Francesco had cut, fingering the bones as if they were sticks of wood from which to choose. Finally he settled on two of them, one a small bone from the lower part of the arm and another that had a minute bit of leatherlike tissue still adhering to a joint.

He pulled them out and thrust them into the sack, then stood abruptly.

''Do you have the glue?'' he asked.

Francesco nodded.

''Then replace the glass and put the box back in place. We've been here too long.''

Francesco's expression was anxious as he went about the task of doing what he'd been told.

''This patch will show,'' he said.

Antonio sneered. ''But not easily, and by the time someone discovers what has happened, we'll be long gone.''

Within minutes, the earthly remains of St. Bartholomew, minus a bone or two, were back in the niche. The trio slipped out of the church and back into the streets with no one the wiser—except God. Hastily, they made for the edge of the village, and when they could no longer see the rooftops, Antonio did a little dance in the middle of the road.

"We did it!" he crowed. "We're going to be rich!"

"We're going to die," Paulo moaned.

"When do we get our money?" Francesco asked.

Antonio smiled, his teeth gleaming brightly in the moonlight.

"We take the left fork in the road and follow the path up to Grimaldi's meadow. He will be waiting."

"Who's he?" Francesco asked.

Antonio shrugged. "I don't know his name… only that he pays well for goods received."

"How much is he paying us?" Francesco asked.

Antonio smiled. "We each get five thousand American dollars."

The amount was staggering for men who had no vocation and who lived by their wits and their lies. Still, Francesco worried.

"You've done business with him before?"

Antonio hesitated. "No, but I can tell these things. He has fine clothes and manicured hands. Men like that have no need to lie."

Paulo snorted beneath his breath, convinced that his life was over. Clean men were killers, too, but he had no intention of voicing his thoughts. If he hadn't been so certain that fate would catch up with him wherever he went, he would have walked away right then. But he had no wish to die alone, and so he followed the other two men to the meeting place.

Before they had time to catch their breaths, a man stepped out from behind a rock. Paulo gasped and stumbled as Francesco stopped short, but Antonio swaggered up to meet him.

"You have it?" the man asked.

Antonio smiled and held up the sack. "We kept our end of the bargain. Do you have the money?"

"I will see the merchandise first," the man said.

"And I the money," Antonio retorted.

The man set down a satchel, then opened it, revealing three substantial bundles of American twenty-dollar bills.

Antonio handed over the sack and then went down on his knees, laughing as he thrust his hands into the satchel and pulled out the cash.

"See?" he cried. "See, I told you. We're rich. We're rich!"

Francesco grinned at his cousin and then dropped to his knees as greed overtook shame.

But Paulo couldn't bring himself to touch the money any more than he would have touched the bones of the saint, and because of his hesitation, he was the first to see the man pull a weapon.

"He has a gun!" he cried.

And because of his diligence, he was the first to be shot. He hit the ground with a thud as a sharp, burning pain began to spread within his belly.

The man fired twice again in rapid succession, killing both Antonio and Francesco before they could look up. He grabbed the money-filled satchel, scattered a few cheap pieces of jewelry upon the ground, as well as a handful of rare coins he'd stolen last week in Cannes. Then he took another gun from his coat and fired it into the air before laying it down on the ground beside the men. He knew their reputation. When their bodies were found, it would be assumed that they'd fought over stolen property and killed each other in a fight. Without looking back, he disappeared into the night.

Paulo clutched at his belly with both hands, trying to hold back the flow of blood, but there was too much, and he was becoming too weak. What was left of Francesco's face was on the ground near his shoe, and the back of Antonio's head was completely gone. His one regret was that both men were no longer alive to see that his prediction had come true.

His voice was weakening, his breath almost gone. But he said it again, if for no one else's benefit but his own.

"See...I told you we were going to die."

Despite all the wrongs that he'd done, Paulo had always been a man of his word.

By the time their bodies were discovered two days later, the killer's payoff was in a numbered account in a prestigious Swiss bank and the goods were en route to the buyer.

Jack woke with a start, momentarily confused by the unfamiliarity of the room. Then he saw the dirty dishes on the tray by the door and remembered the nighttime meal he'd almost shared with Isabella Abbott. He couldn't quit thinking about how sad she'd been, and how beautiful her face was. Shaking off the feeling of miasma, he reminded himself that personal feelings had no place in his line of work. He couldn't afford to feel empathy for someone he was investigating. He only dealt in facts.

As the blessed quiet of the old house permeated the room, he ran through a mental checklist of all the things he needed to do today. First on the list was checking in with the director to let him know he had arrived. With a reluctant groan, he threw back the covers and got up. A few minutes later, freshly showered and half-dressed, he sat down on the side of the bed and reached for his cell phone. With the punch of a few numbers, he was connected.

"Sir…it's Dolan. I'm on the scene."

"Fine. Remember, I want this played loose and easy. It's entirely possible that no one there knew a thing about the old man's background. If that's so, then his reasons for deceit have died with him."

Jack sighed. "Yes, sir, I understand, but in our business, we've always got to look for conspiracy, right?"

"Do I detect a note of ambivalence?"

"Maybe. And maybe I'm just more tired than I thought."

"How are you healing?" he asked.

Jack flexed his stomach muscles, noting that each day brought a little more ease.

"Good. I rarely feel any pain."

"That's good. No need pushing yourself unnecessarily." Then he added, "As a matter of curiosity, what's your first impression?"

*Other than the fact that I almost let myself get infatuated with a ghost?* "Not much. I've only seen a desk clerk. Everyone else was at Frank Walton's funeral. I did meet the owner briefly last night, but I didn't have time to make any kind of connection."

"Did he say anything about Walton's death?"

"He is a she, and she referred to the old man as Uncle Frank. She also mentioned that her father had passed away less than two weeks ago, so she's pretty devastated. I didn't push."

"Hmm, that's quite a coincidence—two people living under the same roof and dying within weeks of each other. Check into the father's passing. Make sure it was from natural causes."

Jack's pulse kicked up a notch. "Do we have any reason to assume otherwise?"

"Company intelligence thinks we've got a visitor."

Jack stilled. "Soviet?"

"Yes."

"How long?"

"Two weeks, maybe more."

"Do we have any background on Walton or, I should say...Waller? What was his line of expertise? Was it nuclear...? Biological...? What in hell did that old man know that would still be of interest after all these years?"

"He was a doctor. If there was a special project, we know nothing about it."

"Yes, sir."

"Dolan."

"Sir?"

"Watch your back."

"Yes, sir."

The line went dead. Jack dropped the phone on

the bed and reached for his shirt. The leisurely week he'd been hoping for had just gone up in smoke.

Up one floor and at the far end of the hall, the uncles had gathered in David Schultz's room. Their demeanor was morose, reflecting their depression. Jasper Arnold scratched his bald head as he looked about the room.

"What about the clinic?" he asked.

"What about it?" Thomas countered.

"Samuel was the heart of it," he said. "David and I have wanted out for more than five years. The staff is well-trained. We've accomplished what we set out to do. I say let them have full authority and we officially retire."

Rufus Toombs smoothed his hands over his paunch, then laid his hands on his knees and leaned forward.

"Samuel had plans, remember? He swore he'd perfected the process even more than before. Things have already been set into motion."

Jasper waved away the comment. "Exactly my point. Samuel had plans...but Samuel is dead." He took out his handkerchief and mopped the nervous sweat from his brow. "I have plans, too, and they do not include being murdered."

David interrupted. "I think you're all overreacting."

Thomas Mowry had been listening quietly, but when he heard what sounded like derision in David's voice, he had to speak up.

"There are facts that cannot be ignored. Please.

We should concentrate on them and not run amok here, worrying unnecessarily and blaming each other for what is, ultimately, inevitable.''

"What are you talking about?" Jasper cried.

"Age has caught up with us," Thomas said. "And...quite possibly our pasts. We knew this could not go on forever. Besides, we have Isabella to consider and protect."

The other four looked at each other and then away, individually nodding or muttering.

"Yes, yes, Isabella," David said. "We have to think of our precious girl."

"Right," Thomas said.

For a moment there was silence, then Jasper asked, "So, what are we going to do about the last project? You know how high Samuel's hopes had been. He kept claiming to have corrected the final flaw in our earlier works."

Rufus sighed. "Speaking of the works...I have news."

The others grew silent, waiting, fearing, yet knowing that their sentence must be that they hear it, if for no other reason than the fact that they were the ones who had set it in motion.

"We have another self-destruct."

There was a collective sigh of frustration and regret that went up within the room and then, moments later, Thomas asked, "Who?"

"Norma Jean Bailey."

"The blonde?" Thomas asked.

Rufus nodded.

Thomas's voice began to shake. "I had such high

hopes for that one. She'd already done some modeling and had enrolled in acting school, remember?''

Each man there averted his eyes from the others, choosing instead to look away, as if afraid to see blame in the other men's eyes. David Schultz simply bowed his head and covered his face with his hands.

Thomas Mowry stood abruptly. ''This leaves only two of the original twenty alive. I find this an unacceptable reason to try once more.'' Then he strode to the window and stared out at the valley and White Mountain beyond.

John Michaels, who up until now had remained silent, cursed beneath his breath, then, oddly enough, began to cry.

The others said nothing. What could they say that hadn't been said before? Finally Jasper broke the silence.

''Does this mean we scrap Samuel's last project?''

''I say we take it to a vote,'' David said.

The five old men looked at each other. Finally they nodded in agreement.

''Then a vote it is,'' Jasper said, and picked up a pen and a pad of paper from beside the telephone. ''Yes means we give the project one last try. No means we quit. Now. With no regrets and no blame.''

''All right,'' they echoed, and then each wrote his decision on a piece of paper and tore it off before passing the pad and pen to the next man.

David took a small porcelain bowl from a bookshelf, folded the paper his vote was on and dropped it into the bowl before passing it around.

One by one, the men dropped in their votes. Jasper Arnold was the last. He dropped in his paper, then set the bowl aside as if it contained something foul.

"It's your bowl. You count them," John said, and handed the bowl to David.

David Schultz felt every one of his seventy-eight years as he moved to his desk with the bowl in his hands.

"Once the count is made, there is no going back. Understood?"

"Understood," they echoed.

He unfolded the first bit of paper.

"Yes. It reads yes."

He laid it aside and picked up the next, unfolding it with methodical precision.

"No."

He picked up the next and the next, until he had two votes for yes and two votes for no. The room was completely silent except for the occasional hiss of an indrawn breath and the faint scratchy sound of paper against paper.

"This is the last and deciding vote. Whatever it—"

"Just do it!" Jasper cried.

David nodded, then unfolded the paper. His nostrils flared. His expression went blank. He looked up.

The men held their breaths.

"Yes."

A collective sigh filled the room, part of it tinged with disbelief, part of it echoing the inevitability of what lay ahead.

"Then that's that," David said. "One more time."

"For Samuel," Jasper added.

"And for Frank," Rufus said.

They nodded, then stood. Without speaking, they left the apartment, adjourning to their own rooms to dress for breakfast. There was work to be done.

Isabella handed the room key to the couple who'd just checked in, directed them to the elevator, then watched them as they walked away. She didn't have to ask. She knew they were here for the clinic. There had been so many over the years that she'd come to recognize the quiet look of desperation they all wore. Saying a silent prayer for their success, she filed away their credit card information, then turned to answer the phone. As she did, she missed seeing Jack Dolan's descent down the stairs.

But he didn't miss her.

He'd heard her voice before he'd seen her, and despite his hunger for a hearty breakfast, he had to see her again—in broad daylight, when he could be absolutely certain she wasn't the ghost he'd first imagined her to be.

"Good morning."

Isabella turned around and found herself face-to-face with the man from the lobby last night. Her first impression was one of surprise. The night before, she'd been so wrapped up in her own grief that she'd failed to pay him much attention. To her, he'd just been a lost and hungry guest whom she'd fed and sent on his way. But now, with the early morning sunlight coming in through the mullioned windows over the entry doors, she had ample light by which to see. She took a deep breath. There was plenty to see.

He was tall—taller even than her Uncle David, who was six feet two inches. His hair was thick and straight, a warm, chocolate brown, and clipped very short. His eyes were blue, with a tendency to squint. She could tell by the tiny fans of wrinkles at the corners of both eyes. He had the physique of a runner—lean and fit, without a spare ounce of flesh. His shoulders were broad, as was the smile he gave her when he leaned across the desk.

"Good morning to you, too," Isabella said. "I trust you slept well after your midnight snack."

Jack's gaze swept the delicate curve of her cheek and neck, then back up to her face, looking for signs of exhaustion. They were still there, behind the smile.

"I think I slept better than you," he said. "Again, I'm very sorry for your loss."

The dull ache in her heart shifted slightly as his concern gave her momentary ease.

"Thank you." Then she changed the subject. "I'm guessing you're headed to breakfast. The dining room is across the lobby and to your left."

Realizing he'd been politely dismissed, he nodded his thanks and turned away from the desk just as an odd assortment of elderly gentlemen exited the elevator and headed for the desk.

"Isabella...darling...you have no business working like this so soon. Where is Delia?"

Isabella blew Thomas Mowry a kiss. "Good morning, Uncle Thomas, and quit fussing about me. She'll be here any moment, I'm sure."

Jack nodded politely as, one by one, the men gave him a studied look. These, he suspected, would be the men she referred to as her uncles.

"Good morning, gentlemen," Jack said.

They nodded and smiled, but Jack could tell they were only being polite.

"I'm Jack Dolan," he said, and held out his hand to the nearest man.

David Schultz hesitated, but only briefly, then accepted Jack's offered hand.

"Dr. David Schultz," he said. "The gentleman to my right is Dr. Jasper Arnold, then Rufus Toombs, John Michaels, and the last one on my right is Thomas Mowry. We are Isabella's uncles. Are you visiting family in the area?"

"Nope," Jack said. "All my family is still in Louisiana. I'm in the area gathering some research for a book."

John Michaels clapped his hands in delight.

"A writer! I always wanted to write, didn't I, Thomas?"

Thomas Mowry shifted his glasses to a more comfortable position on his bulbous nose as he gave Jack a closer look.

"So you're a writer, are you? Are you published?"

"Not yet."

"Ah...I see."

Jack felt a little like he used to feel when his father would look at his report card. The disappointment was always there, even though he had tried hard not to show it.

"So, Mr. Dolan...what did you do before you decided to become a writer? For a living, I mean."

Jack grinned. "The same thing I'm still doing. I run a computer software business in Washington, D.C."

"Enough," Isabella announced. "I'm sorry, Mr. Dolan. I assure you we do not require our guests to undergo such rigorous questioning. Delia is just pulling into the parking lot, so won't you join us for breakfast? I can promise there will be no more questions."

Jack shrugged off her apology by offering her his elbow.

"I'll willingly be grilled any time by an entire room full of uncles just to eat a meal with you."

Isabella hesitated. His gallantry was unexpected, but not unappealing. She glanced at her uncles, who seemed to be waiting for her decision. She surprised them and herself as she came out from behind the desk and slipped her hand beneath Jack's elbow.

There was a faint tremble in her voice, but her gaze was steady. "My father always escorted me to the dining room."

Jack gave her hand a quick squeeze of understanding, then looked at the five staring men.

"Gentlemen...won't you join us?"

It was well that he'd asked, because they wouldn't have let her get away with such a good-looking stranger.

# 5

Leonardo Silvia stood stoically behind his wife, Maria, as the doctor gave them the news. It wasn't as if it was the first time they'd heard the words, but the heartbreak was still the same.

"I'm sorry, Mrs. Silvia, but the procedure did not work. You're not pregnant, and frankly, I can't promise you'll ever be. There are too many factors against it."

Maria Silvia bore the news without blame, but in truth, she was angry—angry at God for denying them the only thing she had ever truly prayed for. Oh, she'd said plenty of prayers in the past, and for lots of trivial things, like praying that Leonardo would get a raise at his job, and praying for forgiveness for various and sundry things. But she'd never prayed from her soul the way she'd prayed for a child, and she'd been praying faithfully for more than five years. Her shoulders slumped momentarily, and then she lifted her chin.

"Thank you for your time, Dr. Worth, but I am not ready to give up."

Dr. Worth sighed. In his thirty odd years of prac-

tice, he'd never seen a woman so determined. No
matter how many times she'd been disappointed, he
had yet to see her break down or cast blame. He
looked from Leonardo to Maria and then back
again, tapping his pen against his desk as he debated
with himself about giving them any kind of false
hope. Still, as a doctor, he considered it his obli-
gation to tell them everything he knew.

"While I am certain that I cannot do anything
more for you than I've already done, there is a place
that has a good record for helping couples like you.
However...I'm not certain of the costs, so it might
be beyond what you could manage."

Leonardo saw the momentary flare of hope on
Maria's face. It was all he needed to see. He laid
his hand on Maria's shoulder and gave her a gentle
squeeze.

"It cannot hurt to inquire, Dr. Worth. If it is beyond our means, then we will decide. We've come
this far. I see no reason not to pursue all our options."

Maria's eyes welled with unshed tears, but her
voice was strong as she met the doctor's gaze.

"This place...where is it located?"

Worth sighed. "Montana."

Leonardo's eyes widened. "So far?"

The doctor nodded. "I know it's a very long way
from Queens, New York, to Braden, Montana, but
if you two are still in the market to take a gamble,

you might just take yourselves on a little trip out West."

"Do we need to be referred?" Maria asked.

"I don't know, but I will be more than happy to call and make the appointment for you. Just let my nurse know when you would be available to travel. Oh, and just so you know...I'd make arrangements to be gone at least a couple of weeks, possibly more. There will be the inevitable tests to be run."

Maria Silvia stood abruptly, clutching her purse against her barren belly, then looked at Leonardo. He smiled and cupped the side of her face. It was all she needed to see. She turned back to the doctor, her voice filled with determination.

"We will call your office tomorrow," she said.

"Fine. As soon as I know your schedule, I can make the call."

Leonardo shook the doctor's hand. "Thank you, Dr. Worth."

"Don't thank me yet," he said. "I haven't done a thing."

Leonardo smiled. "That's not true. You've given us another day of hope."

The next day was Sunday. Leonardo had to work, but Maria was up at the crack of dawn with him, fixing her hair and ironing her best dress.

"What are you doing, Maria *mia?* Going to your momma's for dinner?"

She shook her head. "No. I am going to church."

"But we went to mass last night," Leonardo said.

Maria nodded as she hung the freshly ironed dress on a hanger and unplugged the iron.

"Yes, I know, but I'm going again this morning. There is something I need to tell God."

Leonard sighed and took his wife in his arms.

"Maria...we have already prayed to be led to make the right decision regarding the fertility clinic and also to accept whatever comes. Don't you think God already got the message?"

Her lips firmed as she turned to the dresser in search of her slip.

"Yes, I know He hears," she said, and took a slip from the drawer and pulled it over her head. "But there's something I forgot to tell Him."

Leonard smiled to himself, watching as his wife disappeared into their closet in search of some shoes. Maria talked to God on a regular basis in the same manner as they were talking now. The only difference was, she didn't actually hear His answers. Those had to be deciphered through the events in their lives.

"So, what is the big thing you forgot to mention?" he asked.

She came out of the closet clutching a pair of black leather heels, then leaned over and put them on, holding on to the doorknob to steady herself as she did. When she was shod, she straightened and fixed her husband with a straightforward look.

"I forgot to tell Him that if He will give us a child, the child will be raised as one of His own."

Leonardo's heart skipped a beat. "What are you saying?"

Maria shrugged. "It's simple. Boy or girl... whichever we are blessed to received...we will raise the child for a lifetime of service to God."

Leonardo paled. "Maria! You do not make bargains with God! Besides...what if we do have a child? What makes you think that the child will want to give up a life like ours for the service of others? That means no spouse, no children, no choice other than sacrifice and service to others."

Maria's lips firmed as she reached for the dress.

"I do not bargain with God. I only make promises, and this is mine. Say what you will, Leonardo, but in my eyes, it is a small sacrifice that we make so I can carry your child next to my heart."

Leonardo wilted. As always, his love for his wife overcame whatever reservations he might have regarding this war she waged against her inability to conceive.

"Then so be it," he said softly.

The dress settled on her body, molding itself to her shape as she turned her back to him and lifted her hair.

"Will you zip me up, my love?"

Hiding his heartache, he reached for the zipper. "Of course, Maria *mia,* I'll do anything you ask."

*  *  *

Isabella looked at herself in the mirror, checking one last time to make sure her hair was okay. Satisfied that all was in order, she turned away, gazing instead at the five-room suite within Abbott House that was her home. The door to her father's bedroom was closed, as it had been since the day of his funeral. The last time she'd gone in there was to pick out clothes in which to bury him. She had yet to get up the nerve to go back. She sighed as she moved toward the library, reminding herself that there would be plenty of time later to decide what to do with his things.

Although the decor of the rooms was straight out of the twenties and thirties, she never thought to change it. She'd grown up with ornate fringed lamp shades, flocked wallpaper and Oriental rugs on shining hardwood floors. While she was a woman of the twenty-first century, she often felt more at ease with things from the past. The influences of her childhood had been strongly impacted by the seven men who had raised her. What was comfortable and familiar to them became so to her, as well. She'd grown up listening to big band music from the thirties and forties rather than the youthful music of her time. And while she'd excelled at her studies in school and had been a popular young girl, she'd never felt stifled or cheated by the lack of female companionship at home.

But now, things were changing. She could look into the future and know that within a few short years, there was every chance that she would be entirely alone. The emptiness of knowing she would never see her father's face again, never hear his laughter or groan at one of his silly old jokes, was heartbreaking. She wasn't over the shock of losing him and didn't even know how to begin grieving for Uncle Frank. She'd heard the maids talking about how brave she was and knew the people down in Braden looked at her in the same fashion. But they didn't know how scared she was, or that she lay awake at nights for the first time in her life, afraid of the future.

She knelt in front of the safe and dialed the combination, removed the deposit bag, then locked it again before rising. While she would have loved to wallow in misery for the rest of the day, there was too much to be done. Straightening the crease in her slacks, she headed for the door.

Morning sunlight coming through the windows above the hotel entrance left warm yellow patterns on the floor of the lobby, reminding her of the butter-colored squares from the old quilt on her father's bed. Someone had given it to him many years ago for helping them conceive their first child. Isabella had heard the story many times in her life but had never tired of it. Now there was no one left to retell the tale, and nothing to remind her but the quilt itself. Taking a deep shaky breath, she made herself focus on what she needed to do first, the deposit bag she was carrying uppermost in her mind.

She looked toward the desk and saw Delia in conversation with a rather bedraggled stranger. When Delia saw her, she quickly waved her over.

"You needed to see me?" Isabella asked.

"Miss Abbott, this gentleman is asking about work."

Isabella smiled politely as she turned her attention toward the man. She would guess his age was in the mid-sixties, with a good week's worth of whiskers and dust on his shoes. His clothes were sturdy, but not very clean, and there was a look in his eyes that told her he hadn't always been this way. When he met her gaze, he automatically straightened his shoulders and held his ground, as if expecting to be refused while he had yet to ask. Isabella held out her hand, waiting for the man to shake it. She could tell he was surprised by the gesture, but she'd learned long ago never to judge anyone by appearance alone.

"I'm Isabella Abbott."

The man hesitated, then wiped his hand on the side of his pants before taking what she offered.

"I am honored to meet you, Miss Abbott," he said. "My name is Victor Ross."

"What kind of work are you looking for?" she asked.

"I can do any kind of manual labor. I have no place to sleep, and I've run out of money. I'll do whatever you ask of me."

There was no real need for workers, but Isabella didn't have it in her to turn away a hungry man.

"Well, Mr. Ross, I don't need a regular groundskeeper, but there's about a week's worth of work that needs doing. I'm assuming you know how to use hedge clippers and a lawn mower?"

"I will do what needs doing," he repeated.

There was something about the way he spoke that seemed odd, an almost pedantic rhythm to the words that made her think English might not be his first language. But a good speaking voice was not a requirement for mowing the grass.

"Fine, then. How does eight dollars an hour, plus room and board, sound?"

The man's eyes widened as he did some quick mental calculations in his head, and then he nodded.

"All right," Isabella said. "Do you have any belongings?"

He ducked his head. "A small bag outside the door."

"Good. There is a building on the grounds out back. All the equipment you will need is inside, along with a small room and a shower. You will eat your meals in the kitchen with the rest of the staff."

Victor Ross looked at her then, judging the kindness in her eyes, and knew her to be a woman with a good heart.

"Thank you, Miss Abbott. I will not let you down."

Isabella smiled. "Put up your bag and then go

through the back entrance to the kitchen. You can start work after you've eaten. I'll tell the cook that you're coming.''

''Yes, miss. Thank you, miss,'' he said, and left before she could change her mind.

Delia frowned, angling her heavily painted eyebrows into puzzled arches as she looked at her employer.

''Miss Abbott, what are you going to tell Harve Mosely when he comes to mow next week?''

''Why don't you give him a call and tell him not to come until the week after next?''

Delia sighed. ''Yes, ma'am. You're too tenderhearted, you know.''

Isabella shrugged. ''Maybe so, but at least I'll sleep tonight knowing I didn't turn away a hungry man. Also, please call the kitchen and tell Sarah the man will be eating with them for the week. I'm going into town to the bank. I won't be long.''

''Yes, ma'am. Drive safe.''

''Thank you,'' Isabella said, and was out the door before anyone else could change her plans.

Vasili Rostov pushed his way inside the large metal shed and then stood in the doorway, watching the dust motes shifting in the morning sun. He shut the door behind him as he moved to the back of the building, in search of the place where, for the next few days, he would lay his weary head.

The door squeaked as he opened it. Inside was a

bed just big enough for one, as well as a bureau and a small table and lamp. Except for the lack of a television, it reminded him of his apartment in Leningrad. The comfort was small but welcome, and beat a bedroll and hard ground all to hell.

He tossed his bag on the bed, ignoring the dust he sent airborne, and headed back outside to the hotel kitchen. He hadn't had a hot meal since he'd gotten off the plane in Montana. At least now he was on the premises where Vaclav Waller had hidden himself for the last thirty years. There was plenty of time to figure out what his next move would be while he was mowing grass and clipping bushes.

Isabella was coming out of the bank when she heard someone calling her name. She stopped and turned, unaware of what a picture she made with the sun on her hair and a smile on her face.

Bobby Joe Cage knew a good thing when he saw it, and Isabella Abbott was definitely it. He, along with a good half dozen of Braden's finest young men, had been trying to make time with her for several years, but with little luck. However, with the passing of her father and then one of the old men she called uncle, he figured his chances had just increased. He came across the street at a lope, counting on his good looks to make up for his lack of a job and money.

He took off his Stetson, aware that the sunshine

made his blond hair turn gold, and flashed what he hoped was a sympathetic smile.

"Isabella...I'm so glad I saw you. I've been meaning to come out to Abbott House and pay my respects, but I didn't want to intrude on your mourning."

"Why, thank you," she said. "I haven't seen you in months. Have you been out of town?"

He'd been shacked up with a showgirl from Las Vegas, which hadn't worked out, but he had no intention of telling her that.

"Yes, and I only just heard about your losses after I got home yesterday. I can't tell you how sorry I am. Your father was a real good doctor. If it hadn't been for him, my sister, Lucy, and her husband wouldn't have been able to have a baby."

It wasn't anything she didn't already know, but hearing praise for her father's dedication to his work made her feel good.

"Thank you for saying that," she said. "Right now, it means a lot to hear anything positive. It's been a very rough two weeks."

Bobby Joe frowned. "Yeah, I heard about old man Walton getting murdered in New York. That's a bad place. I sure wouldn't want to be there."

Ignoring the less than respectful manner in which Bobby Joe had referred to Uncle Frank, she nodded, then shifted her purse to her other shoulder.

"I have one more errand to run before I get back

to the hotel, so I'd better be going," she said. "It was good to see you. Tell your parents I said hello."

Bobby Joe grabbed her arm. "Wait!"

She winced from the pressure of his fingers and then slid out of his grasp.

"Sorry," Bobby Joe said. "I just...well, I thought we might—"

Suddenly aware of where the conversation was heading, Isabella interrupted.

"Bobby Joe, right now I'm not up to anything social, but thank you for asking."

Resisting the urge to run, she turned and headed for the post office. Her skin was still crawling, even after she was inside and standing in line. Something about Bobby Joe's behavior had made her very uncomfortable, which made no sense. She'd known him all her life.

While she was waiting to purchase her stamps, Bobby Joe was still working his angle. He watched until she went into the post office, then ducked between her car and the pickup truck parked beside it. After one quick look to make sure no one was watching, he pulled out his knife and squatted beside the back of her car. Without hesitation, he plunged the knife into the rear tire, then stood abruptly, pretending that he'd just picked up something that he'd dropped. After one quick look around to make sure he hadn't been seen, he stepped up onto the sidewalk and walked up the street. The tire would go flat before she got home, giving him the opportunity for one more go at her. Maybe she would be more sympathetic to his request for a date after he'd come to her rescue.

Jack Dolan was standing in the barber shop and looking out the window when he saw Isabella exit the bank. He thought about stepping outside to say hello when a man hailed her from across the street. Curious, he watched as the man ran to meet her, wondering how she would greet him. The thought that he was setting himself up to watch her be hugged, maybe even kissed, was oddly disconcerting. That bothered him more than a little. He shouldn't give a damn about her personal life.

However, when the man pulled off his hat and flashed her a smile, Jack took an instant dislike to him.

Their conversation was brief, which was somewhat reassuring, but when Isabella turned to walk away and the man yanked at her arm, he had an urge to intervene. Before he could react, though, Isabella had made her excuses and disappeared.

Jack's eyes narrowed as the man's face took on a surly expression. Jack was smiling to himself, thinking that Isabella had obviously turned him down, and then realized the scenario wasn't over. He saw the big cowboy move toward Isabella's car, recognized the furtiveness with which he was moving, and wondered what he was going to do next. But when he saw him pull something out of his pocket and then drop down, he suspected the man was up to no good.

"Hey, mister. You still want that haircut?" the barber asked.

Jack hesitated, then shook his head. "I just remembered something I need to do," he said. "I'll catch you tomorrow, okay?"

"Sure thing," the barber said, and motioned to the next man in line.

The man was gone when Jack came out of the barber shop. He stood for a moment, undecided as to what to do next. He raced across the street to the photography shop and picked up the film he'd left to be developed. Taking pictures of the area was part of his cover, and he wasn't ready to blow everything yet. Then he headed up the street to where he'd parked his car. He didn't know what was going to happen, but whatever it was, he wasn't going to be far behind.

When Isabella came out of the post office with her stamps, it was close to eleven. Plenty of time to get home and help set the tables for any customers who might come for an early lunch. While few of the locals ever stayed at the hotel, many of them came to eat. Except for a couple of small cafés and one aging Dairy Queen, it was the only place in the area that served food to the public.

As she drove out of town, she couldn't help but wish her father was by her side. He had always loved the Montana autumns, and although it was only the tenth of September, the nights were already quite cool and the aspens were beginning to turn. Soon their leaves would be a bright splash of yellow against the dark green pines. Snow would appear on the mountain tops, and sunrise would reveal the vast rolling meadows at the foothills to be bright with frost.

Overhead, she saw the great wingspan of an eagle riding the air currents in search of food, and in the distance off to her right she could see a herd of elk grazing at the edge of a clearing. She took a deep breath and then exhaled slowly, savoring the sense of peace she felt at knowing this was where she belonged.

She was more than halfway home when she began to realize it was becoming difficult to hold the car on the road. Nervously, she braked and pulled over to the shoulder, getting out in time to see the left rear tire going flat.

"Oh great," she muttered, and kicked at the tire in frustration.

She knew how to change it, but it wasn't her favorite thing to do. With a muffled curse, she opened the trunk and began removing the jack and the undersized spare. This would mean a trip back to town just to get the tire fixed. Tossing her navy blue jacket inside the car, she rolled up the sleeves of her shirt and grabbed the tire iron. First she would loosen the lug nuts, then she would jack up the car.

She thought about calling Delia just to let her know what had happened and then changed her mind. If she did, Delia would surely tell the uncles, and then they would all show up, taking charge and setting her off to one side, which made no sense. She was definitely younger and stronger than any of them, except possibly her Uncle David, who still presented a commanding figure.

With no more than two lugs nuts loose, she heard the sound of an approaching car. Glad to know help was arriving, her relief shifted slightly when she saw who it was.

Bobby Joe Cage emerged from his truck with a smile and a swagger.

"Hey, honey…looks like you've had a bit of bad luck."

Isabella stood. "Yes, I did."

He took the tire iron from her hand. "Let me have that thing. You got no business trying to change a flat. That's a man's work."

Despite his chauvinistic attitude, she was glad for his help and handed him the tool, standing back as he squatted down beside the flat and finished what she'd set out to do.

Within the space of five minutes, he had the tire off, the temporary spare on, and was loading the flat and the jack back into the trunk.

"There you go," he said lightly, dusting his hands on the seat of his jeans, and flashing her a wide, engaging smile.

Isabella started toward her car to get her purse. "Thank you so much for your help, Bobby Joe. I really appreciate it, and I'd be happy to pay you for your trouble."

He sauntered up beside her, and then, before she knew what was happening, he had her pinned against her own car. He slid a hand up beneath the fall of her hair and tilted her head just a touch.

"The only payment I need is your sweet kiss," he said softly, and lowered his head.

Shock coupled with anger as Isabella thrust her hands between them, shoving hard against his chest.

"Don't, Bobby Joe! I told you before, I'm not in the mood for—"

He grabbed both her hands and quickly pinned them behind her, still smiling, still coming closer.

"Sure you are, honey. You just don't know it yet. Trust me. I can make you feel better."

Isabella's heart skipped a beat. Bobby Joe wasn't stopping, and he wasn't taking no for an answer. She twisted within his grasp, trying to pull herself free, but was unable to push him away.

"Please, Bobby Joe...I thought you were a friend. Don't to this to—"

"Honey, I haven't done anything yet," he whispered, then ground his pelvis against her belly and crushed his lips to hers.

Stunned by his behavior, she struggled to get free, but his grip was firm, and the weight of his body kept her practically immobile. A spurt of fear, coupled with the sudden taste of blood in her mouth, made her moan.

Bobby Joe took it as a sign of passion and reached for her breast.

One moment he was all over her, and the next thing she knew he was in the dirt and Jack Dolan was standing over him.

Blood spurted from between Bobby Joe's fingers as he held them to his face.

"Ju bwoke by dose."

"Then I'd better try that again," Jack growled. "Because I was aiming for your neck."

Isabella rushed between them and grabbed Jack's arm. "Jack, wait! It's all right. He didn't really hurt me."

Jack turned, unaware that the expression on his face had gone cold or that his nostrils were flared with anger. All he wanted to do was hurt the man the way he'd hurt Isabella. His gaze raked her face, then settled on her mouth. A drop of blood was oozing from her lower lip. The sight of it made him sick to his stomach. If he hadn't intentionally stayed so far behind, this could have been prevented.

Bobby Joe began shuffling in the dirt, trying to get to his feet. Jack heard him and turned. All he did was point, but it was enough to keep Bobby Joe on his butt. He turned back to Isabella and took a handkerchief from his pocket, then dabbed at the bruise on her lip. When she winced, he felt the pain all the way to his toes.

"I'm sorry," he said quietly. "Your lip is bleeding."

She blushed and looked away, embarrassed by the whole disgusting episode.

"His teeth, I think...they cut my lip when he tried to—"

"He set you up," Jack said.

Her eyes widened. "No. I had a flat. He stopped to help and—"

"I watched him from the barber shop. I didn't know exactly what he'd done until now, but he did something to your tire. Where is it?"

Isabella pointed to the trunk.

Jack gave Bobby Joe a hard look and then strode to the trunk. Within seconds, he found what he'd been looking for.

"It's been cut."

Isabella gasped and pushed past Jack to confront the bleeding man on the ground.

"Is that true?" she asked.

Bobby Joe moaned. "I din't mean ta hurt...jus' wanna' to—"

"Shut up," Jack said. "It was pretty damned evident what you wanted. However, I'm going to tell you what you're going to get. What you did to her tire could have caused an accident. You can tell the rest of your excuses to the police."

Isabella groaned beneath her breath. The incident was getting uglier by the minute, and if this got out, the repercussions from the community would be humiliating, to say the least.

"No," she begged. "Let him go."

Jack pivoted angrily. "He could have killed you."

She glared at Bobby Joe, who was staring at the dirt.

"He's not a killer. Just stupid. Let him go, Jack. I want this over."

Her lips were trembling, as was her voice. The plea in her gaze was as fervent as her words had been. Despite his better judgment, he finally nodded, then turned and kicked the bottom of Bobby Joe's boot.

"Get up, you sorry bastard, and if you ever come near Miss Abbott again, I'll find out. And when I do, I'll make you sorry. Do you understand me?"

Bobby Joe was on his feet, a handkerchief pressed to his nose as he ran for his truck. He paused at the door, then looked back.

"I'b really sorry, Isabella. Din't mean to—"

"Get going," Jack said.

Bobby Joe jumped into his truck and sped away without looking back.

Jack turned around to find Isabella sitting on the ground, her head between her knees. Her shoulders were shaking, and he suspected she was crying.

"Well, damn," he muttered, and pulled her to her feet, then put his arms around her. Half expecting her to argue about the familiarity with which he was holding her, he was surprised when she wilted against him. "Don't cry, Isabella. It's over, okay?"

"It'll never be over," she said, and then began to cry in earnest.

Jack held her, knowing that her tears had nothing to do with what Bobby Joe had done. It was just the final straw in a life turned upside down.

# 6

It took all Jack had to let Isabella go.

"Get in my car. I'll take you home."

Tears were still welling as she turned away in confusion.

"But my car...I can't just—"

"We'll deal with it later. Right now you just need to go home."

The urge to crawl into bed and pull the covers over her head was strong, but if she did, she was afraid she would never come out.

"I'll be fine," she said. "It was no big deal."

"Then why are you still shaking?" Jack asked.

Isabella frowned. "Okay. Fine. Yes, it rattled me, but I'm a big girl. I can take care of myself."

Her lip was swelling as they stood there arguing, and the sight of it did things to Jack's head that didn't bear investigating.

"Miss Abbott, I have absolutely no doubt that what you're telling me is true. But chalk it up to an overdose of macho or manners or whatever you choose to call it, I'm still taking you home whether you like it or not."

Suddenly Isabella's resistance was gone. All she could do was drop her head and nod.

He took her by the elbow and led her to his car. Wordlessly, she slid into the seat, then leaned back and closed her eyes. The scent of peppermint and something woodsy drifted past her nose, but it disappeared when Jack got in, started the car and turned on the air conditioner.

"Buckle up," he said quietly.

She did as he asked, then tunneled her fingers through her hair in frustration.

"I can't believe I let that get so out of hand."

Jack glanced at her as he pulled around her car and headed for the hotel.

"That man who cut your tire...you known him long?"

"All my life."

"Have you two ever dated?"

She snorted lightly beneath her breath. "No. I've never been that desperate."

Jack savored the news while stifling a grin. "Since we're being a little personal here, I can't help but wonder why a woman like you hasn't married."

Isabella turned to look at him, absently noting that his profile was as hard and unforgiving as the surrounding mountains.

"Exactly what is a woman like me?" she asked, and then thought she saw a flash of color on his cheeks.

"You have to know how beautiful you are," Jack said, and then tapped the brakes as a deer bounded across the road.

"Local hazard," Isabella said, then added, "And thank you for the compliment."

Jack nodded. "You're welcome. So...why aren't you married?"

She smiled. "You're persistent, aren't you?"

"It goes with the job," he said without thinking, then silently cursed his stupidity. He'd been thinking about being a Federal agent when he'd said that.

"Yes, I suppose writers do have to be more persistent than most."

"Right," he said, and relaxed slightly, reminding himself to be more careful about what he said, then added, "But you still haven't answered me."

Isabella laughed out loud and then winced.

"Ouch," she mumbled, and pressed her fingers against the cut on her lip. "Lord! The uncles are going to have a fit."

"As they should," Jack said.

Isabella grinned. "My hero," she said, and this time she knew she saw him blush. "I'm not married because I've never been in love, and I happen to believe that the two go hand in hand."

"Never?"

"Except for Phillip Hanson."

Even before he asked, Jack decided he didn't like Phillip Hanson.

"Who's he?"

"The boy who sat in front of me in second grade. He gave me bubble gum every day for two weeks. I was in love right up until the day Margaret Bailey moved to town. After that, he started giving her what I considered to be my gum, and we fell out of love as quickly as we'd started."

This time Jack was the one who laughed. "It was his loss."

Isabella sighed as she clasped her hands together in her lap. The ugliness of what had transpired was fading, and it was all due to Jack Dolan's kindness.

"Jack?"

"Yes?"

"Thank you."

He frowned. "If I'd been quicker, it wouldn't have happened."

"No, not for that," she said. "For making me laugh."

A wry grin tilted one corner of his mouth.

"You're welcome."

"We're almost there," Isabella said, pointing toward the windshield.

Jack looked past the road to the looming mountain beyond the hotel.

"That's quite a backdrop," he said.

"What? White Mountain?"

He nodded.

Her gaze slid from the three-story hotel in the distance to the massive shift of rock beyond it, and she suddenly shuddered. "Yes, magnificent, isn't it?

Although when I was a child, it gave me the creeps.''

It was the last thing Jack would have expected her to say.

"Why?"

"No good reason," she said, and then shrugged off the chill she'd gotten as she'd looked up toward the craggy peak. "I used to imagine that something wicked lived on the mountain."

"And now?"

"Now I know that wickedness can be anywhere. Let's just say I've learned to adjust."

Jack knew she was referring in part to Frank Walton's murder. It was the opportune time to throw in a few questions.

"You're talking about your uncle's murder, aren't you?"

She hesitated for a moment, then nodded. "I guess I am."

"Was he on vacation?"

She frowned. "I think so. It was all so sudden. One day he just up and announced at the breakfast table that he was going on a trip. Uncle Rufus offered to go with him, but Uncle Frank turned him down. Said he had to go by himself."

"Where did he go?" Jack asked, although he already knew where Frank Walton had been killed.

"We found out later. New York City...actually, a place called Brighton Beach. I suppose he had business there, but I can't imagine what it would have been. He was a retired botanist, you know.''

"No, I didn't know," Jack said. *So she didn't know about his background—or, if she did, she isn't telling.* "I understand he wasn't really related to you."

Her shoulders slumped. "None of the uncles are. My only living relative was my father."

"Interesting, though, how they all consider you their family," Jack said. "I guess they got to know you when they moved here."

Isabella shook her head. "They're part of my earliest memories," she said. "In fact, they were here before me."

"Really?" Jack said. "They must have been fairly young men then, at least in their forties. It's odd that they would all wind up here, practicing their respective professions, isn't it?''

Isabella frowned. It *was* odd, but these were things she had never really considered.

"I suppose," she muttered, then undid her seat belt as Jack pulled to a stop and parked. "Now to face the music."

"But not alone," Jack said, and got out of the car to open the door for her.

*Not alone.* Isabella shivered as she watched Jack Dolan circle the car to help her out. When he slid a hand beneath her elbow, her heart gave a funny jerk and then settled.

They made it into the lobby and past the front

desk; then David Schultz came into the lobby from the veranda and waved. It wasn't until he got closer that he realized something was wrong.

"You've been crying," he said, and gave Jack a hard look.

"It wasn't his fault," Isabella said. "So wipe that glare off your face."

The old man cupped the side of her face, and when he saw her cut and swelling lip, he gasped.

"Isabella! Darling! What happened to you?"

"Oh...it wasn't such a big deal. I just—"

Jack interrupted. "Some local jerk tried to get more from her than she was willing to give."

Despite his years, at that moment David Schultz looked positively deadly.

"Who?" he asked, his voice hard and flat.

Isabella sighed. "Bobby Joe Cage. I had a flat, and he stopped to help me fix it, and then—"

Jack interrupted again, his nostrils flaring angrily. "Damn it, Isabella, quit making excuses for the son of a bitch. He cut the tire to make sure it went flat."

Then he turned to David, making sure that they knew how close she'd come to a possible rape.

"He saw her in town and set her up for his own little party. It was just luck that I saw him messing with her car. I got suspicious and followed, but I wasn't quite fast enough to keep her from getting hurt."

The old man's shoulders slumped. If Samuel had still been alive, it never would have happened. People had too much respect for him ever to do something like that to his daughter. But Samuel was gone, and it was now up to them to make sure Isabella was protected. He straightened slowly, thrusting his chin forward as he embraced Isabella.

"I'm terribly sorry this happened to you, dear, but rest assured that it won't happen again."

Isabella wanted to cry all over again, but not because of what had happened to her. As she rested her cheek against her Uncle David's chest, the unsteady rhythm of his heart was an all too vivid reminder of his waning years. She shook her head and looked up at him.

"No, Uncle David. It's over, and that's that." Then she glanced at Jack and smiled. "Besides, Mr. Dolan has already exacted retribution."

David looked at Jack, suddenly aware that there was more to the story than had yet been told.

"Like what?"

Jack shrugged. "I guess I broke his nose."

David Schultz grinned and then thumped Jack on the back. "Well done, young man. On behalf of the uncles, I thank you."

Jack nodded shortly. "Her car is still on the road. The spare is on, but she needs a new tire."

"Jasper and I will tend to it immediately," David said. "All I need is the keys."

Isabella dug them out of her purse and handed them over.

"Just charge the tire, Uncle David, and tell them to send me the bill."

"I'll do no such thing," David said. "I'm sending the bill to Lawton Cage. It's his fault that boy is so wild and unruly. He can pay for this like he's paid for everything else that boy has done wrong."

Isabella sighed. There was no use arguing any further.

"Fine," she said. "But I'm serious when I tell you that I do not want this reported to the police. The less I have to deal with that man, the better off I'll be."

David nodded in agreement, then patted her on the head as if she were a child.

"You go to your room and lie down now, dear. We'll take care of everything."

Assuming that she would do as she'd been told, he left her standing in the lobby.

She looked at Jack. "I've just been sent to my room, haven't I?"

Jack wanted an excuse to touch her again, but that had come and gone out on the road by her car.

"It's not such a bad idea," he said. "First maybe put some ice on your lip before it swells any more."

"You're probably right," she said, and then glanced at her watch. "Although it's almost noon, and I usually help out in the dining room during the—"

"They'll manage. Besides, if you go in there with a fat lip, then you're going to have to explain what happened at least a dozen times before you're through.''

Isabella made a face. ''Ugh. You're right. I hadn't thought of that. Well, that settles it. I'm off to the kitchen for some ice and then into bed. At least for a while.''

''I'd be happy to get the ice for you if you want to—''

Isabella laid her hand on his arm. ''You've done enough for me for one day. I'll get my own ice. You go have some lunch. You've earned it.''

Jack shifted from one foot to the other, unable to think of a single reason to delay her exit any further.

''Yes...all right, I guess I am a little hungry.''

''Enjoy,'' Isabella said, and then squeezed his arm lightly before walking away.

Jack stood without moving, his gaze fixed on the confident set of her shoulders and the languid sway of her hips as she walked across the lobby. Only after he could no longer see her did he realize he'd been holding his breath. He exhaled slowly as his gaze moved from the doorway to the painting above the stairs.

The woman looked down at him, smiling slightly, as if she knew a secret she wouldn't tell. But there was no secret to what Jack was feeling. He was getting too interested in someone who was part of his investigation.

He started to go into the dining room, and then changed his mind and headed for the stairs instead.

He needed to wash up and change his shirt. He wasn't about to eat a meal with Bobby Joe Cage's blood on his sleeves.

Victor Ross was clipping the hedge at the front of the hotel when two of the old men came hurrying outside. Unwilling for them to see his face, he turned and ducked his head. But he caught just enough of their conversation to realize that Isabella Abbott had been involved in some upsetting incident. They were obviously off to right the wrong, and Isabella had taken to her bed.

His mind raced as he thought back over the morning. Earlier he'd seen one of the men, the one they called Thomas, leaving with a briefcase in his hand, and he still wasn't back. David Schultz and Jasper Arnold had just left the grounds, which meant that John Michaels and Rufus Toombs were the only two unaccounted for. He knew that the men occupied the entire upper floor of the hotel. It was the first time since his arrival that he'd been given an opportunity to search Frank Walton's room. He gave the hedge a few more quick snips, then hurried around to the back of the building. The fire escape was old but sturdy, and would serve his purpose nicely. He stored the tools he'd been using and then washed quickly, anxious to slip into the kitchen for his noon meal. It wouldn't take him long to see whether the other two men showed up to eat. If they did, he would have the upper story of Abbott House to himself for at least thirty minutes, and that was all he would need. If there was anything of interest to his government in Frank Walton's room, it wouldn't take him long to find it. If he came up empty-handed, he was going to contact his superiors, tell them that the old man was dead and buried, and call it quits. He missed his bed and his friends, and was willing to admit he was too old for this spy stuff after all. Besides, what could one old man possibly have known that would be of any interest to his country now?

It had been easier than Vasili Rostov expected. He'd seen the two remaining residents of the third floor enter the dining room and take their seats at a table with several other diners. After placing their orders, they quickly engaged in conversation, assuring him that, for the time being, the top floor of Abbott House was unoccupied.

He'd stuffed down the last bite of his sandwich, then left through the back door of the kitchen, stating loudly that he had to get back to work. Then he'd gotten his clippers, circled the building and gone up the fire escape to the top floor, picked the lock to the access door and stepped inside, leaving the clippers behind to use as an excuse if he got caught walking around the grounds later. It wasn't until he was staring down the long dark hallway that he realized he'd completely overlooked the possibility of an alarm. He held his breath, waiting for something to sound, and when it didn't, he breathed a quiet sigh of relief.

There were six doors. Three on the left. Three on the right. With no way to ascertain which one had belonged to Frank Walton other than trial and error, he began by trying the first on his left. It was locked. As was the next, and the next and the next. It seemed strange to him that six men would claim the entire third floor of a building for more than thirty years and still lock their doors behind them when they left. But, he reminded himself, this was also a public hotel. He supposed they did it as a means of protecting their private property from nosey strangers.

With no time to waste, he picked the first lock and slipped inside. The aroma of coffee was still in the air, and there was a coffee cup on a side table with a few drops still in it. An open book, a pair of slippers by a chair, and he quickly ascertained that this wasn't Frank Walton's room.

Without touching a thing, he backed out the same way he'd come in, locking the door behind him and moving to the next. It wasn't until he'd opened and closed three doors that he found the room he'd been looking for.

The moment he entered, he knew this was it. The air in the suite seemed stale, and there was a faint but obvious layer of dust on the coffee table near the window. The room was neat, the way it might be left when taking a trip. He remembered how his mother used to clean their small cottage before going to bed, as if by the simple act of neatness she would be able to face the next day of privation. But Walton had not been in this room for weeks, and it was inevitable that some dust would appear.

He peered back into the hallway, heard nothing, saw no one, and quietly locked himself inside. Unless someone got a wild urge to suddenly pack away a dead man's things, he should have ample time to search.

He paused momentarily, looking around the place that had been Frank Walton's home and remembering the old man he'd seen in the alley. There had been fear, but Rostov knew that he'd also seen recognition. If Walton was so afraid of being found that he would kill himself rather than be taken back to Russia, there had to be a reason other than mere deportation.

The living room was furnished in dark, somber tones, and there were places on the heavy velvet drapes that had faded from a dark cranberry to a watered-down cherry. The rug on the floor was imitation Persian, and the cushions on the wing-back chairs and sofa bore the indentations of years of use.

He moved first to an oversized highboy that had obviously been used as a desk and began opening drawers. He found nothing more incriminating than some old gas receipts and two unpaid bills. From there, he went to a small kitchenette. It took exactly five minutes to search it without any success. That left only two other rooms. A small private bath and the adjoining bedroom.

Rostov started across the floor, and as he did, a board squeaked beneath his feet. Attributing it to the age of the house, he headed for the bathroom. A few minutes later, he came out, no wiser than when he'd come in, save for the fact that his first impressions of Frank Walton had been right. Rostov had found a bottle of EAP—etoposide/adriamycin/cisplatin—along with a paper listing side effects for the new compound being used in the treatment of some cancers. Knowing this, Walton's actions now made a strange sort of sense. The decision to take his own life hadn't been as drastic as Rostov had first believed. The old man must already have been dying. He'd just chosen his end then and there.

Frustrated, and more than a little worried as to what his superiors were going to say when he called to tell them he'd failed, he started toward a dresser. Once again, the floor squeaked beneath his feet. He looked down, realizing it was in the same place. He frowned at his carelessness. If someone was upstairs now, they might hear the sound. Even if he got caught, they would merely assume he was a common thief, but he would be arrested and fired. Rostov could not afford to have his true identity surface, so he circumvented the area and headed for the dresser. A quick search revealed nothing but clothing. From there he went to the bed, then the mattress, checking between it and the box springs for anything that might be concealed, taking care not to step on the squeaking boards in front of the bed.

To his frustration, he found nothing. He moved to searching behind heat vents and photos, behind paintings hanging on the walls, then looking in vain for any kind of safe. Disgusted that his search had netted nothing of use, he stood in the doorway, giving the room one last sweep before calling it quits.

"Why, old man? What did you know that was worth dying for?"

But Frank Walton didn't answer.

He stared at the room, and the longer he looked, the more he realized that something seemed out of sync. The furnishings were old—of the same period as the living room furniture had been. A high four-poster bed, dark cherry-wood dresser, drapes on the verge of shabbiness. His gaze slid to the braided rug at the foot of the bed, remembering the squeaky floor beneath.

Then he looked at both sides of the bed and back to the rug at the foot, and it hit him. One did not get out of bed by crawling out at the foot, so why would a throw rug be there, rather than on the side of the bed?

Rostov had stayed alive in his business for as long as he had by never ignoring instinct or curiosity, and he wasn't about to start now. He walked back into the room and pulled the rug aside.

At first glance, he thought he'd been mistaken as to a sinister reason for the misplaced furnishings, but the longer he looked, the more he realized the pattern of the wood was not true. He moved closer, then ran his fingers along the seams in the planks. Within seconds, it became obvious that two of these boards had been cut away from the rest and were only lying in place.

He started to smile.

His heartbeat accelerated as he pulled out his knife, using the blade as a pry bar to displace the floor. Within seconds, he had achieved success.

At first glance he saw nothing but a dark empty space below the floor boards, and his hopes fell. But when he thrust his hand inside and began to feel around, something changed. Almost instantly he felt fabric, and then something hard wrapped within it. He grasped it firmly, and pulled it up and out into the light of day.

It was a pouch of some sort, and inside, a book. It didn't take him long to decide that he'd found what appeared to be a diary, but before he could look through the book, he heard voices outside in the hall.

Muttering a brief curse because he'd waited too long, he replaced the boards and slid the throw rug back in place. Then, shoving the book and pouch into his pocket, he hurried to the door, plotting the movements of the two old men who had obviously finished their meals. When he heard one of them announce he was taking a nap and the other one say he would finish a book, he smiled. All he had to do was wait.

Soon he heard their doors open and close, then listened to their footsteps as they moved around within their rooms. A short while later it got quiet. It was then that he decided to exit.

Quietly, he checked the hallway, satisfied to see it was deserted. He slipped out of Walton's room, taking care to lock the door behind him, then headed for the fire escape. Only after he was outside, with the sun on his face and the door locked behind him, did he breathe easy again. Without looking back, he grabbed the clippers and hurried down the stairs. Once on the ground he dared to look up. There was no one there, and the curtains at the windows were closed and unmoving. Patting the parcel in his pocket, he sauntered across the grounds toward the gardener's shed.

One of the cooks stepped outside to toss some vegetable peelings into the compost heap. She saw him and waved. He nodded cordially and waved back, brandishing the clippers, making sure she would think he had just finished some job.

Inside the shed, he tossed the clippers aside and hurried to his room in the back. There was no lock on his door, so he shoved a chair under the knob. Using his bed as a chair, he removed the pouch and then opened the book.

A slow smile of satisfaction spread across the angles of his face as he began to read. He'd been right. It was a diary, and it belonged to Vaclav Waller.

July 12, 1970
Today I died and Frank Walton was born. I am very sad about my demise and second-guessing the wisdom of what we are doing, but it's too late now. What's done is done.

Rostov frowned, then reread the first entry. We? Who was "we"? Gut instinct told him he needed to know more about what Waller/Walton had been working on and why he'd been allowed to leave the Soviet Union at the time of his death. Even more disconcerting was the fact that Waller had not acted alone.

He looked up at his surroundings, at the dust on the floor and the sunlight coming through a dirty, curtained window. He was a very long way from home and seriously out of his depth. Not for the first time, he wondered if he'd been sent because he was expendable. Then he sighed. That was nothing new. A spy was by definition expendable. That much was always understood.

He turned back to the book and began to read.

# 7

Rostov got up to get himself a drink, still reading as he walked. He knew from the entries that Vaclav Waller had made that something big was going on, but the entries were too vague to know exactly what it was. He filled a glass and drank it dry, then returned to his bed. This time he crawled all the way onto the mattress and leaned against the wall, using it for a backrest as he shifted the book a bit more toward the light. The day was passing, but he was so engrossed in what he was reading that he hardly noticed.

September 11, 1971

Well, we've done it. Right or wrong, the first test case is in place, and this time with no rejections. Only time will tell what the outcome will be, but if we're successful, the human race as we know it will never be the same.

Is this right? Are we doing mankind a favor, or are we playing at being gods?

Suddenly Rostov heard the squeaking of a hinge as the door to the tool shed was opened. Then he heard footsteps coming across the concrete floor toward his door. With no wasted motion, he stuffed the book beneath his mattress and moved the chair from beneath the door, then crept onto the bed and closed his eyes.

"Hello in there! Mr. Ross! Are you there?"

Rostov faked a weak voice as he answered.

"Yes, I'm here. Come in."

He looked toward the door, pretending illness as Thomas Mowry peeked inside.

"I say," Thomas said. "Are you all right?"

Rostov rolled to the side of the bed and sat up, then swayed, as if struck by a sudden spell of dizziness.

"I'm sorry, sir," Rostov said. "I'll get right back to work."

Thomas hastened to the bedside. "No, no, that's not why I've come. Isabella was concerned when she didn't see you outside. She asked me to check on you. Are you ill?"

Rostov placed a hand on his stomach and shrugged. "I have nausea."

Thomas shifted his glasses a little higher up his nose as he laid a hand on Rostov's forehead.

"You don't have a fever," he said, more to himself than to Rostov, then picked up Rostov's wrist and began taking his pulse.

"Please, sir," Rostov mumbled. "I can work.

Tell Miss Abbott that I am fine. I do not want to lose my job.''

Thomas shook his head and patted Rostov on the back.

''Lie back down, my friend. You won't lose your job just because you're ill.'' He pushed gently against Rostov's shoulder until the man did as he asked. ''There now,'' Thomas said. ''David is back from town. He's a doctor. I'll have him come check you out.''

Rostov's pulse accelerated. ''Oh, no, sir, there is no need. I'm sure it was something I ate…. Or maybe I just got too hot. I will be fine.''

''Nonsense,'' Thomas said. ''What's the good of having a house full of doctors if you can't get free care when you need it?''

Chuckling at his own wit, Mowry left, leaving Rostov in bed.

Rostov sighed. Further reading of the diary would have to wait while he endured a physical examination from a man who treated infertile women. He snorted beneath his breath and closed his eyes. If he was going to play sick, he might as well get some extra sleep while he was at it.

As he lay there, something about what Mowry had said suddenly clicked. A house full of doctors? Was that an exaggeration, or had it been a slip of the tongue? He'd been told that Frank Walton had been a retired botanist, and yet he knew that in Russia, Vaclav Waller had been a doctor involved in medical research. And there were the constant references in his diary to other people being involved in some big project. The head cook was a talker, and he'd listened more than once to her rattling on about how important the uncles had been in their younger days. How Mowry had been a chemist and John Michaels a geologist. That Rufus Toombs had been an archaeologist and worked in some great museum back East. He knew that Jasper Arnold and David Schultz were doctors, because they, along with the recently deceased Samuel Abbott, had founded that fertility clinic in Braden. But he'd assumed that the entries in Waller's diary had been entered in another place and time, before Waller had grown old. He had assumed that this was a place where the old men had come to retire. What if he was wrong? What if the "house full of doctors" were the others that Walton/Waller kept referring to in his entries? Rostov discarded the thought almost instantly. It seemed too far-fetched to be believed. However, he knew that to get his answers, he needed to do some research of his own. If he only knew the details on how Waller was supposed to have died. What could he possibly have done to fake his death and get away with it for all these years? But Rostov was in over his head, completely disconnected from the powers that be back home. If he called asking too many questions, they would assume that he had failed. He wasn't ready to give up just yet.

And so as he waited for David Schultz to appear, another idea began to form. One more radical than anything he'd ever considered. With the discovery of the diary, his expectations of finding something that might interest his government were over, but maybe his findings would be of interest to somebody else. The first chance he got, he was going to call his contact and tell him the old man was dead.

The thoughts raced through his head as he began to smile. Vaclav Waller wasn't the only one who knew how to fake a death. Rostov loved his country, but he was getting old, and he wasn't a fool. After all the years he'd given to her, she'd given little in return. His pension was paltry, his room hardly better than this gardener's shed. He'd seen plenty of opportunity for a man with his background while he'd been in Brighton Beach. It would be easy to assume a new identity. All he needed was something to get him started on the right track. The diary had possibilities. Maybe there was something in there with which he could work a little blackmail. He wouldn't be greedy. Just enough to set him up in an apartment in Brighton Beach. All he had to do was make a call.

He was still smiling when he heard someone approaching his room. Reassuming a weakened demeanor, he closed his eyes as David Schultz knocked and then entered.

Isabella slept through lunch and then busied herself in the office with some overdue bookkeeping, thereby removing herself from curious stares. The swelling in her lip was almost gone, but the cut was still evident, as was a darkening bruise. Bobby Joe Cage had certainly done a number on her. It would be a long time before she forgot the panic she'd felt in knowing things were out of her control. She paused at the computer, her fingers on the keyboard, and almost immediately Jack Dolan's face, dark with anger, popped into her mind. He had appeared without warning, like an avenging angel. If it hadn't been for him, this evening might have taken on a whole different character.

Her expression twisted angrily. Was this something every woman had to go through when cast into the world on her own? She wouldn't know. Before her father's death, she'd taken her security for granted, but after today, she wasn't sure. Dejected, she slumped forward and covered her face with her hands.

"Oh, Daddy, why did you have to die? I wasn't ready to let you go."

The words were little more than a whisper, but spoken just the same. Isabella shoved the keyboard aside and stood abruptly, her eyes filling with tears. She strode to the windows overlooking the front grounds and pulled the curtain aside. A couple of unfamiliar vehicles were in the parking lot. Probably more clients for her father's clinic. Only it wasn't her father's clinic anymore.

Loneliness swamped her as she let the curtain fall into place. Granted, those couples yearned for a child of their own, and she wasn't denying their right or the intensity of their desire to make it happen. But she wondered if they knew how truly blessed they were? At least they had each other. She had no one. She knew it was foolish, but her heart ached for something she'd never known.

*Brighton Beach P.D.—The Same Day*

Detective Mike Butoli's broken toe was getting better, but his attitude wasn't. Even though the John Doe who'd been found murdered in the alley behind Ivana's Bar and Grill now had a name, Butoli still didn't have a clue as to who had done it. One of his snitches had claimed the rumor on the street was that it had to do with the Russian Mafia and the dead man's past. He knew it was a possibility, especially after the dead man's prints had come back from Interpol. Granted, it had become quite a puzzle after they'd proved conclusively that the dead man's prints belonged to a Russian doctor who had supposedly died back in the seventies. And there was another odd but pertinent fact. The autopsy had confirmed that while the old man had died from the stabbing, his days had already been numbered. He was suffering from an advanced case of stomach cancer. Traces of a chemical compound called EAP had been in his system, a drug that was now being used in such cases.

At that point the Feds had gotten involved and Lieutenant Flanagan had told him to back off, but Butoli wasn't buying it. The man had died on their beat, and he wanted the man who'd killed him, which was why he was still following up leads. And after the phone call he'd just finished, he had discovered some very unusual facts.

Fact number one:

Walton/Waller was definitely dead. He'd died on a Saturday night right before the storm front that had blown through and toppled the old lifeguard tower out on the beach.

Fact number two:

Butoli had been in the morgue, watching as the coroner sliced the old man open from stem to stern.

And given that set of facts, then the question still remained as to fact number three:

How had Frank Walton been on an American Airlines passenger list the next day, with a destination of Braden, Montana?

Butoli got up from his chair and circled the desk, heading for Flanagan's office.

"Hey, Lieutenant. Got a minute?"

Barney Flanagan waved him in. "Barely," he said. "What's up?"

"You know that dead defector we found?"

Flanagan frowned. "Damn it, Butoli, I thought I told you to—"

Butoli held up his hands. "I know, I know. But just hear me out."

Flanagan's face was as red as his hair, but he held his tongue, waiting for the detective to speak.

"Okay," Butoli said. "It's like this. The investigation was already rolling when the Feds stepped in, right?"

Flanagan crossed his arms over his belly without giving Butoli the satisfaction of a nod.

Butoli ignored the pissed-off expression on his lieutenant's face and kept talking.

"So what was I to do? I mean…you can't just cancel something that fast once it's in motion. So…I had already put in a call to LaGuardia, as well as the bus terminals and the train stations. You know…checking to see when the old man had come in. The way I figured it, the Georgian Hotel might not have been the first place he stayed, and to know for sure, I had to know how long he'd been in the city, right?"

Flanagan shrugged. Butoli was a good detective, thorough, and as honest as his mother's priest. So what he was saying did make some sense.

"Yeah, so?"

Butoli grinned. "So I just got a call from La-Guardia. According to their manifest, a man named Frank Walton had flown into LaGuardia about two weeks before the day he was killed."

"That doesn't tell us anything new," Flanagan said.

"No, but this does. Either Frank Walton's nasty little habit of resurrecting himself after death is still ongoing, or we've got a rat in the woodpile."

"What the hell are you talking about?" Flanagan muttered.

"The day after his body was discovered in that

alley, someone named Frank Walton boarded an American Airlines plane on a return ticket to Braden, Montana.''

Flanagan came out of the chair, his eyes wide with disbelief.

"You're sure?"

"Dead sure...and pardon the pun."

"Holy shit! There's a good chance that this is something the Feds don't know. It's my understanding that they've sent a man to Braden. He needs to know that the killer might be there, too."

Butoli sighed. "I figured you were going to say that."

Flanagan picked up his phone and started to dial.

"Sit," he ordered. "You're going to tell them exactly what you just told me, you hear? And then you're going to file that case away and get to work on something you can fix. Understand me?"

Butoli hesitated, then shrugged. "Yeah, Lieutenant, I understand."

And he did. There was every chance that the man who'd gotten on the plane as Frank Walton was the man who'd killed him, and if he was, he had more of an itinerary than they had believed.

Flanagan handed him the phone. He took a deep breath, introduced himself to the Federal agent on the other end of the line and started to talk.

Jack stepped out of the barber shop, rubbing the back of his neck and feeling the short strands of his hair. It was a good thing he'd told them to just take off a little. Any more and the old barber would have given him a buzz cut.

He glanced across the street, remembering how the last time he'd been in Braden, he'd watched Isabella come out of that store. His gut knotted as he imagined her coming toward him with that long, lanky stride. Her dark hair swaying with the rhythm of her body as she moved closer to where he was standing. Her eyes lighting up in recognition, her mouth widening in a smile. Her arms sliding around his neck as she leaned...

A horn sounded on the street beside him, and he jumped as if he'd been shot, then turned and glared at the teenager behind the wheel.

*Damn kid...the least he could have done was waited until my fantasy was over.*

Disgusted with himself, he turned and began walking up the street. The more people he visited with, the more information he was gleaning about the permanent residents of Abbott House. He now knew that all seven men had arrived in Braden together, which he found very odd. And that Samuel Abbott had been the only one who was married. A few of the older people remembered his wife, Isabella, commenting on the tragedy of her death as she'd given birth to their only child.

He thought of Isabella, growing up without knowing a mother's love, then remembered the adoration with which the old men treated her and decided they had more than made up for her loss.

As he turned the corner, a tall, angular man with a mop of long black hair stepped out of an alley and started walking toward him. His appearance was strange, his behavior even stranger. When they drew abreast of each other, the young man started to talk, moving his hands in short, jerky motions as his hair swung across his face.

"I'm gonna get me a guitar and go to Memphis," he said.

Jack's heart went out to the man. Despite his obvious problems, he still seemed to have a dream.

"That's good," Jack said, and started to walk on by. To his dismay, the man turned and followed.

"I can sing," he said. "I can sing real good. I always sing for my momma."

Then he grabbed a handful of his hair and suddenly pulled. Jack knew it must hurt. The action was hard and brutal.

"Hey, buddy," Jack said. "Take it easy there."

The man sighed. "I can't find my momma. Is this Memphis? I gotta find momma."

"No, buddy, this isn't Memphis. You're in Montana. Real pretty country here, don't you think?"

The man raised his head, but even then, Jack could not get a clear view of his face for the hair in his eyes. He might as well have been wearing a veil.

"See that store over there?" the man said. "They sell guitars. I'm gonna get me a guitar and go to Memphis."

Knowing that any further conversation was going to be a repeat of the last, Jack tried to walk away.

"Okay. Good luck," he said.

The man was still talking as Jack started across the street.

"I can sing! I can sing real good. I sing for my momma. She likes to hear me sing."

The bell jangled over the drugstore door as Jack walked inside. The woman behind the counter looked at him closely, as had nearly everyone else that he'd met. They weren't unfriendly, just cautious, as was the way in so many small towns.

"Afternoon," the woman said. "I see you met John."

Jack looked back across the street, watching the black-haired man as he shuffled off into an alley.

"Is that his name? I didn't know."

"Yeah, John Running Horse."

"He's Indian?" Jack said. "I didn't realize."

"The Blackfeet Reservation isn't far from here, but he wanders off all the time."

"He said he was looking for his mother."

The woman shook her head. "His mother is dead. Has been for more than ten years, I guess."

"What about his father?" Jack asked.

"Killed in a car wreck about a year ago. John's been sort of lost ever since."

"Isn't there anyone to look after him?"

"Oh, he's got family all right, but they're all kind of scared of him, I think."

Jack turned, staring at the woman in disbelief.

"Scared? Because of his mind?"

"No...because they say he's not one of them. They say he's a spirit that doesn't belong."

Jack frowned as the woman continued.

"Who's to say?" she muttered. "He's lost in his head, whatever else is wrong."

"He kept talking about a guitar."

She nodded.

"That's all he talks about…that and going to find his mother. Isn't that crazy? He's never been out of Montana in his whole life, and he thinks his mother is in Memphis. Poor thing."

The lost sound of the man's voice was haunting him. Suddenly he didn't want to talk about John Running Horse any longer and made his purchases without bothering to linger.

As he drove out of town a short while later, he saw the man again, walking in the opposite direction on the side of the road. He thought about going back and picking him up, then decided against it. Something told him that the only place John Running Horse wanted to go was to Memphis, and Jack was going in the wrong direction.

Later, after getting back to Abbott House, he went to his room to go over his notebook and the bits and pieces of Frank Walton's life that the townspeople of Braden had been willing to share. All he had learned that he could easily verify was that the man had been here for years, and that he had claimed to be a botanist. Also, while no one knew all that much about his profession, everyone agreed that Isabella Abbott had called him Uncle. That was all well and good, but it told him absolutely nothing about why he'd faked his own death and hidden out here. Had he come on his own, or was there an accomplice? He'd had to get fake identification from someone, somewhere. And the bigger question was why? For some reason, Jack had gotten the impression from the director that Vaclav Waller had been involved in something valuable at the time of his disappearance. Something that, even now, would be worthy of rediscovery. Jack shook his head in disbelief, unable to think of even one thing that other doctors and scientists had not already discovered—even perfected—in the ensuing thirty years. What possible knowledge could an old man have that would warrant his murder?

Nothing occurred to him. And he was still bothered by the fact that he was deceiving Isabella Abbott. It shouldn't matter what she thought. She wasn't his concern. But knowing that and accepting it were two different things, and he was having difficulties with living the lie.

While Jack was struggling with his moral dilemma, his cell phone rang. He glanced at the ID screen and frowned when nothing came up. When he answered and heard the director's voice, he knew that their call was being scrambled.

"Sir?"

"Dolan, we've come by some interesting news that you should know."

"Yes, sir?"

"We have reason to believe that the man who killed Walton used the old man's return ticket to Braden."

Shock spread slowly through Jack's system as he absorbed the news.

"You're sure, sir?"

"As sure as we can be without an actual sighting."

"Do we know what he looked like? The man who used the ticket?"

"No."

"Are we still assuming it was a foreign hit?"

"Yes."

"Shit, sir."

There was a low chuckle on the other end of the line.

"My sentiments exactly," the director said, and then was all business once more. "In light of these facts, I am telling you to use extreme caution. We have no way of knowing exactly what he or she is after."

"Yes, sir, but do we know who might be in danger?"

"No."

There was a moment of silence on Jack's end, and then he sighed.

"Okay, thank you, sir. That clears up a lot of questions I was going to ask."

"Do you have your laptop and printer with you?" the director asked.

"Yes. No self-respecting writer would be caught dead without them."

"Good. I'm having an attachment sent to you that contains everything we know about Vaclav Waller, including all the pictures we have on file of him. Unfortunately, there are only three, the last of which is of him boarding the plane on which he supposedly went down. I don't know if it will be of any use to you, but at least you'll know everything we know.''

"Thank you, sir, and if you find any pictures of Russian assassins, don't hesitate to send them, too. I can always use a little midnight reading." Then he added, "I suppose I'm still undercover?"

"Yes, until the situation warrants a change. As for now, you're going to have to settle for a good paperback instead of a photo album. Keep in touch."

There was a dial tone in Jack's ear; then he hung up the phone. He sat down with a thump and thrust his fingers through his hair in frustration.

Christ Almighty. Working this case was like sending a blind man into a room with no walls. There were no boundaries or starting places, no matter where he turned.

It was fifteen minutes to seven when Leonardo Silvia got home from work. His back was aching, and he'd smashed his thumb in a drill press just before noon, so he was looking forward to a home-cooked meal and an early night. Yet when he walked in the door, he could tell his expectations were slightly off.

Maria was lighting candles on the dining table. There was a bottle of wine chilling on the sideboard, and he could smell pasta sauce simmering on the stove. His mind began to race, going through every anniversary they shared, certain that he'd forgotten something important.

Maria heard the door open and looked up. When

she saw Leonardo, a wide smile spread across her face. She opened her arms, and he walked into them, burying his face in the sweet curve of her neck and closing his eyes. For a few brief moments his weariness and pain were forgotten.

"I have forgotten something important, haven't I, *cara mia?*"

Maria laughed at her husband's woeful expression.

"No, no. You forget nothing. I made us a special celebration meal because today the doctor called."

Leonardo went limp with relief. At least he wasn't in trouble, and then his mind shifted gears as he realized what she was saying.

"You mean the doctor from the Montana clinic?"

"Yes!" Maria cried, and wrapped her arms around his neck. "We have an appointment for next Tuesday. Is that all right? You said all you needed was a couple of days notice."

Leonardo could feel the trembling in her body as he held her close.

"Yes, it's all right. I've already talked to Gus. He says I can have up to two weeks off if need be."

Maria kissed him hard on the mouth and then spun out of his arms as she danced around the room.

"This is it," she said, waving her arms over her head as she made dainty pirouettes. "I can feel it, Leonardo. This time it will be different."

Leonardo made himself smile, although he wanted to cry. They'd been through so many disappointments before, he wasn't sure he could bear seeing her heart break again.

"Just don't get your hopes too high," he said softly.

She stopped abruptly, her hands clasped beneath her chin.

"You don't understand, Leonardo. This time it will happen."

"How can you be sure?" he asked.

"Because I promised God, remember?"

"Yes, I remember."

"Good!" she said, hurrying from the dining room toward the kitchen and calling out behind her as she left, "Go wash your face and rest your feet a bit. I'll call you when dinner is ready."

Leonardo smiled at her as she hurried away, but his steps were dragging as he left the room.

It was almost dark. Sunset had come and gone, and there was nothing to be seen beyond the terrace of Abbott House but the silhouette of White Mountain against a navy blue sky.

Isabella hugged herself against the chill and resisted a shiver as the night breeze lifted the hair from her neck. Even though she was wearing wool slacks and a heavy cable-knit sweater, she could feel the cold through her clothes.

Behind her, the dinner hour was in full swing. Patrons from the two surrounding communities often patronized Abbott House for its food, as well as the ambiance of reliving a gentler time in the nation's history. If it were not for the computer at the check-in desk and the occasional ring of a diner's cell phone, one could almost believe that time had passed this house by. Samuel Abbott had transferred his love for old-world, understated elegance to both his hotel and his only daughter. Even wearing the most recent fashions, there was an air of reticence about Isabella, a quiet dignity that was foreign to most young women of her age. It was as if she'd been born a generation too late.

Isabella ran her tongue along her lower lip, testing the cut that she'd incurred in her altercation with Bobby Joe and wondering how he had explained his broken nose to his father. Thanks to Uncle David and Uncle Jasper, her car was back in the garage, complete with a new tire. And, thanks to Jack Dolan, she had nothing worse to show for the incident than a fat lip.

As she stared up at the heavens, a falling star suddenly streaked across the sky, burning out before her eyes as it hit earth's atmosphere and disappeared.

"Daddy? Is that you?" she whispered. "I don't know what to do. How can a world as perfect as ours seemed to be come apart so fast?"

She started to cry, huge, quiet tears that streaked down her cheeks as swiftly as the star that had burned out in the sky. Despite her tears, she continued to talk as if her father was standing beside her in his usual manner, with his head tilted to one side and a half smile on his lips.

"Uncle Frank is dead, too, you know. I'm guessing that the pair of you are somewhere deep in a game of chess.'' She swiped her hands across her face, clearing her cheeks of the tears as she managed to smile, remembering their heated debates over the chess board during the long winter nights. "Can you argue in heaven? If not, you're both in for a big shock, aren't you?''

She paused and looked up, as if waiting for an answer, but it never came. Finally she dropped her head and then covered her face, her shoulders shaking as she stifled her sobs.

That was how Jack Dolan found her—standing in the moonlight at the edge of the terrace, her head bent in sorrow. The only other witness to her misery was a nightbird calling from a nearby tree. He hesitated, considering whether to go back inside, when she suddenly stiffened and then turned.

He cursed beneath his breath, angry with himself for waiting too long. The last thing he wanted to do was embarrass her further. Today had been more than enough.

"I'm sorry," he said. "I was just coming out to get some air. I can go—''

"No," she said shortly. "Don't apologize. You're a guest. You have every right to all of the amenities Abbott House has to offer.''

The pain in her voice was palpable. It drew him toward her like fire to tinder. Even in the darkness, he saw the trembling of her lower lip and the dampness on her cheeks, and something deep within him tore loose and fell free.

"Miss Abbott...''

Her lips twisted wryly. "I think we've moved beyond that formality."

His gaze centered on her bruised mouth. He thought of the blood that had been there earlier. Now it had been tracked by her tears.

"I know there's nothing I can say that will make your grieving easier, but if there's anything I can do, all you have to do is ask."

Isabella's stare cut through the shadows as she judged the big man's face. Her father had always said she was a good judge of character. She hoped he was right, because she was about to do something quite out of character for her.

"Yes, actually, there is."

Jack was surprised but secretly pleased.

"Name it," he said.

She walked into his arms.

"I need to be held."

His first and last thought was Sweet Jesus, and then her arms slid around his waist. When the weight of her cheek hit his chest and he smelled the sweet citrus scent of her shampoo, he wrapped his arms around her and did as she asked.

# 8

Time ceased as Jack's awareness centered on the woman in his arms. Not even the bulk of her sweater could disguise her fragility. He pulled her close, and as he did, the weight of her hair on the backs of his hands was like warm silk against his skin. He felt her sigh and then shudder. Instinctively, he braced himself, readying for her collapse, but it didn't come.

Her fingers dug at his back, clutching the knit fabric of his pullover for leverage as her breasts pillowed against his chest. He felt her inhale deeply, then pause, and he caught himself holding his breath, waiting for her to exhale. When she finally did, his breath flowed from him in unison. He laid his cheek against the crown of her head.

"I'm sorry," he said.

Then she answered, her voice so soft he had to bend his head to hear.

"Everything is coming undone."

Thankful she couldn't see his expression, he slid his hand beneath the hair on her neck, gently massaging the strip of skin between her hairline and her sweater. If she knew what was really going on, she would know it was already undone. The only question that remained was whether there would be anything left of her life to fix when Jack's investigation was over.

"Not really," Jack said. "It's only changing."

Isabella stilled and then slowly lifted her head.

"Changing? That's an understatement, don't you think?"

Resisting the urge to brush the hair from her forehead, he had to be satisfied, instead, with the scent of her perfume.

"Nothing ever stays the same, Isabella. We're born. We live. We die. And if you think about it, those are also the most painful things we encounter. We are thrust abruptly into a world without warning, torn from the relative comfort and safety of our mothers' bellies. Then we struggle through the business of living, rejoicing in the highs and weeping through the lows, and just when we think we're about to get the hang of it, we find ourselves at the end, looking back over the years and wondering where the hell the time went. My philosophy is to try and cram as much into the living part of it as possible, so that when the dying comes, my regrets are few."

Isabella stared at him, absorbing the way the moonlight and shadows lay soft upon his face, and hearing the tenderness and empathy in his voice. Finally she spoke.

"How old are you?"

Jack was surprised by the question but answered without hesitation.

"Thirty-eight."

She nodded thoughtfully, repeating what he'd said. "Thirty-eight. Your wisdom seems more suited to someone of my father's era." Then she smiled. "I will say this. My father would have liked you. He would have liked you a lot."

Before Jack could answer, Isabella rose up on tiptoe and brushed a kiss across his mouth.

"Thank you," she said. "For everything."

She walked away then, leaving Jack alone in the moonlight with the taste of her strong on his lips. Unwilling for the moment to end, he turned abruptly to call her back, but she was already inside and out of sight. He leaned back against the retaining wall around the terrace, his shoulders slumping with defeat. He was getting in over his head with this woman. The problem was, if it came to choosing her welfare over his duty, he wasn't sure what his choice would be.

Frustrated, he cast one last look at the surrounding area, noting absently a faint light in an outbuilding on the edge of the grounds. He stared at it for a moment and then shrugged off the momentary concern as he stepped off the terrace and headed into the shadows. Thinking of the killer who'd used a dead man's plane ticket, he started to circle the hotel, expanding the perimeter of his search as he walked. It wasn't much, but right now, it was about all he could do. If they only knew why Frank Walton had been murdered, then they would have a place to start looking for clues. As it stood, there was, literally, nothing to go on but false identities and assumptions.

A short while later, satisfied that all was well at Abbott House, Jack went inside and up to his room. He needed to check his e-mail for the information the director was going to send, then go back over the notes from the interviews he'd had today with some of the citizens of Braden. One way or another, he had a job to do, and the sooner he got at it, the better off they would be.

Rostov sat cross-legged in the middle of his bed with the diary in his lap. An empty soup bowl was on the end table by his bed, as was a partially filled and melting glass of iced tea. Thanks to his ruse at playing sick, he'd been served supper in bed. But as soon as he'd finished the soup, he'd resumed reading the diary, convinced that it was going to be his ticket to a new life and identity in the United States.

He turned the page, noting the date as well as the brevity of the entry, and frowned.

January 31, 1973
    One Isabella dies. Another Isabella is born.

That would be about the right age for Isabella Abbott, the woman who'd hired him. He'd seen the painting in the hotel lobby, but he'd assumed it was the same woman. If it was her mother, instead, then he supposed that she'd died giving birth to her child. He shrugged. It wasn't uncommon, especially in his country, where medical attention was not the best.

His gaze slid to the opposite page, and his frown deepened.

February 3, 1973
     Isabella was buried today. Samuel is distraught, blaming himself needlessly. There was no way to foresee the complications of childbirth, but he is not dissuaded. He spends night and day in the laboratory, leaving his baby daughter to the care of others. It is a tragedy.

Rostov turned the page, hoping for something more volatile than the musings of an old man, but it wasn't until a notation made about six months later that things began to get interesting.

July 29, 1973
     We've done it. Samuel is ecstatic, as are we all. The woman is pregnant, and with the new method of implantation. We'll keep track of her progress, of course, but technically, our job is over. The birth of her child will also mark

the birth of a new project. If this succeeds as we predict, we have changed the world.

Rostov's heart skipped a beat. Ah, now it was beginning to make sense. Waller was a doctor. They ran a fertility clinic. His mind raced. How could helping women get pregnant change the world? It wasn't as if they were the first. This had been going on for years. But the notation was unmistakable. Somehow, they were implanting women in some manner that was life-altering.

He thought back to the days when Hitler had been in power. His desire for a pure and perfect Aryan race had taken him higher than any man in government power had ever gone, although in the end, he had also fallen farther than any man before him. The little he'd been given on Waller's background said that the old man had been involved in genetic research. So what if they had learned how to manipulate DNA? What if they had implanted the woman with her own fertilized eggs as usual, but changed in some manner so as to create a perfect child? It made sense to Rostov. If any part of this was true, then it was no wonder his country had still wanted the old man back. But if this was so, then why hadn't the world seen the evidence firsthand? More than enough years had come and gone. This child, if it had lived, would be in its late twenties—plenty of time for an exceptional person to make a mark on the world.

He frowned. What if it had already happened?

The world was filled with geniuses of all kinds. Men and women who manipulated the computer industry and the Internet as easily as he tied his shoes. And what if it wasn't just mental superiority that they'd been striving to achieve? There were Olympic medalists and military heroes—professionals of all kinds who were unique in their own fields. And if the men who had created them had a piece of that action, the possibilities were endless.

His frown deepened. Even if this was so—and he had yet to prove his hypothesis—it still remained for Rostov to find a way to cash in on the information.

Quickly he scanned the rest of the diary, noting mention of at least nineteen other "projects," as Waller had called them, and then in 1992 the entries ceased.

He flipped through the pages, hoping for something to explain the further lack of entries. He found nothing but a single notation on the very last page.

December 2000
   In trying to play God we have, instead, created Hell. No one knows why, but Isabella is the key.

Rostov closed the diary and then shoved it beneath his mattress before turning out the light. Without bothering to remove his clothes, he rolled over on his side and closed his eyes. He didn't know what it all meant, but the longer he thought about it, the more convinced he became that he had an agenda of his own. Tomorrow he would make contact with his superiors and tell them the old man was dead. After that, the world was his for the taking—and he was going to take all he could get. And—according to Vaclav Waller—Isabella Abbott was the key to his success.

Isabella slept curled up on her side, her face to the window and the moonlight shining through. In her dream, she was in London, lost on a dark street with no end in sight. As she walked, thin fingers of fog swirled at her feet, yet as afraid as she was, she resisted the urge to run. Behind her, the sounds of footsteps on the cobblestone streets could suddenly be heard, and she turned in fear, terrified of who was behind her.

Someone called her name! Her breath caught between a gasp and a scream as a figure emerged from the shadows. She went limp with relief.

*"Daddy! Oh my God, Daddy, it's you! I got lost and was so afraid."*

*Samuel Abbott paused beneath the gaslight, the moisture from the fog heavy on his clothes, his breath coming in quick gasps as if he'd been running.*

*"You're not lost, Isabella. Look up."*

*Isabella looked. There was a street sign right*

above her head. *Braden, Montana? That didn't make sense.*

"But, Daddy, I thought this was London."

Samuel shook his head. "You've never been to London."

"But I have," she argued. "I remember."

Samuel smiled. "That's not your memory," he said softly. "Let it go. Let it go."

Isabella woke with a start, half expecting to see the room filled with fog, and instead got moonlight in her eyes. She rolled over with a groan, bunched her pillow beneath her chin, then closed her eyes, willing herself not to dream. She'd had all the nightmares for one night that she could handle.

Jack lay wide-eyed and sleepless, staring up at the pattern on the ceiling, trying to make sense of what he'd just read. Frank Walton, aka Vaclav Waller, had been involved in DNA research when he'd "died." Rumor had it that the Russian government had been about to pull the plug on what they considered flawed research and send him to a lab involved in chemical warfare. But somehow he'd wound up on a private plane, on his way to a world-class medical convention in the Bahamas, instead. And the plane had gone down two hours after take-off, with no survivors.

Jack shifted where he lay and bunched a couple

of pillows beneath his head before refocusing his thoughts.

Odd thing about that plane crash. Besides Waller, there had been six other doctors, one with a wife, and two pilots on board. No bodies or wreckage were ever found—only an oil slick in a vast ocean of blue to indicate their passing.

But Waller hadn't died then. That was now a given. So had he somehow faked getting onto that plane and then made a getaway at the airport before it took off? Jack chewed the edge of his lower lip as he considered another option. Considering the fact that no wreckage or bodies were ever found, then the possibility existed that the plane had never gone down. And if that hypothesis was true, then what had happened to the other doctors?

The agency had sent him the three known pictures of Vaclav Waller, but the images had come across the Internet too grainy for him to tell much about the faces. He needed to see a real one and had indicated as much by return email. Knowing the Bureau, there would be one waiting at the check-in desk tomorrow morning, so for now he was going to have to settle for a night of supposition.

Finally he closed his eyes, and when he did, his mind was awash with the memory of Isabella Abbott walking into his arms, of the feel of her body pressed to his, and of the kiss she gave him when she left. Cursing himself and the weakness of the flesh, he crawled out of bed and strode to the bathroom, stripping off his sweats as he went. He'd already showered once, but another was overdue, and this one was going to be quick and cold. He was hard and hurting, with no other way of alleviating the pain.

He stepped beneath the shower, gritting his teeth as the cold water needled his skin.

''Son of a bitch,'' he muttered, and ducked his head beneath the spray.

Minutes later he was spread-eagled on the bed on his belly, trying to sleep, but something kept getting in the way of oblivion. He didn't have to focus hard to know what it was. It was Isabella, and even though he knew she was asleep on the floor below, he imagined he could smell the scent of her perfume.

Isabella stepped out of the hotel onto the terrace, then down the steps, following the sound of the weed-eater on the south side of the building. Her Uncle David had told her the gardener was going to be fine, but she wanted to see for herself. As she walked, she couldn't help but admire how neatly Victor Ross had been keeping the grounds and wondered if he would be interested in a permanent job. She rounded the corner just as Victor Ross turned around. He killed the weed-eater when he realized she wanted to talk.

Isabella smiled. ''I'm sorry to disturb your work, Mr. Ross, but I wanted to see for myself that you were all right today. If you're not feeling up to par, you're more than welcome to take another day of rest."

There was a brief moment of guilt as Rostov absorbed what she was saying. Things were certainly a lot different here than they were back home, and this woman had been nothing but kind to him. However, he didn't feel enough guilt to change what he was going to do.

"Thank you, Miss Abbott, but I am fine."

Isabella picked a dead leaf off the perfectly clipped hedge and tossed it aside, then gave the man another considering look.

Rostov waited for her to speak.

"Mr. Ross...I was wondering, do you have any immediate plans for your future?"

The irony of her question was not lost on the big Russian. She was part of his future; she just didn't know it yet.

"Not really, Miss."

Isabella nodded. "Then I have a proposition for you...if you're interested, of course."

"Yes?"

"You're doing a wonderful job here."

An odd spurt of satisfaction came and went. "I have found this job to be quite enjoyable."

Isabella hesitated. It wasn't the first time she'd noticed his rather stilted form of speech and wondered if English was a second language, rather than learned from birth.

"Well, it shows," she said, then added, "Which brings me to the point I was going to make. If you are interested, I would like to hire you permanently, with a raise in pay. In the winter months, when there is little to be done outside except shovel snow, you would be available as a handyman in the hotel proper. You would live on the grounds, of course, but not in that shed. We would find a room for you in the hotel. There are a couple just off the kitchen that were once maids' quarters. They're not being used, because all our housekeeping staff live off the premises in their own homes. Maybe we could take out a wall or connect them in some way so that you could have a private suite of your own."

Rostov was stunned. He took off his hat and wiped his brow while giving himself time to think. There was a moment when he actually considered doing just that. It was simple work. He would have a place to call his own. But he thought of the diary and the possibility that he might be recognized. Frank Walton had known him for what he was, even though they'd never met. And were it not for the beard he'd been growing and the fact that he'd stayed as far away from the old men as possible, he might already have been recognized again. He also had to consider the fact that Isabella Abbott was worth far more to him as a hostage, rather than an employer.

"This comes as a surprise," Rostov said, and made himself smile to show appreciation. "I haven't stayed in one place for a very long time. May I have a couple of days to think about it?''

Isabella nodded. "Certainly. In the meantime, I'll let you get back to work.''

"Thank you, miss. I do appreciate the offer.''

Rostov bowed before he thought, then straightened abruptly and shoved the hat back on his head. People did not bow to their superiors in America. He knew that, but he'd done it without thought. Angry with himself for slipping up again, he restarted the weed-eater and began attacking a clump of grass that had escaped the lawn mower's blades.

Isabella watched for a moment, then turned away. She was halfway to the terrace when it occurred to her that the man had actually bowed, as if she were some kind of royalty. Not that it mattered, but if she was a betting woman, she would lay odds that Victor Ross had not been born in the United States.

Jack was at the check-in desk when Isabella walked into the lobby. The photos from headquarters had arrived, just as he'd expected. Anxious to view them, he still hesitated, wanting a reason to talk to Isabella again, so he waited, telling himself that remaining on speaking terms with her and the staff was just part of his cover.

She circled the counter. "I'll take it for a while, Delia. Why don't you go finish that report on my desk?''

"Yes, ma'am," Delia said, and went into the office, leaving Isabella alone with Jack. She made herself act calm, when in actuality she was more than a little bit rattled by his presence.

"Good morning, Jack."

Her smile ripped right through his conscience, but he hid it well.

"Good morning to you, too."

Faint color spread across her cheeks as she remembered that she'd not only asked to be held but had kissed this man without conscience. Searching for something inconsequential to talk about, she pointed to the packet he was holding.

"I see you have mail. Something from your publisher?"

For a moment he couldn't think what she was talking about, and then he realized he was supposed to be a writer.

"More in the way of research," he said.

Before Isabella could follow up on his answer, the front doors swung suddenly inward. When she saw who it was, she groaned beneath her breath.

"Oh great," she muttered. "Just what I need."

"Who's he?" Jack asked, as he watched the overweight and graying cowboy stride toward the desk.

"Lawton Cage. Bobby Joe's daddy."

"Is he going to give you trouble?"

"Most likely," she said.

At that point Lawton Cage had arrived and their conversation was over.

"Miss Abbott."

Isabella lifted her chin, giving him full access to the damage his son had done to her face.

"Lawton. Haven't seen you here in a while. Have you come to dine with us?"

He pointed a finger in Isabella's face. "You know why I'm here Missy. I want to know what happened between you and my son yesterday, and I want to talk to the sorry son of a bitch who broke his nose."

Jack stepped between Cage and the desk.

"That would be me," Jack said, and smiled without humor as he casually pushed Lawton's arm aside. "Didn't your mother tell you it isn't nice to point?"

Lawton Cage had been riding roughshod over anyone who'd gotten in his way since the day he'd turned twenty-one. To say he was pissed about Jack's attitude was putting it mildly.

"Who the hell are you?" he growled.

"I'm the sorry son of a bitch. Nice to meet you."

Jack heard a snort behind him and wasn't sure if Isabella had laughed or choked off a cry of alarm.

Lawton's face turned as red as his shirt as he doubled his fists.

"You're gonna pay for what you did to—"

"No. I'm not the one who owes Miss Abbott, and since you've come to clean up your son's messes, then it's you who's going to pay."

"What the hell are you talking about?" He pushed past Jack and then leaned over the desk. "Isabella! I've known you since the day you were born and thought highly of your father. But I'm not going to ignore what happened to my son just because—''

Again Jack stepped between them, saving Isabella the task of trying to explain things to a man who was obviously out of control.

''What you should be doing is thanking her,'' Jack said. ''Because if it wasn't for her, I would have had your son arrested.''

Lawton's eyes widened. His nostrils flared. He stared at Isabella in disbelief.

''Is this true?''

''Yes, Lawton, it is. And I would like for you to leave now before you say something we'll both regret.''

''I'm not going anywhere until I get some answers.''

''Fine, then,'' Jack said. ''I watched from the barber shop window while your son cut a tire on Miss Abbott's car. Then he followed her out of town, for whatever purposes he had in mind. When I drove up, she was trying to fight him off. Her lip was bleeding, and she was begging for him to stop. I helped him make up his mind.''

''You broke his nose,'' Lawton said, but the tone of his voice was weaker than it had been moments before.

''He was lucky it wasn't his neck,'' Jack said.

An angry flush spread slowly up the big man's neck and face.

"There was a time in these parts when what you did would have gotten you shot."

"Yeah?"

Lawton nodded. "Yeah."

"Well, where I come from, there was a time when a man like Bobby Joe Cage would have wound up as gator bait in some Louisiana swamp for what he did."

Lawton stared, judging his opponent carefully.

Jack looked back, waiting for the man to make the next move.

Suddenly Cage's mood shifted. He took a deep breath and, for the first time since he'd come into the hotel, removed his Stetson and nodded to Isabella.

"Miss Abbott, you have my apologies for what happened. I trust you'll send the bill for the tire to me."

"I believe Uncle David has already done that," she said.

A muscle twitched at the corner of Lawton's mouth, but to his credit, he didn't argue.

"Then my business here is done," he said. He started to leave, then looked back at Jack.

"You. What's your name?"

"You mean besides sorry son of a bitch?"

"Jack, for Pete's sake," Isabella muttered, anxious for this to be over.

Jack heard her and grinned, but waited for Lawton to ask.

"Yes, besides that," Lawton said.

"My name is John Jacob Dolan, but everyone calls me Jack."

Lawton took a deep breath and then nodded, slapped his hat back on his head and strode out as forcefully as he had entered.

"Good Lord," Isabella said, when the door had swung shut.

Jack turned and winked.

She started to laugh when Delia came out of the office and interrupted.

"Oh, Miss Abbott. A special delivery package came for Mr. Rufus about a half hour ago, but I can't find him. What should I do with it? It's marked Fragile, and I'm afraid if it's left up here at the front desk something will happen to it."

Isabella looked beneath the counter where Delia was pointing, for the first time seeing the long wooden box with international postage.

"Probably more of his archaeological stuff. I should probably take it to his room."

"I'd be happy to carry it for you," Jack said.

Isabella hesitated. "Are you sure? I don't want to delay your own work."

"This is part of my work," Jack said.

"What do you mean?"

His gaze slid past her mouth, then settled on her eyes. "Well…if you let me carry this for you, then I will have a legitimate reason to spend some more time with you."

Her blush heightened, but she laughed. "Far be it from me to deny my knight in shining armor his one desire."

"Oh…it's not the only desire I have, but it's a good start," he said softly, then handed her his FedEx pack. "If you don't mind?"

She took the packet as he circled the desk and picked up the long bulky box.

"After you," he said, and let Isabella lead the way.

"We'll take the elevator," she said. "No use carrying that all the way up three flights of stairs."

Jack waited for her to get in the elevator and then angled the box slightly as he entered after her. At once the tiny car started to climb, creaking and groaning as it lifted off the first floor, then passed the second. When it stopped, Jack was none too reluctant to get out.

"Are you sure that thing's safe?" he asked, as Isabella started down the hallway.

"Certainly, or we wouldn't be using it."

"It makes a lot of noise."

"Right now, so are you," she said.

Jack grinned, but Isabella didn't see it. She had stopped at the second door on their left and was knocking. No one answered.

"Uncle Rufus, it's me, Isabella. Are you in there?"

Still no one answered. Satisfied that she would not be intruding upon his privacy, she began digging in her pocket for the passkey. Just as she was about to put the key in the lock, the door at the end of the hallway opened and David Schultz looked out.

"I thought I heard people out here," he said. "Were you looking for Rufus?"

"Yes. A package came for him. It's marked Fragile, and Delia was afraid something might happen to it, so Mr. Dolan volunteered to carry it up here for me."

The curiosity on her uncle's face was impossible to miss.

"A big box at that, isn't it?" he said, as he ambled out of his room.

"Yes. I was just going to put this inside the door. I don't think he'd mind, do you?"

"Certainly not," David said. "Here, you unlock it and I'll hold it aside." Then he smiled at Jack as the door swung inward. "Quite a cumbersome thing. Careful you don't scrape your knuckles as you come through the door."

"Right," Jack said, and carried the box inside. "Where do you want me to put it?"

Isabella hesitated. "I'm not—"

"Put it here," David said, indicating the floor near a small dining table. "Otherwise it might scratch the furniture."

"You're right," Isabella said. "Here, Jack. Let me help you."

Together, they lowered it carefully to the floor. At the moment when they let go, they both happened to look up and found themselves almost nose to nose.

Jack's belly tightened. One inch farther and he would be kissing her.

Isabella saw her own reflection in Jack Dolan's eyes and for a moment felt as if he'd stolen her soul.

"Well now," David said. "I wonder what Rufus has gone and gotten for himself this time."

His question broke the tension between Jack and Isabella. They stood abruptly. Again Jack was disconcerted by the emotions he kept feeling when he was around this woman, while Isabella was struggling with confusion of her own. She didn't know whether these things she was feeling for him were just remnants of gratitude for his coming to her rescue, or if it was something more.

Before Jack could think of what to say, Rufus Toombs entered, a jovial smile on his face.

"Have I missed my own party?"

Isabella laughed and wondered if it sounded as fake to everyone else as it did to her.

"Almost," she said. "You had a special delivery, Uncle Rufus. I asked Jack to carry it up for me."

Rufus looked past them then, for the first time seeing the long wooden box lying on the floor.

Jack thought he saw an odd expression come and go on his face, and then the old man clapped his hands together as if he'd just been given a gift.

"Wonderful! Wonderful! I'm thinking this might be the find a colleague of mine was going to send."

"What kind of find, Uncle Rufus?"

"Now, Isabella, how on earth could you ask such a question? You know me. It's bound to be a parcel of old relics." He put his hand on Isabella's back and gently urged her toward the door, chuckling as he went.

Jack had no option but to follow, and before they both knew it, they were outside in the hallway, while the two old men were still inside together.

Isabella raised an eyebrow and then grinned wryly. "Why do I feel like we've just been given the brush-off?"

Jack was of the same opinion, but more suspicious of the reason why.

"Does stuff like this happen often?" he asked, as they got back on the elevator.

"Stuff like what?" Isabella asked.

"You know...packages of old relics and the like?"

"It used to a lot when I was a child. Actually, it's been ages since it's happened. Of course, he's much older now. It only makes sense that he would cut back on the work."

"Exactly what does he do with them...the contents, I mean?"

Isabella gave him a look that was almost accusatory, making Jack afraid that he had asked too much. Then she seemed to discard whatever she'd been thinking and answered.

"They have a lab or a workshop or whatever you

want to call it down in the basement. Uncle Frank used to catalogue and sketch his botany finds. Uncle Rufus's speciality was in Egyptology. He used to get all sorts of things that other people either couldn't identify or else needed confirmation that their suppositions were correct. Uncle John was a geologist. Even though they've all retired, he usually keeps a rock tumbler going, polishing some of his latest finds."

"Interesting," Jack said. "But what about the others?"

"They used Daddy's lab at the clinic for their infertility work. This is just a place for the others to putter. Most of their real work was done on-site."

The elevator stopped. The door opened. Jack stood back for Isabella to get off first. When she didn't immediately move, Jack looked over to see what was wrong. She was standing without moving, watching his face. His heart sank. *Damn it. I asked too many questions.*

"Is something wrong?" he asked.

She stared for another moment longer, then finally shook her head.

"I hope not," she said quietly, and walked out of the elevator, pausing only long enough to thank him one more time.

"You're welcome," Jack said, mentally cursing himself up one side and down the other. "Oh... Isabella!"

She stopped. "Yes?"

"I'm going to do some research on the geography of this place today. Is there anything you would recommend that I see?"

The niggle of worry in Isabella's belly began to relax as she reminded herself that curiosity was probably part of a writer's mentality, but before she could answer him, he added another question that made her heart skip a beat.

"I don't suppose you'd want to go with me?" he asked. "We could take a picnic, and you could show me the sights as we drove."

She started to refuse, then remembered how gently he'd held her last night, and how his mouth had felt beneath her lips when she'd kissed him.

"I'll be on my best behavior," he added.

Even as she was thinking of a way to say no, she was wondering what it would be like if his best behavior ever slipped? She'd seen a glimpse of his passion when he'd put Bobby Joe Cage in the dirt, and again just now when he'd stood between her and Lawton Cage. After a lifetime of perfect behavior, Isabella knew she was changing. Maybe it had been coming all along, but she'd been more aware of it than ever since her father's death. She wanted to love—and be loved. And how was that ever going to happen unless she took the occasional risk?

"Now?" she asked.

"Yes."

"I need to change my clothes."

"I'll wait."

"And I need to tell the kitchen to fix us some sandwiches."

"I can do that while you change."

Isabella's eyes narrowed thoughtfully. "Do you always get your way?"

Jack shoved his hands in his pockets.

"Are you coming?"

She hesitated, then nodded.

He smiled. It was a slow, gut-burning look that went all the way to Isabella's toes and back, and in that moment she knew this man was someone who could matter to her—matter a great deal.

She'd been in love once, or thought she had, when she was in her teens. About four months into the relationship, they had made love. It had been her first and last attempt at misplaced passion. The boy had dropped her within weeks, and she'd been ashamed and in a panic until her period had come and gone. After that she'd sworn never to put herself in that position again unless it was with someone who mattered.

And now there was Jack Dolan.

She wasn't a child any longer, but the risks were still the same.

"Wait for me in the lobby. I won't be long."

"I'll wait."

The quiet certainty in his voice was her undoing. She shuddered as she walked away, wondering if he would wait long enough for her mind to wrap itself around the fact that one day she would lie naked in his arms.

# 9

They had been driving for almost two hours before Isabella felt relaxed. Jack's manner had ranged from cordial and interested in what they were seeing to playful and teasing. Slowly the tension she'd been feeling had begun to disappear. She had almost convinced herself that she'd imagined the sexual tension between them.

Almost.

But not quite.

Jack stood on the rim of a canyon, looking down into the narrow valley below. What had once been lush, high country grass was already turning brown, evidence of early killing frosts. The ponderosa pines under which they had parked were straight and tall, pointing persistently heavenward against the constantly prevailing winds. The mountain peaks across the valley were already white-capped, with some of the higher crevasses filled with drifted snow. Areas of spruce, fir and pine grew as far as halfway up the mountains, but after that there was nothing but intermittent outcroppings of unyielding rock, fit for nothing but an eagle's eyrie.

The grandeur of the place was overwhelming to a man like Jack, who'd grown up in the thick humidity of the Louisiana bottoms. Here, it was like standing at the top of the world. He took a deep breath and turned to the wind, relishing the sharp, cleansing feeling.

Beside him, Isabella stood silently, grappling with her own emotions. Initially, their trip had started out strained, but the farther they'd driven, the more relaxed she'd become. Now Jack sensed the scenery was settling to her, as well.

"You okay?" he asked.

She nodded.

"Glad you came?"

She looked at him then, but he couldn't read her expression.

"Yes, I'm glad."

"How high do you suppose we are?" Jack asked.

Isabella turned to look out across the valley to the peaks beyond.

"I don't know, probably between eight and nine thousand feet above sea level. Why?"

"Because my ears are ringing."

She grinned. "I don't hear anything."

Surprised by her teasing, he pulled her hair and grinned.

"Oh. That's very funny, Tinkerbell."

The look on Isabella's face was priceless. It was somewhere between shock and indignation.

"What did you call me?"

Now he was the one who was grinning. "What? You never had a nickname?"

"Never."

"You mean some bratty little boy in school never called you Izzy...or Bella...or—"

"Never."

He shook his head. "I'm thinking you've led a very sheltered life."

Isabella turned abruptly and strode to the car, then began digging through the trunk for the food that they'd brought. Jack knew almost instantly that he'd said the wrong thing. He followed her, gently sliding his hand across her back.

"Isabella...I'm sorry. I wasn't thinking about...I shouldn't have said..."

She straightened, her eyes bright with unshed tears.

"Don't apologize," she said. "It's just something I'm going to have to get used to. My life *was* sheltered. Until a few weeks ago, I never realized how much." She tried to smile through the tears. "Besides, I always liked Tinkerbell. She was a woman...er, fairy...who knew her own mind. Not a bad role model after all."

"Isabella..."

"Yes?"

"I very much need to kiss you."

*Oh God. This soon?*

She looked at his mouth, wondering how it would feel against her own. When he came closer, she tensed, thinking there was something she should say, like no, or please do. But then his hands cupped her face. When he traced the edges of her lower lip with his thumbs, her eyelids fluttered shut. She felt his breath on her face, and then he was there, his mouth against hers, searching gently at first, then harder.

Shock ricocheted through her defenses, making her weak with a longing she'd never known. Before she was forced to make another decision, he let her go, then enfolded her within his embrace.

"Easy," he said softly. "This is what we call a hug."

Isabella hid a smile against the front of his jacket.

"Really? It's what I would call making a move."

He ruffled her hair and then kissed the top of her head before making himself let her go.

"Yeah, I suppose that's another way to look at it. Now, what do we have to eat?"

She arched an eyebrow and smiled. "Just like a man."

And that quickly, the tension between them disappeared. Isabella was still smiling as she took an old blanket from the trunk and spread it beneath a sheltered stand of pines. Jack followed with the picnic basket, and soon they were sitting cross-legged on the blanket, talking amiably as they dug through the food the cook had prepared.

"Looks like we have bacon and tomato sandwiches, or ham and cheese."

"How many do we have?" Jack asked.

Isabella looked up to see if he was serious. He was. She smiled.

"Plenty."

"Then I'll have one of each," Jack said, and held out a paper plate.

She loaded it up, adding pickles and a big spoonful of potato salad.

"How does that look?" she asked.

"Like it might hold me for a couple of hours."

Her eyes widened. "Are you serious?"

"No."

Her laughter pierced him as he took the first bite of potato salad, and he knew that for the rest of his life he would remember this moment and the sound of her joy echoing across the canyon.

As they ate, they talked about everything from favorite Christmases to school bullies, and somewhere between the last bite of sandwich and her first bite of cookie, Isabella knew something was happening between them. After that kiss, he hadn't touched her again, but she saw the wanting in his eyes and felt his gaze on her face when he thought she wasn't looking. She felt guilty for being happy when her father and Uncle Frank were dead, but she had not been brought up to play the martyr. Being raised by seven very pedantic and logical men had ironed out any feminine wrinkles she might have developed in that respect. She didn't have it in her to play games with emotions, especially her own. She was falling for Jack Dolan. Plain and simple.

"Want another cookie?" she asked, as she began to pack up their leftover food.

"No room," Jack said, and rubbed his stomach.

"That's something I didn't expect to hear you say."

Jack grinned and tossed a wadded up napkin at her before stretching out on the blanket.

"If you need any help with the dishes, just let me know," he mumbled, as he folded his hands behind his head and closed his eyes.

Isabella snorted lightly. "That would mean you'd have to be upright and awake."

He crossed his legs at the ankles and shifted to one side without opening his eyes.

"You're a good cook, Tinkerbell, but don't ruin it by trying to make me feel guilty. Better people than you have tried—with no success."

She was smiling to herself as she tossed the last of the picnic stuff into the basket and put it in the trunk; then she glanced at her watch, taking note of the time. It was a little after 2:00 p.m. Plenty of time to get down from the mountains before dark. She glanced behind her. Jack looked awfully still.

"Jack?"

He didn't answer.

She shut the trunk lid and then walked to the blanket. He was already asleep. She stood for a moment, staring down into his face, studying the strength in his jawline and the length of his body. He was a very big man whom she had known for less than a week. The only things she knew were what he'd told her, and every bit of it could have been a lie. Good sense told her to go slow where this man was concerned, but her heart was telling her differently. The past few weeks had brought home to her how brief life could be and how swiftly it could end. She was twenty-eight years old and had never been truly in love. If this man stuck around long enough, she might find that was no longer the case.

Hesitating only briefly, she knelt down on the blanket. No big deal. They'd been sitting on it together during their meal. Just because the food and plates were gone, it didn't change all that much. And all that food and mountain air were making her sleepy, as well. She would lie back for just a few minutes to rest her eyes. Then she would wake Jack and start for home.

She stretched out on the blanket, then rolled to her side with her back to where Jack was lying. Overhead, she could hear the high-pitched screech of a foraging eagle, as well as the wind whistling through the pines above. She took a deep breath and then closed her eyes.

\* \* \*

Jack woke abruptly, his mind searching for answers to a series of confusing questions, including where in hell was he? How had he gotten here? And why was his left leg almost numb? Then the wind blew a strand of Isabella's hair across his lips and he remembered it all—standing on the rim of the canyon with her breath on his face and then holding her close in his arms, sharing food and laughter and the promise of so much more. He shifted slightly and looked down. She was fast asleep in his arms, with her leg across the lower half of his body and her cheek pillowed against his chest.

He looked at his watch. It was almost four. They'd been asleep for the better part of two hours. The sky was no longer clear and sunny; it looked to be threatening rain. Rising on one elbow, he scooted Isabella off his chest and then watched her wake up. The shock he saw on her face was as inevitable as the kiss she was about to receive.

"You are so beautiful," he said softly.

Isabella's thoughts were still slightly unfocused, but there wasn't any doubt in her mind about what was going to happen. What startled her most was how much she wanted to lie in his arms with nothing between them but passion. She lifted her hand to his face, feeling the faint prickle of whiskers as well as a muscle jumping near his jaw.

"I'm not very experienced at this," she said softly.

Jack brushed a kiss across her chin, then traced the curve with the tip of his tongue.

"I am," he answered.

"I'm not protected."

Jack shook his head as he kissed one of her eyelids, then the other.

"Yes, you are. You have me."

"I meant—"

Jack put a finger across the middle of her lips, shushing her explanation before it went any further.

"I know what you meant." He kissed the bridge of her nose, then cupped her face. "This isn't going to go that far."

Isabella sighed. "Just take me somewhere I haven't been."

Jack slid his arms around her and rolled, pulling her on top of him and then burying his face against the curve beneath her chin as her hair curtained around them. When she raised herself above him, his heart swelled with tenderness. He wanted to hold her and cherish her and never let her go.

"God, you feel like heaven in my arms."

"Can I trust you?" she asked.

Guilt struck. He wanted to look away from that wide, naive stare and instead found himself backed into a mental corner.

His hesitation was unexpected, and suddenly Isabella was nervous.

"Jack?"

"I can't do this," he muttered. "Not like this. Not without the truth."

If he'd slapped her, she couldn't have been more shocked. Embarrassed and hurting, she bolted to her feet and then turned her face to the wind.

"We need to go," she said briefly. "It's late."

Jack was up within seconds and standing behind her. The pain in her voice was unmistakable. He hated himself for letting this go too far, but when he reached for her, she shrugged off his grasp, yanked the blanket from the ground, then strode toward the car.

"Isabella...don't."

She tossed the blanket into the trunk and then turned. The wind was sharper now, blowing harder and lifting her hair like a long black veil.

"Don't what? Feel stupid? It's too late for that. Now please, get in the car before we get snowed in up here."

Without waiting to see if he would follow, she got into the car and slammed the door.

Startled, Jack glanced nervously at the sky and then headed for the car.

"Are you going to let me explain?"

She looked at him once, then looked away.

"There's nothing to explain," she said. "You came for local color, didn't you? Obviously you've already gotten all you need. Do you want me to drive?"

Cursing beneath his breath, Jack started the car

and turned around, retracing the route they'd taken. They rode in complete silence as the day continued to darken, stopping only once to refuel and use the bathrooms. By the time they arrived at Abbott House, it was night and the hotel was lit against the darkness like a beacon for the lost.

"We're home," Jack said, as he parked and killed the engine.

"No," Isabella said. "*I'm* home. You're just passing through."

She got out of the car, took the basket and blanket from the trunk, and strode into the hotel, leaving Jack to find his way alone.

He stood beside the car, judging how much anger she had left by the length of her stride, then decided his best bet was to wait until morning. Maybe then he would have figured out a way to explain why they hadn't made love. Then again, maybe not. To do that would mean blowing his cover, and that made no sense. He'd come to look for answers to a murder and instead had fallen in love with the shadow of a ghost. What was even worse was the fact that the murderer was probably living among them, and he had no way of knowing who he might be. One thing was certain: he needed to talk to the director.

As he started toward his room, he remembered he had yet to study the packet of photos he'd received earlier. Had that been only this morning? It seemed like a lifetime ago.

The desk clerk was a man, someone Jack had never seen before, and he nodded at Jack as he strode up the stairs to his room. The scent of food from the dining room wafted through the air, but he had no appetite. He was still locked into the image of Isabella's face. She'd turned off as certainly as if he'd flipped a switch. All he could do was hope that when this mess was over, he might still have a chance to work things out. Then he reminded himself that when this was over, his face might possibly be the last thing she would ever want to see. If he discredited her beloved Uncle Frank, or any of her other "family," he was as good as gone.

He unlocked his door and then entered his room. The bed had been made, and there was a bouquet of fresh flowers on a table by the window. He tossed his jacket on a chair and headed into the bathroom to wash up. When he came out a few minutes later, he was barefoot and bare-chested, wearing nothing but a pair of aging gray sweatpants with a tiny FBI logo near his ankle.

He picked up the FedEx packet he'd received early that morning and dumped the contents onto the bed. There were only three shots. One, a studio photo of a thirty-something Vaclav Waller, similar to what might be attached to a résumé. The second was a dark, grainy image accompanying a story clipped from a Russian newspaper. A translation of the text had been attached to the story. Jack scanned it quickly, noting that the bulk of the story was about the strides the man was making in researching DNA. The last picture was a copy of a real photo. He turned it over and read the brief notation on the back. It had been taken by an AP reporter in July 1970. In the photo, seven men, all of whom were doctors, were getting on a chartered plane that was bound for a medical symposium in the Bahamas. There was also a woman, whose face Jack could not see, and two pilots standing on either side of the stairs as the doctors were boarding.

Jack turned the picture back over, looking carefully at each of their faces. Three of them were bearded; one was wearing sunglasses; one's face was only in silhouette; and the other two were waving at the camera. The one in sunglasses was noted as Vaclav Waller. He studied the face only briefly. It was the others who interested him most. Waller was finally dead. That was a given. But what about the others? Did they really go down with the plane, or was the whole thing an elaborate ruse? And if so, then why? He could understand the ramifications of Waller's deception. If he had wanted to defect and feared repercussions from his country, he might have considered faking his own death to eliminate that risk. But the other doctors were not from communist-ruled countries. He turned the photo over again, reading off the names. Dr. John and Mary Rhodes, U.S.A. Dr. Vaclav Waller, Soviet Republic. Dr. Anton Spicer, Great Britain. Dr. Henry Jamison, U.S.A. Dr. Conrad Garner, Belgium. Dr. Somner

Craner, Belgium, and Dr. Orman Rhinehold, France. Only Waller might have had a possible yearning to defect. The others would have had no reason to go along with such a scheme.

He reached for his cell phone and put in a call to Quantico. He had a buddy in research who might be able to help. The phone rang seven times before Jack remembered the time. On the verge of hanging up, he was startled when he heard Steven Randolph's voice.

"Hello?"

"Steve, it's Jack Dolan."

"It's also almost eight o'clock at night. This is a recording. Call back during our regular office hours."

Jack grinned. "Shut up and listen for a minute, okay?"

"What the hell do you want, Dolan?"

Jack picked up the photo he'd been looking at. "A favor."

"I knew that when I heard your voice. What I'm asking is...*what* favor do you want?"

"Get a pen."

For the first time since Steven Randolph had answered the phone, Jack heard him chuckle.

"Hell, Dolan, didn't you know those grow out of my fingers? I'm always ready. Fire away."

"John Rhodes, Vaclav Waller, Anton Spicer, Henry Jamison, Conrad Garner, Somner Crane and Orman Rhinehold."

"Got 'em. Now what?" Steven asked.

"For starters, they all died in a plane crash in 1970…or at least that's what we were led to believe."

"What's up with that?"

"Well, Vaclav Waller turned up murdered in Brighton Beach a few weeks ago. Quite a trick for a man who was supposed to have died in a plane crash over thirty years ago."

"What's our interest?" Steven asked.

"Waller was a Russian doctor, and we got some info that indicates a Soviet visitor entered the country right before the old man was killed. It's a long story, but we have reason to believe that whatever the Russians are after, they didn't get it from Waller."

"How do you know?"

"We have it on good faith that the killer has moved to the place where the old man had been living. We don't know what he's after or who else might be in danger. And the more I know about this man, the better off I'll be."

"Yeah, okay, but what's with the other names?"

"They were doctors who were also on the plane that supposedly crashed. I want to know everything there is to know about what they were working on. Oh yeah, and except for John Rhodes and Henry Jamison, the others are European, so look elsewhere, too."

"Got a number where you can be reached?"

"Yeah, but why don't you e-mail me the stuff instead?" He gave Steven Randolph his e-mail address, then, a few minutes later, disconnected.

Weary in both heart and body, he tossed the pictures on a table and crawled into bed. He was still thinking of Isabella when he fell asleep.

By the time Isabella got into her room and undressed to take a shower, she was shaking. She reached for the soap as she stepped beneath the spray, but it slipped through her fingers and fell to the tub.

She stared down at the pink orb as it lay between her feet, watching the faint flow of melting soap slide toward the drain. In that moment, she saw her life in the very same way. The foundation that had been her life was sliding out from under her, just as the soap had slipped from her hands. No matter how hard she tried to stay focused, things kept getting in her way.

The logical part of her said that she couldn't really care for Jack Dolan—that she was just transferring her emotions to a living, breathing man because the other men in her life kept dying. But the emotional part of her knew that if Jack Dolan were only willing, she could very easily give him her heart. Unfortunately, he had not only refused her willingness to make love, but, in essence, had refused her, as well. And therein lay her pain.

She tried to laugh, but it came out as a sob.

Weary all the way to her soul, she went to her knees, covered her face with her hands and started to cry. Water pelted her head, running down her face and mingling with her tears. She cried until her eyes were swollen and her head was one giant ache. Finally she dragged herself to her feet and scrubbed herself raw. Even after she emerged from the shower, she knew what she'd done had been symbolic, rather than resulting from a need to be clean.

As she was drying off, the phone in her living room began to ring. She started to answer it, then thought of Jack and changed her mind. Finally the ringing stopped. She toweled her hair until it was partially dry, then wrapped herself in a thick cotton robe, stepped into her favorite house shoes and went into the tiny kitchen.

As she began to brew a pot of coffee, a gust of wind blew against the windows, rattling the panes. She glanced toward the windows, shivering as she did. The approaching storm they'd seen over the mountains was finally here. It was too early in the year for snow in the valley, but she knew the rain would be cold, making for a dreary day tomorrow, which suited her mood just fine.

It was just before sunrise when Vasili Rostov rose. He dressed hastily, then dug through his pack for his phone. He glanced outside, trying to judge the time by the brightening aura on the horizon, then shrugged. It didn't matter what time it was here in

Montana, he was about to call home, and he'd been gone so long that he'd lost track of the time difference.

He sat down on his bed, punched in a series of numbers, then waited for his call to be answered. To his relief, it didn't take long. He spoke softly, not wanting to be overheard speaking in his native tongue.

"This is Rostov."

"You have news?"

Rostov grunted. "He is dead."

There was a long, pregnant silence, which did not alleviate Rostov's anxiety.

"Are you there?" he asked.

"This is not what we wanted to hear."

Rostov sighed. "It is not what I expected, either."

"How did this happen?"

Again Rostov hesitated, uncertain how to explain what had gone wrong. Finally he decided on the truth.

"He killed himself as we spoke."

"Explain!"

There was anger in his superior's voice, but the distance between them gave him a courage of his own.

"He took one look at my face and knew."

"He recognized you?"

"Only in the capacity in which I was sent."

"And for that he chose to die?"

"He knew I would take him back. He chose not to go. It is that simple."

"When did this happen?"

"A week ago. I am now in the town where he was living. I have searched his home and found nothing that would lead me to believe he was anything but an old and dying man."

"Dying? I thought you said he was already dead."

"I have reason to believe he was suffering from cancer. I found medicine in his belongings that someone suffering from cancer might take. It is why I think he chose to end his life here rather than in an interrogation center in Russia."

"Was anyone living with him?"

Rostov's heart skipped a beat. This question could have meant anything, but something told him the man was not referring to a wife.

"There is an entire hotel full of people. He had rooms alone on the top floor of a rather quaint hotel. I've been in it. There was nothing of consequence."

"Then it is over. You know what to do next?"

"Yes," Rostov said. "I know what to do next."

"When you get back, come to my office."

"When I get back," Rostov repeated, knowing full well that would be never. His failure to produce the desired results would not be looked upon with favor, which was another reason to proceed with his original plan. He hung up the phone and then packed it away. A man without a home, such as he was pretending to be, would have no use for such a thing, and for the time being, he needed to stay in his disguise.

David Schultz got up from the table where he'd been eating breakfast and went to the table where Isabella was sitting. He leaned over and kissed the top of her head before sitting opposite her. There were shadows on her face, and her eyes were red-rimmed and swollen. Seeing her this way made him feel old and helpless. Surely there was something he could say that would help her get past this grief.

"Good morning, dear. We missed you earlier," he said, indicating the other uncles, who were still finishing their meal.

Isabella shoved aside a piece of fruit on her plate and then laid down her fork.

"I know. I'm sorry, I should have—"

"No apology necessary. We were merely concerned."

"I'm fine," she said, and took a sip of her coffee.

He laid his hand on her arm and gave it a squeeze.

"You don't look fine."

He thought he saw her chin quiver, and when she suddenly looked away, he knew he'd been right. Her eyes were swimming with unshed tears.

"Isabella...darling...you are breaking my heart. I know you are missing Samuel, as well as your Uncle Frank, but you have to know they're in a better place. Samuel's heart attack was sudden, but it was massive. There was nothing that could have been done to save him, no matter where it happened. As for Frank's passing, it, too, was out of our control. He became a victim of circumstance, didn't he?''

Isabella sighed. She was ashamed to admit that most of her tears were selfishly directed at her own disappointment and not for the loss of her father and Frank.

''Yes, Uncle David. I know that, and truthfully, I'm getting better every day.''

He frowned. ''Then what's all this about?''

She shrugged, then looked away. At that moment she saw Jack walk into the dining room. She flinched, and David saw it. Suddenly her behavior was starting to make sense.

''How was your trip yesterday?''

She looked startled. ''What trip?''

''I was looking for you yesterday afternoon. Delia said you were gone. She also said that you'd taken that writer, Jack Dolan, on a sightseeing trip. So how was it? Did he get everything he needed…for his book?''

Isabella's eyes flashed, but she stifled her anger. It wasn't Uncle David's fault that she'd set herself up for disappointment.

''I suppose so. I took him into the Lewis and Clark National Forest.''

David smiled. ''It must be beautiful up there this time of year.''

"It was cold," she said, and poured some fresh coffee in her cup, then busied herself by stirring in a spoonful of sugar.

"It must have been late when you returned. I didn't see you at dinner."

"It wasn't all that late. I just wasn't hungry," she said.

"Darling…"

She looked up. The concern on his face was her undoing. Besides, she'd never been able to lie. She lowered her voice as she answered.

"He didn't do anything, if that's what you're worrying about."

"Then if he didn't make a pass, why are you angry?"

Stunned by his perceptiveness, she struggled for an answer she didn't have.

"Do you like him?" David asked.

"Of course. He's a likeable man, but I hardly know him," Isabella muttered.

"Oh…love has been won and lost in less time than you've known Jack Dolan."

She shrugged, refusing to comment.

At that moment David wished that Samuel were still alive. This was something that a father should be dealing with, not an uncle—and only an honorary one, at that.

"You've never dated much. The uncles and I have often worried that you're too confined by this hotel to get out as much as a young women such as yourself should.''

''I've gone out as often as I wanted. Besides, it's not like there's a huge gene pool of eligible males here. There are only six thousand people in Braden, and more than half of them are senior citizens. Most of the others are married or spoken for, and the few who aren't, aren't worth the dirt it would take to bury them.''

David frowned, remembering the incident with her tire.

''Bobby Joe Cage definitely falls into the latter category.''

''My point exactly,'' Isabella said.

''Jack Dolan is not from here.''

''Which means he won't be staying, doesn't it?'' she said, and then stood abruptly. ''I'm sorry, Uncle David, but I just remembered something I need to do.''

She left without waiting for him to tell her good-bye. David stood, watching her sail past Jack Dolan's table with her head held high. And judging from Dolan's expression, he was in no better mood than Isabella had been.

He sighed as he thought of what lay ahead. The biggest relief they could know was that Isabella had found someone to love her when they were no longer around. With one last glance in Jack Dolan's direction, he went back to the table to gather the others.

It was time to set the last project in motion.

# 10

Isabella was already at the front desk, checking in new guests, when David exited the dining area. Thomas and Jasper lingered behind to visit with an acquaintance from Braden, but John and Rufus were at David's heels. The two old men were head-to-head, talking animatedly with each other as they walked. John Michaels's thin, lanky body was a complete opposite to Rufus's tall, portly figure. Samuel Abbott had often lovingly referred to them as their very own Laurel and Hardy.

When Isabella saw them coming, she flinched. The last thing she wanted was more of her Uncle David's third degree.

"Miss?"

She quickly returned her attention to the couple who were just checking in.

"I'm sorry. What did you ask?"

Leonardo Silvia repeated his question.

"Do you have a phone book we might borrow? I need to look up the number to White Mountain Fertility Clinic. We have an appointment there this afternoon, but I want to confirm the time."

"There will be one in your room, but I know the number. It's 555-1212."

"You are sure?" Leonardo asked.

Isabella smiled. "I've called it every day for most of my life."

Maria Silvia leaned across the counter, fixing Isabella with a sympathetic stare.

"You, too, are trying to have a child?"

"No, nothing like that. My father, Dr. Samuel Abbott, was one of the founders of the clinic."

Maria's eyes widened. "Oh! How proud you must be of him that he is devoting his life to helping people like my Leonardo and me."

"Yes, I was very proud. Unfortunately, he passed away recently."

Maria gasped and then moaned. "No...oh no! We have come too late!"

The terror on the little woman's face was evident. Isabella quickly added, "Oh, no! I didn't mean to imply that there was no longer a clinic. The clinic is run by a fully trained staff." Then she waved her Uncle David over to the desk, anxious that he help calm the woman before she went into hysterics. "Uncle David, I want you to meet Leonardo and Maria Silvia. They've come to visit the clinic. In fact, they have an appointment this afternoon. Maria, this is Doctor Schultz, another one of the founders."

David Schultz saw desperation in the woman's face and gently took her hand in his own.

"Maria, is it?"

She nodded quickly, but her heart was still pounding out an irregular rhythm.

"Yes, Doctor. I am Maria Silvia. This is my husband, Leonardo. You can help me have a baby?"

David smiled. "We can certainly try."

She began to relax. "Oh…it will be successful. This I know."

It was good to know that her confidence in their facility was high, but David worried that her expectations were even higher. He didn't want to dispel her hopes, but he also didn't want to mislead her.

"Well, we do all that is humanly possible and then say a few prayers. After that, it is up to a higher power."

Maria's smile widened. "I have already prayed to God many times, but this time I know my prayers will come true."

Leonardo put his arm around his wife and tried to pull her away.

"Please…Maria *mia,* don't bother the doctor right now. Leave all our explanations for our appointment this afternoon at the clinic."

But Maria wasn't through. She couldn't let go without being sure the doctor understood. She patted Leonardo's cheek, then turned to David once more.

"I do not wish to bother you," she said. "I only want you to know that I have promised my child to God. This is how I know it will happen."

The hair on the back of David's neck suddenly

stood on end as he looked down into the woman's eyes.

"You promised a child to God?"

She nodded. "Son or daughter...it does not matter. What matters is that I have promised God that I will raise our child to serve others as His disciples served Him."

"That's a very noble thing to do," he said. "But what if your child chooses otherwise?"

Maria shook her head. "It will not happen."

Curious now, the other two uncles were also listening closely to this small, dark-headed woman's unusual theory.

"How can you be so sure?" David asked.

"Because if God gives me the child, He will certainly also give the child the calling."

He stared at her closely, seeing a faith that almost shamed him. And knowing the last project that still lay ahead of them, David felt as if his meeting with this woman had been predetermined.

"Yours is a most remarkable faith," he said.

She smiled. "My God is a most remarkable god." Then she patted Leonardo's hand. "My husband has already picked out a name if it's a boy."

David chuckled. "That's what I call planning ahead."

Maria nodded. "It will be after his grandfather, you see. Tell him, Leonardo."

Leonardo gave David an apologetic look as he answered.

"It's true. I have always said I would name our first son after my grandfather. His mother was English, his father Sicilian. He spent his whole life in Italy but considered himself too old to emigrate when my family left for America."

"So what was your grandfather's name?" David asked.

Leonardo shrugged. "Bartholomew Silvia. The family called him Barto. An odd combination of names, I grant you, but I loved him dearly."

David nodded cordially, but his mind was racing.

"Someone will be seeing you this afternoon?"

"Yes, and it will be none too soon, right, Leonardo?"

"That is true," he said, then picked up their suitcases before leading her toward the elevator.

David glanced at John and Rufus, who were watching him intently. He looked back at the woman, his eyes narrowing thoughtfully as the pair began to cross the lobby. Suddenly he called out. "Maria!"

She stopped beside the stairwell, then turned, unaware that the light from the mullioned panes above the entry had formed a halo above her head.

"Yes, Doctor?"

When David saw that, he took it as their own blessing to proceed.

"What is the doctor's name who you're going to see?"

"A Doctor Bennett, I believe."

"Yes, yes, Aaron Bennett. A fine doctor with a very high rate of successes, but how would you feel about seeing me, instead?"

Maria beamed. "I would like it very much…to consult with a doctor we have already met. And one of the founders of the clinic! It is more than we expected."

David nodded. "Then it's agreed. I'll call the clinic myself and notify them of the change. As for now, you two get settled in your room. Get some rest. Have a good lunch. We'll see you at three."

"Thank you, Doctor Schultz. Thank you very much."

"No, Mrs. Silvia, I suspect it is we who should thank you."

His cryptic comment was as surprising to Isabella as his offer had been. It had been more than five years since any of the three founders had taken regular patients. She wondered what was so special about this particular woman that would make him come out of retirement. But when she looked at the aging trio, they seemed blithely unaware of her curiosity.

They had started up the stairs when David stopped and turned.

"Isabella, I think you should take the day off."

"What on earth for? I never take a day off."

"That's exactly why you should do it," he said. "And while you're at it, get your hair done. Have a manicure. Get a massage from that…that…what's her name at the beauty shop.''

"Lola Bryan, and I'm not going to do something so frivolous for no reason.''

Jack Dolan came out of the dining room just as David started to answer. He gave the man a studied look and then turned to Isabella.

"You've got a reason, and you know it.''

Irked by their interference into what she considered a personal issue, she stubbornly refused to comment as they walked up the stairs and then out of sight. When she turned back to the desk, Jack Dolan was there. The sight of him standing there did things to her heart that were better left unsaid. Torn between the urge to hit him or kiss him, she took a deep breath instead.

"How may I help you?'' she asked.

The frigid tone of her voice cut all the way to Jack's conscience, but he wasn't going to play the blame game right now.

"Are there any hiking trails around here?''

His question took her by surprise. Her answer gave away what she'd been thinking.

"Didn't get enough sightseeing yesterday?''

The moment she asked it, she could have cut out her tongue. She rolled her eyes, then took a deep breath.

"Excuse me while I rewind my mouth.''

A muscle twitched at the corner of Jack's lips,

but he managed to stay a smile. Something told him it wouldn't be wise to laugh right now.

"Yes, there are a couple." She reached beneath the counter and then handed him a map. "They're easily identified by the red lines. I assume you've had backpacking experience?" Then she added, "I ask only because we have had the occasional hiker get lost up in the mountains, and I wouldn't want it to happen again."

Jack took the map. "Yes, I know what I'm doing."

*Well, good, because I certainly don't.* "That's fine, then," Isabella said. "Be sure to pack enough water. You aren't planning to stay out overnight, are you?"

Jack shook his head. "No. Just a day trek."

"Then dress warmly and enjoy your hike."

Jack sighed. God, he hated the way he felt.

"Isabella?"

The look in her eyes would have fried eggs on a cold sidewalk.

"What?"

"Yesterday I—"

"There is nothing to explain. Your message was sent and received."

He sighed. "It isn't what you think."

"Nothing ever is."

"Damn it, that's not what I meant."

She leaned forward, lowering her voice so that their conversation was not overheard.

"I do not intend to speak of this again, Mr. Dolan. Do you understand?"

He leaned forward, too, his voice full of misplaced anger.

"I hear you, but it doesn't mean I'm paying attention. Do *you* understand?"

Isabella glared.

Jack stared back.

The phone rang. Isabella turned to answer it. When she looked around, Jack was staring out the window. The moment she hung up, he pointed.

"Who's that man?"

She leaned across the desk to see where he was pointing.

"Oh...that's the gardener. Why do you ask?"

"He looks familiar."

"You've probably seen him out mowing."

"No."

She shrugged. "I don't see how you can be so sure."

Jack turned. Fixing her with a cold, intent stare.

"I don't forget faces."

"That's good to know," she snapped. "So when you're gone, I will rest easy knowing mine won't be forgotten."

Jack glared, alternating between the urge to shake her or kiss her senseless. The knowledge that there was a killer in their midst—one who was most likely a Soviet spy, to boot—was making him antsy. And the fact that he couldn't come right out and confront these people about Frank Walton's deception was making his job even more difficult. What made him feel even worse was the possibility that Isabella was involved in the lie, and if she was, she could also be in danger. However, his frustration with her was secondary to the warning that had gone off in his head when he'd seen the man outside.

"What's his name?" Jack asked.

"What's whose name?"

"The gardener."

"Victor Ross, and he's a good worker who minds his own business, which is what I suggest you do."

Having said that, Isabella flounced into the office and slammed the door. Seconds later, Delia emerged through the same door, a little wild-eyed and nervous as she quickly took up a position at the check-in desk.

"Good morning, Mr. Dolan. Is there something I can help you with?"

"I doubt it," Jack muttered, and headed for the door.

Despite Isabella's assurance, he still wanted a closer look at the gardener, but when he got outside, the man was no longer in sight.

Frustrated with women and the world in general, he went back into the hotel, then hesitated as he stared at the closed door to the office. After a moment of indecision, he headed to his room. There would be time to talk to Isabella later, because he was almost positive that he'd seen that man before, or someone who looked an awful lot like him. If he could just remember where. Maybe it would come to him later.

The hiking trails that he'd asked Isabella about were not for sightseeing. He was convinced that the man who'd killed Frank Walton was somewhere in the area. But, because of the clinic, there was a constant influx of strangers, so isolating one particular individual was proving difficult, if not impossible. And there was always the possibility that the killer was hiding somewhere in the mountains, biding his time. Jack's idea was to hike some of the area surrounding the hotel. He couldn't cover all of it alone, but he could eliminate some of the most obvious possibilities.

Isabella stared at the papers on her desk for all of two minutes before she picked up the phone, punching in the numbers with angry jabs. The moment her call was answered, she knew that what she was going to do amounted to nothing more than running away. But facing her life as it was today was more than she could handle.

"Marcy, this is Isabella Abbott. Do you have time to cut and style my hair today? You do? Great. Oh, one other thing. Is Lola working today? Good. Is it possible that I might get a massage before you do my hair? Fantastic! I'll see you at eleven."

She hung up the phone, then took a deep breath and exited the office.

"Delia, I'm going to Braden. I won't be back until sometime this afternoon."

"Okey-dokey," Delia said.

Isabella smiled grimly as she strode down the hall toward the family suite. Okey-dokey indeed. She needed to take a feather from Delia's happy cap. Lighten up a bit. The world was still going to revolve even if her own personal life was wobbling, so to hell with Jack Dolan.

The uncles had gathered in David's room in preparation for the beginning of their last project. While they were waiting for John to arrive, they were having coffee and watching the news.

"Did you hear that?" Rufus asked, as he pointed to the television screen. "Some man in Florida was wrestling an alligator and got his nose bitten off. What must he have been thinking to do such a thing to begin with?"

Jasper chuckled. "Not the best donor for the gene pool, is he?"

The others laughed. Moments later, the news anchor switched from local to world news. Suddenly David raised his voice above the din.

"Listen!" he cried, then picked up the remote and turned up the volume.

"On a stranger note...a theft was discovered this morning in a remote Italian village. Some of the bones of a long-dead monk known only as St. Bartholomew have been stolen. Sainthood was ordained by the Pope some eighty years ago after people began praying to the monk's remains and claiming to have been healed.

"The discovery was made after a cleaning woman bumped the container in which the bones were being displayed and a piece of the glass fell off. It's not known how many were taken, only that some are missing.

"Last week the bodies of three local men who were reported to have made their livings in less than honest ways were found dead in a farmer's field. It was thought at the time that they had fought among themselves and killed each other, but now, with the discovery of this most recent theft, there is talk that there might be a connection between the two incidents.

"More later."

"My God," David said, and turned off the TV. "What has Samuel done?"

The others looked as horrified as he did. Never in all their years of working together had they crossed that kind of a line.

"Did you know?" Jasper asked.

David gasped in dismay. "No! Of course not. Did you?"

The others denied knowledge, as well, leaving them to ponder the lengths with which Samuel Abbott had been willing to go to see his work come to fruition.

"What do you think we should do?" David asked.

"We can't give them back," Rufus said. "We'd have to explain how we got them, which would lead to why, and, well…you know."

"Did you catch the monk's name?" John asked.

David frowned. "Yes. Why?"

"Do you remember the Silvia woman?"

David nodded. "I'm not likely to forget."

"The name they plan to give their baby if it's a boy…didn't the husband say they were going to name him Bartholomew, after his grandfather?"

"Yes. So?"

"The bones. They belonged to a monk named St. Bartholomew."

There was a moment of shock, followed by a buzz of voices.

"Hush!" David said quickly. Then he looked at John. "What are you thinking?"

"That it's a sign to proceed."

Even though the vote had already been taken to proceed, David sensed ambivalence within the group.

"Rufus…I can tell you're having reservations."

Rufus nodded, absently rubbing his paunch as he paced.

"More than one, yes, more than one."

Thomas Mowry took off his glasses, then blew his nose. "He's not the only one," he said, and sat down with a thump. "I can't believe we're going to try this again—and after all these years. I don't care if this is a sign. If we've learned anything from the other projects, it's that they did not succeed.''

''They didn't all fail,'' David said.

They looked at each other, then nodded.

''That one was different,'' Jasper said.

Thomas shook his head. ''That's the point. The one successful implant was different, but we don't know why.''

''Samuel said—''

''Samuel is dead,'' Thomas said shortly. ''And so is Frank. I think nature is trying to tell us something here, but we're not listening. We have had only one success out of twenty projects. That is not good odds.''

''But Samuel said he had perfected the process, remember?''

Thomas slapped his hand on his knee. ''How many times must this be said? Samuel is not here. Do you know enough about what he was doing to replicate it?''

David nodded. ''Yes...and we have already found the perfect woman. The woman John referred to before.''

Jasper and Thomas looked startled. ''But how—''

''It was fate,'' David said. ''Ask John and Rufus.''

The pair of men looked at each other and then turned to the others.

''It's true,'' John said. ''We talked to her only a

short while ago. She has an appointment with David at three o'clock this afternoon. If she's physically able to carry a child, then I say, yes.''

Rufus nodded in agreement, then leaned forward and lowered his voice.

"She has promised her child to God.''

Jasper frowned. "She what?''

"She says she prayed to God to give her a child, and in payment, she will raise the child to live its life in the service of God's teachings…sort of like the disciples.''

"Is she nuts?'' Thomas asked.

David smiled. "No. Just determined.''

They sat, absorbing the news and weighing the obstacles. Rufus got to his feet and stared at the wooden box on the floor, weighing what he knew it contained against what they'd been told. Finally he turned to the others.

"If we're going to make this work, we need to get busy. John, you get one end of that box, and, Jasper, you get the other. And be careful with the contents. We don't have much to work with.''

David locked his door from inside, putting on the safety chain as well as a dead bolt, then gathered up an armload of lab coats and led the way into his bedroom. He opened the door to the walk-in closet, shoved aside a large stack of sweaters and pressed down on the shelf. Instantly a large panel of wood separated itself from the closet and slid inward into a pocket in the wall.

"After you," he said quietly.

Then, one after the other, the men stepped into the opening. David was the last to enter, pressing another switch as he did. The wall slid back into place, and the hidden elevator car in which they were standing began a near-silent descent. Moments later, it stopped. The door opened, and the five men walked out into a tunnel and headed toward a phalanx of battery-powered carts lined up against the wall.

They got in without comment, two to a cart, with David taking the lead cart alone. With a turn of the key, he drove forward, guided by recessed lights in the ceiling and the familiarity of having come this way before. The others followed, silent now, as they traversed the tunnel, their thoughts on the task ahead.

Their journey ended a mile from the elevator, deep within the bowels of White Mountain. They got out of the carts and proceeded to a massive steel door. There were no windows or knobs through which to gain access. Only a small black box with a keypad of numbers that had been mounted on the wall. David punched in the access code, and immediately the door swung inward. As it did, the room was illuminated, light spreading from an array of fluorescent fixtures suspended from the ceiling.

They stood for a moment, eyeing the different lab stations they had long ago created, as well as the state-of-the-art equipment on gleaming, stainless steel tables.

David was the first to move. He hit a power switch that turned on all the computerized equipment, then handed each of the men a lab coat.

"You know what to do," he said. "I'll be back later, after I've met with Maria Silvia."

"What if she—"

"It's too late for what-ifs," David said. "Just get started. Something tells me we're running out of time, and in more ways than one."

When he left, the others were bent over a lab table, watching Rufus removing two ancient bones from the oblong wooden box. David shut the door behind him and then took a cart back to the hotel. He didn't want to be late for his appointment with Maria.

It was eighteen minutes after three in the afternoon when Jack reached what amounted to a small plateau on the valley side of White Mountain. He'd been hiking for the better part of five hours and still hadn't come across anything that would convince him the man he was looking for had been hiding in the hills. Added to that, the altitude was killing him. His heart was pounding, and his vision kept going in and out of focus. No matter how badly he wanted to continue, this was obviously as high as he could go. Cursing himself for not thinking to pack a portable bottle of oxygen, he sat down on a boulder, shrugged off his backpack and lowered his head between his knees.

Slowly his heart rate regulated itself and his vision steadied. As he sat, he heard a shrill cry from high above him in the sky. He looked up to see an eagle circling. He watched the great bird's wings fan in perfect symmetry, catching the air currents, then riding them higher and higher.

"So I'm not the only one out hunting today," he said, then picked up his backpack and pulled out a bottle of water.

He drank long and heartily, then set it aside, popped a few nuts in his mouth and began to chew. Slowly his equilibrium began to return. Satisfied that he was ready to start down, he repacked his things and shouldered his pack. He started to retrace his steps and then stopped. He'd come this far without finding anything. It seemed a waste of time to go back the way he'd come, knowing full well there was nothing there that would help his case. He pulled out the map of the hiking trails that Isabella had given him and calculated his approximate location. At that point he realized if he went a quarter of a mile east he would cross the other trail that she'd marked. Even if his hunch had been wrong in thinking the killer had taken to the woods, at least he would see new territory on the way down.

Checking his compass, he aligned himself in the correct direction and started walking. Within thirty minutes he had found the other marked hiking trail and started down, guessing that he would arrive back at the hotel just before dark.

About an hour later he stopped to take a drink, and as he did, he realized that he could see the roof of the hotel from where he stood. Curious, he took out his binoculars, adjusted them to his sight and began to scan the area. Within a couple of minutes he saw a tiny figure emerge from a shed and knew it must be the gardener, Victor Ross. Frowning, he watched until the man had gone into the back of the hotel, then replaced the binoculars in his pack and resumed his trek.

Later, he would think back, knowing that if his shoelace hadn't come untied, he never would have seen the small bit of shiny metal half-hidden in the leaves. Curious, he brushed aside the debris and found a small pocketknife, similar in style to what was commonly referred to as a Swiss Army knife. There was a multitude of small blades suited for different purposes, even one that served dual duty as a can opener and a screwdriver. It wasn't until he began closing the blades that he noticed an odd, unfamiliar mark. He tilted the knife sideways for a better view, and within seconds his head came up and he pivoted sharply. He neither saw nor heard anything that would lead him to believe he was being watched, but that didn't settle his thoughts. The knife that he'd found wasn't remarkable, but the manufacturer certainly was. It was Russian made, and the likelihood that the knife had been lost by someone other than the man he was looking for was nil. Jack Dolan wasn't a gambler, and he didn't like the odds. Finding this knife changed everything. A possibility had just turned into a probability, which meant he needed to contact Washington at once.

He pulled out his cell phone, but to his disgust no signal was available. Anxious to notify the director of what he'd found, he started down White Mountain in haste, mentally sifting through everything he knew so far, which wasn't much.

As he came out from beneath a canopy of trees, a large bird flew across his line of vision in a steep, unyielding dive. He didn't know what it was, but from the speed and the size, it looked like a falcon. Knowing their propensity for hunting, he could only pity whatever target the falcon had fixed upon.

He glanced at his watch. It was almost five o'clock. In an hour or so, it would be dark. Not wanting to be caught on White Mountain at nightfall, he lengthened his stride.

To his left, he saw a blur of feathers and realized the falcon had caught its prey. Within seconds of the thought, a memory surfaced and his heart skipped a beat.

Hawk! Not a falcon—a Hawk. Oh God...that was what he'd been trying to remember ever since he'd seen Victor Ross.

Back in the sixties, there had been a famous Soviet spy known only as the Hawk. He had been relentless and personally responsible for the deaths of many, including ten American agents during a government cleansing. To this day, it was a mystery as to how he'd learned their names. There had been only one known photograph of him, taken at an airport in France. The image had been faint and grainy, but the Slavic bone structure of his face had been as remarkable and unique as a fingerprint.

Jack's stomach turned. If he was right about Victor Ross's identity, this was bigger than any of them had suspected. Settling his pack more securely, he started to run.

David Schultz took a sip of coffee, then picked up the lab tests and bloodwork they'd just done on the Silvias. His initial examination had been hopeful, even more so than he'd expected. Years ago Maria had had a bout with endometriosis, but her scarring was minimal, definitely not enough to preclude her as a candidate for implantation. He leaned back in his chair, smiling to himself as he continued to read. It kept getting better and better. She was thirty-nine years old, enjoyed good health and, if what she said was true, lived a healthy lifestyle, eating foods that were good for her and exercising regularly. Her family health history wasn't so great. Both of her parents had died young, of heart disease, but obviously Maria had taken measures to see that she didn't repeat their fates.

He took another sip of coffee, then kicked back in his chair, contemplating the necessary sequence

of events. The day after tomorrow, he would recommend taking Maria into surgery where they
would stimulate her ovaries, then harvest the eggs.
After that it would be a matter of collecting Leonardo's sperm and then proceeding from there. Tonight he would know for certain if Rufus had been
able to gather any viable DNA from the bones. Until
that time, what would happen with Maria and Leonardo Silvia was anybody's guess.

Isabella kept looking at herself in the rearview
mirror on the drive back home. It was the same face
that had always been there, but the hair was definitely a change. Instead of the long straight sweep
that she'd worn most of her adult life, the beautician
had cut it short to her chin, then layered it all over,
leaving her with a ragged, slept-in look that she
wasn't sure she liked. She kept thinking that she
looked as if she'd just gotten out of bed and dressed
without combing her hair. The short, layered ends
caught the breeze coming through the partially
opened windows, whipping them madly as she
drove, but the farther she went, the freer she felt. It
was as if, in cutting her hair, she'd cut her ties with
the past. Part of who she'd been was buried with
her father and her Uncle Frank. Some more of her
had been left behind on the beauty shop floor. Now
it was up to her to discover exactly who was left.
With one last glance in the rearview mirror, she ac-

celerated swiftly, leaving a wild trail of dust in her wake.

About two miles from the hotel, she saw a man walking toward her on the side of the road.

John Running Horse. Bless his heart, what could he be doing all the way out here?

She slowed down, then stopped and rolled down her window.

"John...it's me, Isabella. Do you want a ride back to town?"

He shook his head, almost in slow motion, peering at her through the curtain of hair falling over his face.

"Can't go with you. I'm going to Memphis. Gotta find my momma."

"I wouldn't take long," she said.

"Can't go," he repeated. "Do you have a guitar?"

"No, I don't, John. I'm sorry."

"I can sing," he said. "If I had a guitar, I would sing. My momma likes to hear me sing."

"All right, then," Isabella said. "Goodbye."

She accelerated slowly, unwilling to stir up any dust until she was farther away. She glanced once in the rearview mirror before she turned the curve. John was just a tiny speck in the distance, but she could tell he was still moving.

It hurt her heart to think of a man that strong in body who had the mind of a child—and a lost one, at that.

# 11

Isabella turned off the road into the parking lot of Abbott House and then drove her car around back, parking it in the unattached garage. She grabbed her purse as she got out and slung the shoulder strap over her neck, leaving her hands free to carry her other purchases. She had just shut the door and was turning around when Victor Ross suddenly appeared in the doorway.

"Victor! You startled me," Isabella said.

"I'm sorry. May I help you carry your purchases, Miss Abbott?"

Isabella smiled. "Yes, that would be great. Thanks."

She handed him the heavier of the two bags and, together, they started toward the service entrance of the hotel.

"So, Victor, have you given any more thought to staying on here?"

"Yes, I am still considering it," he said. "It was a most generous offer."

She smiled again. "You're doing a most remarkable job."

Victor nodded. "Thank you."

They entered the hotel through the kitchen, then proceeded through the lobby.

"Where do you want me to put this?" Victor asked, as they paused at the registration desk.

"Would you mind carrying it a bit further? The family quarters are on the ground floor, just beyond the staircase."

"I would be honored."

Isabella laughed. "I'm afraid it's not much of an honor to be carrying toiletries, but it is much appreciated."

He almost smiled, leaving Isabella with the impression that smiling was not something that came naturally to him.

"Here we are," she said, and took out her ring of keys, then fumbled and dropped it before she could get the key in the lock.

"Allow me," Victor said, and had the keys in hand before she knew what was happening.

To her surprise, he flipped through the keys and chose the right one without asking, then slid it into the lock and gave it a turn. The tumblers clicked silently as the door swung inward.

Victor took the key from the lock and then stepped aside.

"You first, miss," he said.

Isabella was so taken with his manners that she walked inside without retrieving her keys. She was all the way into her small kitchen when she realized

Victor was not behind her. She turned around. He was still standing in the doorway, holding her sack.

"Just put it on that chair over there," she said. "And thank you very much for your help."

"You're most welcome, Miss Abbott," he said, and turned to leave.

"Wait!" Isabella cried.

Victor stopped, cursing his luck. He hadn't had time to slip her room key from the ring.

"Since you're here," Isabella said, "I might as well give you your pay. I assume you would prefer it in cash, since you don't have an account with a local bank?"

He turned around. "Yes, miss."

The moment she turned her back to go to her desk, he slipped the room key from the ring and into his pocket, then laid her keys on a small table by the door. As he waited for her to count out his money, he scanned the layout of the apartment for future reference.

When she turned around with his money, he was looking at a painting hanging by the door.

"Do you like that?" she asked.

He nodded. "It reminds me a bit of my home."

"You grew up on a farm?"

He hesitated, then nodded. That much of a truth could not finger him.

"What did you grow?"

"Barely enough to eat," he answered, and then held out his hand.

A little startled by his abruptness, Isabella laid the money in his palm, then patted his arm.

"Think about that job, will you?"

"I will think on it some more."

He was almost out the door, when once again, she called him back.

"Oh, Victor?"

Anxious to be gone, he gritted his teeth as he turned around once more.

"I don't suppose that farm was in Louisiana?" she asked.

"No, miss. Why do you ask?"

She shrugged. "Just that the other day one of our guests thought he recognized you, and since he grew up in Louisiana, I thought that might be the connection."

Rostov felt the blood drain from his face, but he stood his ground, pretending that her comment hadn't rocked his world.

"I've never been in that place," he said gruffly. "Will that be all, Miss Abbott?"

Isabella knew instantly that she'd made him nervous and regretted the impulse that had made her ask. Lots of homeless people were protective of their personal histories. It made sense that he might resent questions.

"Yes, Victor. That's all. Have a good day."

He nodded once, and then he was gone.

"Odd man," she muttered, and closed the door,

then saw her keys on the table and dropped them in her purse.

Victor made it to the gardener's shed without running, although with every step he'd taken he'd expected someone to shout out his name. He had no way of knowing which guest she had been referring to, or if it had been one of the old men. Either way, his time at Abbott House was over. He had to get out now, before he came face-to-face with a nemesis from his past.

He fingered the money Isabella had just given him and then shoved it deep in his pocket. This was nothing to what he was going to get after he abducted her. She was certain to have inherited her father's interest in the fertility clinic, as well as now owning the hotel and the land on which it sat. The old men would be willing to pay up to get her back, and not just because she was a surrogate daughter. After all, according to Frank Walton's diary, she was the key to their success.

But first things first. He started throwing his belongings into his suitcase, careful to leave nothing behind that would identify him as anyone other than the itinerant he was pretending to be. He was going to have to find a place to hide with Isabella until the ransom had been paid. Once he had the money in hand, he would disappear as easily as he'd come. In the old days, he'd been the best. There was no reason for him to assume he'd lost his touch. It was unfortunate that Isabella Abbott's life would have to be sacrificed, but in his business, the first rule of perfection was to leave nothing and no one behind.

Rostov slipped out of the shed and around the hotel with his pack in hand, then headed for the trees at the western edge of the hotel. He looked back only once but was satisfied that he had not been seen. Just as the sun was sliding behind the uppermost peak of White Mountain, he disappeared into the forest.

It was twilight by the time Jack got off the mountain. With about a mile of clear valley between him and the hotel yet to go, he wanted to slow down. Every muscle in his body was burning, including his lungs. He'd been running on adrenaline for more than an hour, the fear of knowing who the Soviets had sent keeping him moving.

When he got to the grounds of the hotel proper, his body still wanted to run, but his legs wouldn't cooperate. It was either slow down or fall down, and Jack knew that if he stopped, he wouldn't be able to get up again.

When he reached the terrace, his anxiety increased. What if he was too late? What if the Hawk had already made his move? He scrambled up the steps, stumbling on the second from the top, and caught himself with both hands to keep from falling flat.

A couple of guests were admiring the sunset and

gave him a wary look as he passed them by. He could only imagine how he must appear—a wild man invading their space. But if his suspicions were correct, it wasn't the wild man they should be concerned with—it was the killer who'd been mowing the lawn.

He burst into the dining room, frantically searching the diners for sight of Isabella. She wasn't there, and neither were the uncles. He told himself that there were any number of reasons why they might not be there and kept weaving his way through the tables on his way to the lobby.

No one was at the front desk, and only a couple of women were sitting in the lobby, talking quietly among themselves.

"Miss Abbott! Have you seen her?" he asked.

Startled by the abruptness of his appearance, they didn't answer.

"Jack?"

He turned. Isabella was coming out of the office. Or at least he thought it was Isabella. She looked different—sexier.

"Isabella?"

But he wasn't the only one startled by a change of appearance. Isabella took one look at the condition of Jack's clothes and then his face, and knew something had happened.

"What's wrong?" she asked, and ran toward him, thinking he'd been injured. "Are you hurt? Sit down in this chair and I'll get Uncle David."

He grabbed her shoulders. "Nothing's wrong with me. Where's Victor Ross?"

"I don't know. Probably in his room."

Jack took off his backpack, then pulled a handgun from one of the inner pockets.

"Jack! Have you gone mad? Put that gun down or I'm going to call the police."

"Don't do that! You've got to trust me," he said, and dropped the backpack in the lobby floor. "Just lock the terrace doors after me and stay away from the windows until I get back."

"Are you crazy? I'm not going to let an armed guest run wild through my hotel. Put that gun down now or I swear I'll call the police."

"I *am* the police, Isabella. I'm a federal agent. Now do as I say, so that no one gets hurt."

Stunned by what he'd just said, Isabella froze. By the time she came to herself, he was already in the dining room and heading for the terrace. She glanced at the women in the lobby, who had obviously overheard everything.

"Stay put," she said. "And stay quiet."

They nodded quickly, then clasped each other's hands as Isabella ran into the dining room. It was more than half-full of diners in the midst of eating their evening meal, and while she hated to frighten them, she would have regretted even more not following Jack's orders should one of them get hurt.

"People, if I could have your attention for just a few moments," she called.

The steady murmur of voices ceased at the unusual request.

Someone chuckled, and then a man called out from the back of the room, "What's the matter, Isabella? Did the cook set the kitchen on fire?"

She held up her hands and made herself smile as she quickly moved to the terrace. Thankfully, it was empty. She locked the doors and then turned.

"I need you all to move into the lobby for just a few minutes. There's a situation outside that might get out of control, and we don't want anyone to get hurt."

One man stood up. "I've got my gun in my car," he offered.

"No, no, please. Just do as I asked."

Suddenly the sounds of dozens of chairs scooting along the polished hardwood floor filled the room, followed by a nervous murmur of voices as the diners hurried out.

Isabella sighed, hoping she'd done the right thing. With a quick, backward glance toward the terrace, she headed for the front of the hotel.

The people had gathered at the fireplace at the back of the room. Most were standing, though a few of the more elderly were seated.

"What's happening, honey?" one of the elderly women asked.

"I wish I knew," Isabella said.

The gardener's shed was dark, the front door standing ajar. Jack knew before he entered that the man who called himself Victor Ross was gone. Still, he slipped inside, standing in the dark and listening, just to make sure, before he proceeded. The only thing he could hear was the sound of his own breathing.

"Damn, damn, damn," he muttered, as he switched on a light, then proceeded to the back of the shed where the man had been staying.

The room was empty but smelled of smoke. The bed was made, the bathroom devoid of any personal articles, and the small metal can that had served as a waste basket had nothing but a pile of ashes in the bottom. Another clue to prove that Jack's suspicions had been correct. Burning personal refuse was a trick right out of the Cold War. It was a sure-fire guarantee against being traced. Still, he felt obligated to search the place, though he came up with exactly what he'd expected, which was nothing.

Wanting to call the director, he reached for his cell phone and then realized he'd left it in his pack.

Cursing fate and everything in between, he headed back to the hotel at a lope. Knowing that Isabella would have locked him out, he entered through the service entrance and quickly moved into the lobby, where he came face-to-face not only with her but with two dozen curious people, as well.

The moment Isabella saw him, she jumped to her feet.

"Jack?"

"He's gone."

"But I just saw him this afternoon. He helped carry some things to my room, and I paid him for the week."

"What did he say?" Jack asked.

People were crowding around them now, anxious to hear what was being said, but Jack wasn't in the mood to broadcast.

"Send them back to the dining room," he said.

"But they have as much right to—"

"Isabella...please."

She frowned at him, but did as he asked.

"Okay, everybody, you can go back to your meals. If they've gotten cold, the staff will gladly heat them up for you, and everyone will have dessert on the house."

They muttered en masse as they trooped back into the dining room, and Isabella knew that the story would be all over town before morning. Either it would bring out more diners in droves or scare them off completely, and there wasn't a thing she could do to change the outcome. Only time would tell.

Once they were alone, Isabella turned again, her voice sharp with anger and frustration.

"What was that all about? And don't give me the runaround anymore, Jack Dolan...or whatever your name is. This is my hotel, and I have a right to know what's going on."

He pulled out his badge. "My name is Jack Dolan, only I'm not a writer. I'm a federal agent."

When she saw the shield her heart sank. "I don't understand. Why the mystery?"

"Right now I'm not at liberty to tell you everything, but I can tell you that the man you called Victor Ross was no gardener. I'm fairly sure that he's the man who killed Frank Walton."

Isabella felt suddenly sick to her stomach. It was the last thing she had expected to hear. She swayed where she stood, thinking of how close she'd been to that man—of how she'd fed him and laughed with him and even given him money.

"Oh God...I paid the man who killed Uncle Frank? I sheltered him and fed him and—"

Jack shook her gently before hysteria set in.

"Listen to me," he said. "He's gone, and I need to know what you two talked about. Did he say anything that would lead you to believe he'd been planning to leave?"

She started to cry. Quietly. Without sobs or screams. Just huge, silent tears pouring out of her eyes. The sight was enough to make a man come undone.

"Ah, God, Tinkerbell, don't do that," he begged, and led her to a nearby chair. "Here, honey, sit down. But for the fact that I'm filthy, I'd give you a hug. You came through for me back there with flying colors."

"I don't care about dirt," she said softly, and fell into his arms.

"Hell," Jack mumbled, and then held her close,

letting her cry out the shock of what he'd told her. "Where are your uncles? I would have thought they'd be all over the place by now."

"I don't know," she said. "They didn't come down to dinner."

"Maybe they're gone."

"No, no. They would never leave without telling me."

Then she gasped. "You don't think that Victor Ross did something to them, too?"

Jack had been wondering the same thing, but he wasn't going to let her know.

"No way, honey. There's no way he could make five men disappear without causing a big fuss. You know how they are. They're probably together in one of their rooms, watching TV or playing cards."

"Maybe," Isabella said. "But I'm going to check."

"Good idea," Jack said. "I'll go with you."

"I'll just call their rooms and tell them to come to mine." Then she touched Jack's face. "You're bleeding, you know."

He shrugged, only then feeling the faint sting of the cuts he'd gotten as he'd run through the trees.

"Just scratches," he said.

"They need to be cleaned."

He grinned, hoping to ease her mind. "Hell, honey, my whole self needs to be cleaned."

"Then go shower," she said. "After which you will come to my room. By then Uncle David will be there, and he can disinfect those cuts. A couple of them are pretty deep.''

He hated to leave her, but he needed to call Washington now. It was time to spread a wider net.

''If you throw in a sandwich and a beer, it's a deal.''

Isabella nodded, but when Jack started to leave, she grabbed his arm. He stopped and turned.

''What?''

''Is this why you…why we didn't—''

Jack sighed. ''Yes.''

She stood there for a moment, absorbing the truth, and felt lighter than she had in days.

''All right, then,'' she said softly.

Jack touched her face, then her hair, running his fingers lightly over the shaggy cut.

''Do you like it?'' she asked.

''Hell, yes,'' he growled. ''It's too damned sexy for a Tinkerbell. I'm going to have to come up with another name for you now.''

Afraid he'd said more than he should have, he turned sharply and took the stairs up, two at a time.

Isabella watched until he was out of sight; then she headed for her room. It wasn't until she got to the door that she realized she'd left her keys inside in her purse. Backtracking to the office, she got a spare key and let herself in, then headed for the phone.

David had just emptied one of Maria Silvia's eggs of its nucleus, leaving only the outer membrane and the cytoplasm, when a red light over the outer door began to flash. He jerked, accidentally destroying the fragile egg, and then cursed beneath his breath.

Jasper, too, had seen the light and was already removing his lab coat.

"David, someone's trying to reach us."

"I see. I see," he said. "Damn it. One of us should have stayed above to prevent this from happening. We're so short on time, and I just didn't think."

The other men were also scurrying about now, shutting down their lab equipment and shedding their coats.

"We've got to hurry," Thomas said.

Within seconds they were out the door and in the carts. It took eight minutes to get from the lab to the elevator. Not long at all, but an eternity when secrecy was at stake.

Isabella's hands were shaking as she hung up the phone. None of the uncles had answered. She couldn't begin to consider what that might mean. The thought of them being gone from her life seemed impossible to consider, but the past few weeks had taught her a hard lesson. Bad things came to you in life, whether you were ready for them or not.

She tried the phones once more, telling herself that maybe they'd been in the shower, or in another room. But common sense told her that they wouldn't all have been out of pocket at once.

She called Jack's room, but when he didn't answer, she figured he was still in the shower. Unwilling to wait for him to accompany her, she ran for the front office, grabbed a pass key and then headed for the elevator.

"Hey, Isabella."

*Not now.* But she stopped and turned, finding herself face-to-face with a couple of old ranchers who'd been dining earlier.

"What was that all about?" one asked.

"It was just a precaution," she said. "Thankfully, it proved unnecessary, but you know what they say. 'Better safe than sorry.' "

The other rancher chimed in. "Safe from what?"

Isabella didn't hesitate to lie, not if it meant keeping her loved ones safe.

"I think the authorities were looking for some escaped criminal or something. Anyway, it was a false alarm, so you two should be fine going home." Then she winked. "However, I wouldn't pick up any hitchhikers if I were you."

They both blustered and frowned. "We ain't afraid," the first rancher said. "Like I told you before, I got my gun in the pickup."

"Just don't shoot Charlie," she teased.

The other rancher snorted. "He's not gonna shoot me, because I'm unloading that rifle before we get in the truck."

They were still arguing as they exited the hotel.

Isabella breathed a sigh of relief and headed for the elevator again. This time she made it inside without being detained.

As always, it rose slowly, creaking and groaning as it moved to the top floor, and for Isabella, the ride was endless. The moment it stopped, she was out on the run and banging on the first door she came to as she put the key in the lock.

David was the first out of the tiny elevator as he dashed through his closet into his room. He started to pick up the phone and call Isabella, then froze. Someone was in the hallway, calling their names. It was too late to call. She was already up here looking for them.

"Hurry," he said. "We don't have much time. He ran to the door and took off the chain, unplugged his phone and then scurried back to help the others set up the long-practiced ruse.

Jasper grabbed a folding card table as Thomas and John started dragging chairs from around the room and placing them at the table. Rufus yanked open a desk drawer and pulled out a deck of cards and a box of poker chips. Within seconds, the five men were seated around the table, ostensibly immersed in a game of poker.

"I'll bid five dollars," Jasper said, just as the door banged inwardly.

All five men looked up with expressions of pretend surprise.

David stood, his cards still in his hand.

"Isabella! Darling! Is something wrong?"

Isabella went limp with relief. Poker. They were all in Uncle David's room playing poker.

"I called you—all of you—and no one answered. I thought something had happened to you, too."

David laid down his cards and went to her, taking her in his arms.

"We're so sorry we worried you, dear, but my phone didn't ring."

"I called and I called," she said.

Jasper got up and went to the phone. "Look," he said. "It's unplugged."

David frowned. "Probably the cleaning staff accidentally unplugged it. I'm so sorry you were concerned, but as you can see, we're fine. Why don't you come sit with us? You can help me play my hand, just like you used to when you were small."

"No, no, you don't understand. I didn't make myself clear. It's not just that I couldn't find you. I thought you were all dead, just like Uncle Frank."

"But why would you think that?" David asked.

"I don't know where to start," she said.

"At the beginning is usually best," Thomas said, and offered her a chair.

She sat, because her legs were still shaking, and then looked at the five aging men who meant so much to her.

"You are all I have left in this world," she said softly.

"And we love you as if you were our own child," David said.

"I know," she said. "But a situation has developed since we talked this morning."

David ruffled her hair. "I see you took my advice. I like the new style."

"Yes, but that's not what I mean." She took a deep breath and then spat out the words like a bad taste. "Jack Dolan isn't a writer."

David frowned. "He hasn't trifled with your affections, has he? Because if he has, I'll—"

"No, no...oh, Lord, I'm saying this all wrong."

"Then let me help," Jack said.

They turned as one, looking with surprise at the man in the doorway.

"Jack, I was just about to—"

"I heard," he said, and entered the room, closing the door behind him.

"Sir, I believe you owe us an explanation," John said.

Jack frowned. "No, sir, I don't. But even so, I will tell you what I told Isabella. I'm a Federal agent."

Five men stared without speaking, each locked into his own set of horrors.

Isabella interrupted.

"Uncle David, he thinks Victor Ross is the man who killed Uncle Frank."

There was a collective gasp of horror, and then all of them were talking at once.

"Wait…wait…" Jack said. "One at a time… please."

"I'll ask the most obvious question first," David said. "Why would Frank's killer come all the way to Montana? We were given to understand that his death was the result of a mugging."

Jack hesitated, debating with himself about revealing Frank Walton's true identity, then decided against it.

"We're not sure," Jack said. "All we know is that the killer cleaned out Mr. Walton's hotel room, making it appear as if he'd checked out on schedule, then used his plane ticket."

"And I hired him," Isabella wailed. "I gave that man shelter and food and money."

"You couldn't have known," David said. "None of us could have. Why, I even treated him that day he was ill, remember? Just because he deceived us, that does not make us culpable in Frank's death."

"I know," Isabella said. "But still…" Then she shuddered. "I can't get over the fact that he was in my home, standing in my own living room and commenting on art as if he hadn't a care in the world."

"What art?" Jack asked. "And why was he in your room?"

"I told you earlier. He helped me carry some

things from my car, then he waited so I could pay him.''

''Did you give him cash?''

She nodded.

Jack's mind was racing. If Ross *was* the Hawk, money was the last thing he would need. He had a way of procuring whatever was necessary without buying it, and leaving bodies in his wake.

''Mr. Dolan...what made you think that Victor Ross was the killer?'' Thomas asked.

Again Jack guarded his words. ''He was a stranger.''

''Yes, but you said you thought you recognized him, remember?'' Isabella said. ''I even commented on the same thing to Ross myself when he was looking at the painting.''

*Shit.* ''Exactly what did you say?'' Jack asked.

''The painting is of a farm scene. He said it reminded him of where he grew up. I asked him if that was in Louisiana. He said no, that he'd never been there and wanted to know why I asked. I said a guest had seen him earlier and thought he looked familiar. That was all I said. I had no way of knowing it would alert him.'' She looked up at Jack, her expression drawn. ''It was me, wasn't it? What I said made him run.''

Jack laid his hand on her back and gave her what he hoped was a reassuring pat.

''We don't know that, and besides, it can't be helped. If I'd been thinking, I would have kept my comments to myself. I'm the one who knew there was a killer in the area, not you, so don't blame yourself.''

''But I still don't understand,'' Jasper said. ''Why would a New Yorker commit a crime in Brighton Beach, then come all the way to Montana where his victim lived? It makes no sense.''

''Ross isn't from New York,'' Jack said.

''Then where *is* he from?'' David asked.

''Russia.''

Isabella sighed. ''That makes even less sense than ever,'' she said. ''We have no ties to Russia, do we, Uncle David?''

Jack's attention slid from Isabella to the aging doctor, and the moment he looked at his face, he knew. He looked at the others, and while they were doing their best to hide it, he could tell they were in shock.

*That settled it. They knew Walton's secret. He could see it in their eyes.*

# 12

When Isabella saw Jack touch his cheek and then wince, she remembered they had yet to doctor his face.

"Uncle David...I told Jack you would put something on his scratches."

The old man seemed to shift mental gears as he looked at the wounds.

"Of course," he said. "Please, sit here. I'll get my bag."

Jack sat willingly, glad for the excuse to stay in their midst.

"How did this happen?" Jasper asked. "Did you fall?"

"No. I was running down White Mountain. Didn't pay close enough attention to where I was going, I guess."

David set down his medical bag, then took out some sterile swabs and a bottle of disinfectant. "White Mountain isn't a very good place to jog," he said.

Jack looked up, meeting the doctor's gaze. "I wasn't jogging."

David didn't question him further, which Jack thought strange. It was almost as if he knew why Jack would have needed to hurry.

Isabella suddenly straightened and turned to Jack.

"Jack, I just remembered something."

He winced as the disinfectant ran into one of the deeper cuts.

"Like what?"

"Remember when you ran into the lobby and were shouting for me?"

"Yes?"

"Why the panic?"

He shifted slightly so that he could see her face.

"I needed to see that you were all right."

A frown knitted her forehead above her brows.

"I'm just not following all this. If Ross killed Uncle Frank—and I have no doubt that you believe he did—then why would you assume I'm in danger? What happened up on the mountain that made you so sure it was him? He's been here for quite a while. You'd seen him more than once and never said a thing. Why now?"

David had finished cleaning the cuts and scratches and was listening intently, as were the other old men.

"I didn't go to White Mountain to hike. I went looking for the man who used Frank Walton's plane ticket home. I didn't find him, but I found a camping knife with Russian markings. As I was coming down the mountain, I remembered where I'd seen Victor Ross's face."

Jasper Arnold leaned forward, his eyes wide and filled with shock.

"Where?" he asked.

"It was in Quantico, Virginia, during my training days. We were studying…well, for lack of a better word, what amounts to espionage. One of the trainers showed a film about the Cold War, and we were discussing some of the more famous spies of that time and the tactics they had used then that were now out of date. There was a picture of a man, a Russian agent, who was believed to be a spy they called the Hawk. The face just stayed with me. I'm pretty sure Victor Ross is the same man, only I can't be positive. Age is bound to have changed him some, and he's gone now, so I can't look at him again. But…" He shrugged.

"It still doesn't make any sense," Isabella said. "Even if Victor Ross was the Hawk, and even if he did kill Uncle Frank, are you saying he's turned into a common criminal? And why did he come to the United States, anyway? Wouldn't he still be in Russia, savoring his reputation and retirement?"

"There isn't much left of the old Russia," Jack said. "And I'm not implying, nor do I believe, that he's here just robbing and killing for the hell of it."

"Then what *do* you believe?" Isabella asked.

Jack stood, nodded a thanks to David for the

treatment, then made a unilateral decision to reveal more of what he knew.

"I believe he was sent to find one certain man. I believe he found him, but not everything else he expected. I think that's why he came to White Mountain. He came to Frank Walton's home looking for something, and until he finds it, anyone regarding themselves as Walton's family might not be safe."

"My God!"

They turned. Thomas Mowry was clutching his chest.

"And he found us," the old man muttered. "He found us all."

Immediately, everyone rushed to his side. Jasper was closest and was already easing Thomas down to the floor and loosening his clothes. David had his medical bag in hand and went to his knees.

"Thomas...Thomas...are you in pain?" he asked.

"No...just felt faint," he muttered.

"Help me get him in bed," David said.

"Let me," Jack said, and lifted the old man in his arms.

"In there," David said, and led the way to Thomas's bedroom.

Jack laid him down, then stepped back, letting the doctors do their thing. He stood for a moment, seeing the fear and concern on their faces, as well as the bond that years of companionship had woven.

He hated being the one to upset their quiet little world, but if they had knowingly harbored a defector, it was bound to come out eventually.

It wasn't until Thomas began coming around that Jack realized Isabella was missing. He turned to look for her and saw her, pale and shaken, standing in the doorway. He went to her.

"Honey, he's okay. I think it was just shock."

She stared at him as if he were a stranger.

Jack frowned. "Isabella?"

She shrugged out of his grasp and then walked out of the room. He caught up with her at the head of the stairs.

"What?" he asked.

"There's something you're not telling us."

"I've told you everything I can."

"Frank Walton was nothing to you, but he was part of our family. You have no right to keep us in the dark."

He took a deep breath and then exhaled slowly.

"Ask your uncles," he said. "They know more than they're telling." Then he added, "If you need me, I'll be in my room. I have some calls to make."

"What do you mean...they know more than they're telling? Are you insinuating that my uncles are somehow involved in what happened to Uncle Frank?"

"I'm not implying anything."

He walked away, leaving her to digest what he'd left unsaid.

Isabella turned and stared down the long hallway to the last room on the right, then started walking. Halfway there, she stopped, her heart pounding, her hands damp with sweat.

*Oh God…please…I can't take much more.*

Then David came hurrying out of the room.

"Isabella, we're going to take Thomas into Braden. I think he's all right, but to be on the safe side, I'm going to put him on a heart monitor for the night."

"Can I help?"

David paused, then smiled gently and pressed a kiss on her cheek.

"No, darling, we can manage just fine. You hold down the fort here, okay?"

"What if that man comes back? The one Jack Dolan says killed Uncle Frank?"

Something flickered in the back of David Schultz's eyes. When Isabella saw it, her faith in the uncles quietly died. For the first time in her life she felt alone in the world, and she knew that if he answered, it would be a lie.

"Never mind," she said softly. "You take care of Uncle Thomas. I'll take care of myself."

She walked away, her back straight, her stride long and purposeful, and David had never felt as guilty or as old as he did at that moment. They were deceiving her, and she sensed it. Not in a way she would ever imagine, but somehow she knew there was a secret that she didn't share.

"Lord help us all," he muttered, and went downstairs to meet the ambulance that was already on its way.

Jack slammed the door to his room because it was his only outlet for the frustration he was feeling. He strode to the bed and sat down with a thump. The urge to lie back and sleep was strong, but there were things he had to do first. If only he'd come to the realization a day earlier, Victor Ross might still be here. He needed to confirm his suspicions, but had no way to—no, wait.

He came off of the bed in a leap and ran to the dresser where he'd tossed the pictures he'd been taking as part of his cover. He'd taken numerous pictures of the hotel as well as the surrounding area. If he was lucky—and he was due for some luck—the gardener could have been in some.

Grabbing the fistful of photo packets, he tossed them on the bed and then kicked off his shoes. His belly was growling from hunger, but there was too much to do to bother with changing and going downstairs. Room service wasn't offered, but he figured if Delia was on the registration desk, he could talk her into getting him something from the kitchen. At least it was worth a shot.

He dialed the front desk and then counted the rings. About to hang up on the eighth ring, he finally heard Delia's breathless voice.

"Front desk. How may I help you?"

"Delia, it's Jack Dolan in 200. I know Abbott House doesn't offer room service, but I was wondering if I could talk you into getting me some food. I'm not picky. I'll eat anything."

"Certainly, Mr. Dolan. I would be happy to see that you get some food. In fact, I'll bring it up myself."

"Thanks, Delia. I'll leave the door unlocked."

He disconnected, then reached for the first packet of pictures and quickly shuffled through the prints. Victor Ross was in none of them. He looked through the second, then the third, and was halfway through the fourth packet when he started to smile.

"Bingo," he said softly, and turned the photo he was holding a little closer to the light.

It was a morning view of the back terrace, and none other than Victor Ross was coming out of the service entrance. Jack remembered thinking at the time that the man had been in a hurry but had paid little attention. If only he'd looked at him then as closely as he was seeing him now, things might have been well on their way to being over. He flipped through the rest of the photos quickly to make sure there wasn't another that was better, but there was not.

Tossing the pictures aside, he hurried to the desk, scanned the picture into his laptop, then reached for his cell phone. Within moments, the director answered.

"Dolan?"

"Yes, sir. Sorry to be calling so late but—"

"I only pretend to have office hours. What's up?"

"I think I've identified the man we've been looking for. Unfortunately, I missed apprehending him. He got spooked and ran before I could get to him."

"I can get a team there P.D.Q. Do you know where he went?"

"No, although I'm guessing he went back to the mountains. Aside from Braden, which is too damned small to hide out in for long, it's the only place close by in which to hide."

"Maybe he figured out that Walton had nothing of value and has headed for home."

"I don't think so," Jack said.

"Why not?"

"Because he left without answers, and I don't think that will be acceptable to the people who sent him."

There was a moment of silence, and then the director spoke.

"What haven't you told me?"

"I think it was the Hawk."

"Who are you—?" Jack heard the director's swift intake of air and then a shift in the timbre of his voice. "*The* Hawk?"

"Yes, sir."

"I thought he was dead...or at the least living somewhere in relative obscurity on a government pension."

"The man I saw was far from dead."

"I don't know...that's a big stretch. If it was him, then the scope of this is broader than we thought."

"Yes, sir. I was thinking the same thing. I have a snapshot. It's not a closeup, but his face is pretty clear. I've scanned it into my computer, and I'm sending it to you now."

"Give me a second," the director said. "I'm not in my office."

Jack could hear him walking, then a door opening, then closing firmly. Seconds later, he heard the squeak of a chair.

"Okay, I'm in. Just give me a minute to... yeah...here it is. The download is complete. I'm printing it now."

"What do you think?" Jack asked.

"I'll have to give the Company a call and run this through their files. Of course, age enhancement will play a part in this, too. I'll let you know in a couple of hours."

"Yes, sir. I'll be waiting."

"Is there anything else?" he asked.

Jack sighed. It had to be said.

"They know who I am."

"How did this happen?"

"I told them."

There was another moment of silence, this time longer than the first.

"I assume you had your reasons?"

"Yes, sir, I did."

"What do they know about why you're there?"

"Only that I was trailing the man who killed their friend and that we knew he'd used the dead man's plane ticket to come to Braden. Also...I told them he was Russian."

"Do you think that was wise?"

"Right now, sir, I don't know what I think, but I know what I saw. The five old men whom Isabella Abbott calls her uncles were scared out of their minds when I told them. One may have been in the throes of a mild heart attack when I left to come to my room. Oh...I forgot to tell you that I've got a friend in research at Quantico getting me information on all the people who were on the same plane with Vaclav Waller. The one that supposedly went down."

"Really? What are you hoping to find?"

"I'm not sure, but I think I'm on the right track. There were seven doctors on that flight, along with a couple of pilots and a woman, who was supposed to be one doctor's wife. And, up until a few weeks ago, there were seven old men living in Abbott House. The names aren't the same, and I can't tell anything about the faces because the picture is too old and the men are too young, but it's quite a co-incidence, just the same."

"Let me know what you find out from Quantico."

"Yes, sir."

"I'll be in touch."

The line went dead, but Jack was already checking his e-mail, hoping for answers from Steven Randolph. He scanned down the list of new messages quickly, then stopped at the second from the last and grinned.

Dubloh7.

That would be Steven, all right. 007 indeed.

"So, you think you're James Bond, do you, buddy? Let's see what you've found for me."

He opened the message and started to read, and the longer he read, the more he realized that Frank Walton had been the tip of a much bigger iceberg. Every doctor on board that plane had been involved in DNA research and the theory that human genes could be manipulated as a means of everything from preventing birth defects to healing incurable diseases. And what was more telling, according to what Steven had pulled from the archives, they were all in the process of being pulled off their research when the crash had occurred.

He replied to the e-mail, typing in the names of the men who were or had been living here now, including Samuel Abbott. Walton had pulled a scam by living under a dead man's name. He wondered what they would find out by running the same check on these men.

A knock sounded on his door as he hit Send. Finally. His food had arrived.

"Come in," he called, and folded down the screen on his lap top.

He stood, stretching as the door swung inward. But it wasn't Delia who entered with his food. It was Isabella.

He jumped forward, taking the tray from her hands and then quickly setting it aside.

"Is there anything else you'll be needing?" she asked.

"Forgiveness? Understanding? A hug? I'm not picky. I'll take any of the above."

She sighed, blaming herself for her weaknesses. She'd known when she'd offered to bring up the food that he would confront her like this, and she knew, if she was honest with herself, that was why she'd come.

"I can understand about working undercover. I know there are things within your job that are bound to be highly sensitive."

"Yes, and—"

"I'm not finished," she said, holding up her hands and backing up so that there was still space between them.

Jack braced himself for the but he heard coming.

"Then get it said."

"But you can't just throw down a verbal gauntlet like you did upstairs and expect me to ignore it. Do you know what I'm feeling right now? I feel like the orphan I really am. You've made me mistrust the only family I've ever known. I look at those five dear old men and see strangers. I'm scared, Jack, and it's all your fault."

He frowned. "No, Isabella, it's not my fault. I was just the messenger. Whatever is going on with them started long before we were born."

Her lower lip trembled, but she refused to cry.

"What is it, Jack? What's going on? Why are they afraid? And don't tell me they're not, because I saw it in their eyes."

"Did you ask them?"

"No, and I won't."

"Why?"

The words burned her mouth like acid, but they had to be said. She turned away to stare out at the mountain, and as she did, the flesh on her skin suddenly crawled.

"Because I know that whatever they tell me would be a lie, so if I don't ask, they don't have the guilt of that on their consciences."

"I'm sorry."

"God, Jack...so am I."

"Isabella...look at me."

She turned, her eyes wet with tears.

Knowing it was wrong didn't stop Jack from cupping her face and then lowering his head. A second later he was kissing her. Gently. Tenderly.

Then she moaned, and his hands slid from her face to her shoulders, then under her arms and around her back, holding her tighter, pulling her closer, until there was nothing between them but growing need.

Heat built, bodies burned, aching with only one

way to stop—and it wasn't going to happen. Not when she was this vulnerable. Not when the possibility existed that he was going to destroy what was left of her world.

''Oh God,'' Isabella moaned, as she tore herself from Jack's arms.

She dropped to the side of the bed and covered her face with her hands.

''This is crazy, isn't it? Why am I doing this? I must be mad, thinking of you when I should be trying to save myself from this ongoing hell.''

One step and Jack would have been in bed with her, and there would have been no going back. Because he knew his limits, he stayed where he was—his shoulders ramrod straight, his stance braced against temptation.

''You can deny me and yourself and everything in between, but you do not have to save yourself from anything, because I will not let anything happen to you. It's what I do.''

Her hands dropped to her lap as she looked up, and he could see more in her eyes than he needed to see. If he asked her, she would say yes. Sweet Jesus. That wasn't helping him at all.

''So, my white knight still rides,'' she said, but the smile on her face was anything but friendly. ''However, I'm wondering something.''

''What?''

''When you ride off into the sunset...do you always go alone?''

"Damn it, Isabella, you know I can't make promises right now."

She stood too quickly, changing the subject before he could say more.

"I don't know what I was thinking," she said. "You were hungry, and now your food is getting cold. Here…I'll move some of these things on the desk and you can eat there. Or would you rather eat in bed? You could watch TV, although I don't guarantee too many channels. We don't get very good reception because of the mountains."

Before Jack could stop her, she was at his desk, carefully moving papers aside to make room for his tray. Suddenly she paused, then picked up a paper. It wasn't until after she started talking that he realized it was the old photo of the seven doctors as they were boarding the plane.

"Where did you get this?" she asked.

*Shit.* "It's just an old photo."

"But where did you get it?" she asked.

Suddenly Jack knew there was more than curiosity behind the question.

"Why?"

"Because my father is in it…and I think that's Uncle Frank on the left and Uncle David beside him, although I can't be sure. I've never seen Uncle David with a beard."

When Jack didn't answer, her voice started to shake.

"Jack, why do you have a picture of my father?"

Suddenly it all began to make sense.

*Well, son of a bitch. Of course.* ''I didn't know I did,'' he said. ''I've never seen his picture.''

''Oh.'' She handed it to him. ''I suppose you had it because of Uncle Frank?''

''Yes.''

She nodded. ''I'm sorry. I guess I'm seeing the boogey man everywhere now.''

She had turned to leave when Jack called her back.

''Would you do something for me?'' he asked.

''Maybe.''

It wasn't what he wanted to hear, but it would have to do.

''Would you not say anything to the others about this picture...at least for now?''

''It's more of the lie, isn't it?'' she asked, and then waved her hand in abject dismissal. ''Forget I asked. I'm sure that's just more of the part you can't talk about.''

She was all the way to the door when she suddenly froze. When she turned around, new horror was on her face.

''Oh my God.''

Jack knew what was coming, and there was nothing he could say to make it better.

''My father is in that picture.''

''So you said.''

''He was part of the lie, wasn't he?''

''I don't know,'' Jack said.

"But you're going to find out, aren't you?"

"It's why I came."

She started to cry. "What does it matter? Whatever you think you're after, it's bound to have been over for years. They're old and they're weak. You saw what your news did to Uncle Thomas. Are you willing to have all of their lives on your conscience?"

"Are you willing to let a man get away with your uncle's murder?"

"That's not fair," she sobbed.

"Life is not about being fair."

"Then what *is* it about? Make me understand, so I don't hate you." Her voice broke as she leaned against the door. "Because I don't want to hate you, Jack Dolan. Oh God...I don't want to hate you."

Her pain gutted him, shattering resolve and honor and everything in between.

"Then don't. It's your decision, and that's what life is all about...living by the decisions we make."

"You don't make it easy, do you?"

"There is nothing easy about my job, Isabella, but do not mistake my feelings for you as weakness. No matter what, I will do what I have to do."

"Then enjoy your food and sleep well, Jack Dolan. If you can."

She was gone as quietly as she'd come. Jack looked at the tray on the table and knew it was going to go to waste. Something was suddenly wrong with his throat. There was no way in hell he could swallow.

# 13

It was thirty minutes past two in the morning when Vasili Rostov reached Abbott House. Careful to stay in the shadows of the surrounding shrubbery, he made his way toward the back of the hotel and then paused behind a large Dumpster. The only lights on inside the hotel were the night lights in the lobby and in the hallways, the same ones he'd seen every night from his bedroom window.

He wondered if they knew he was gone yet. Chances were they did not. They would have had no reason to go looking for a gardener after the sun had gone down and he'd finished the work that had been set out for him before he'd stopped for the evening. Finishing a job was something he prided himself on. Even if it had been nothing more than clipping hedges and mowing grass, he'd given his word.

He thought of the man who'd sent him here. He expected Rostov to keep his word, too. But Rostov had not survived as long as he had without learning a few things about communist rule. When a project failed, someone had to shoulder the blame and suffer the consequences. The way he looked at it, he wasn't the one who'd let a top-notch scientist get away to begin with. He'd kept his word. He'd found Vaclav Waller. It wasn't his fault that the old man had chosen to die rather than acquiesce.

Circumstances had forced Rostov to take this path. It wasn't one he would have chosen, but he was on it just the same. And to survive the transition, he would need money to make himself disappear.

Fingering the key in his right pocket, he went through a mental checklist of the ground floor of the hotel, including the fire exit at the end of the hall. He had four choices for leaving with Isabella Abbott in tow: the front entrance, the fire exit, the service entrance off the kitchen, or the doors exiting onto the terrace. The odds were in his favor, and he could think of no one who would threaten the success of his mission. The only guests in the hotel were the five old men and a handful of couples desperate for babies, plus the writer. Rostov dismissed them completely.

He patted his left pocket, feeling the hypodermic syringe within the folds of fabric. It was something he'd intended to use on Waller, but it would serve the same purpose for the woman, instead. Careful not to move out of the shadows, he circled the grounds until he was at the service entrance. Within seconds he had picked the ancient lock.

Inside, he stood without moving, listening for

signs of activity, but he heard nothing that would lead him to believe anyone was stirring. It was fortunate for him that the hotel operated more like a home than a place of business. The front doors were locked at midnight. No one stood night duty on the front desk, and the kitchen closed at 11:00 p.m. The guests and residents of the old house should be sound asleep, which suited his purposes completely.

Moving silently on rubber-soled shoes, he slipped from the kitchen into the dining room, then from there to the lobby, staying in the shadows until he was certain he was alone.

Confident that all was going according to plan, he hurried past the registration desk, then the stairwell, heading down the hall to the family suite. He considered it fate that Isabella had asked him to help carry her things earlier. It saved him from having to search for her room tonight, not to mention that now he had her key.

When he reached the door, he paused, his eyes narrowing as his expression went flat. He looked down the long hallway, then back behind him. Nothing moved. No one spoke. It was just as well. He would have killed them without compunction.

Satisfied that all was well, he laid his ear against the door, taking comfort at the silence within. Then, with one last glance around, he took the key that he'd stolen from Isabella's key ring and slipped it into the lock.

* * *

Isabella had cried herself to sleep and for the past hour or so had been locked into a repeat of the same awful dream. In the dream, Jack kept running into the lobby, shouting her name. Only when she saw him, it wasn't sweat on his clothes and face, it was blood. And every time she tried to ask him what was wrong, he kept pulling his gun and telling her they all had to die.

She rolled onto her back, then to her right side, thrashing beneath the covers as she struggled to stop the sequence from recurring. And then, suddenly, her father was there, standing between her and Jack.

"Daddy...I'm so glad you came. Everything is out of control." She pointed at Jack. "He says the uncles have a secret, but no one will tell me what it is. It's not fair, Daddy. Make them tell me what it is."

"Forget the secret, Isabella. Someone is at your door! Wake up. Wake up now!"

Isabella sat straight up in bed, her heart pounding, her eyes wide with fright. Shoving her hair from her face, she held her breath, listening. Listening.

Then she heard it. A faint rattle at the front door of the suite, then a squeak, as if someone had stepped on a loose board in the floor.

*Oh my God...it wasn't a dream! Someone was really trying to get in.*

She crawled out of bed, taking the phone with her as she went, and locked herself in the bathroom. Without turning on the lights, she started to dial the police, then realized it would take them too long to arrive. It was then that she thought of Jack Dolan. Since there was a Federal agent on the premises who was meddling into her life, the least he could do was save it before he tore it all to hell. Seconds later, she was dialing his room.

Jack had fallen asleep on top of the covers, still wearing his socks and sweats. When the phone rang, he rolled instinctively toward the side of the bed and was reaching for his shirt as he answered.

"Hello."

"Jack...it's me. Someone is trying to get into my room."

The voice was barely a whisper, but he knew immediately it was Isabella.

"Where are you?"

"I locked myself in the bathroom."

"Stay there. I'm on my way."

He dropped the phone without hanging it up and grabbed his gun on the way out the door.

Running in his sock feet, he made little noise, but when he started down the stairs, there was no way he could disguise the fact that he was coming. Boards on the stairwell squeaked in several different places, but there was nothing he could do except keep moving. Seconds later, he cleared the last step and headed down the hall to her room.

The night lights in the hallway were off. Another sign of foul intent. The door was ajar. The rooms dark. Holding his gun with both hands, he held it forward in shooting position and slipped inside.

Instantly he saw a shadow passing between him and the window. It was too tall and too broad for Isabella. His belly knotted. Son of a bitch. It had to be Rostov, but why Isabella? What did he think she knew?

He slipped along the wall now, moving quickly but carefully, unwilling to give himself away.

He heard a door rattle, then a soft chuckle.

"Isabella...come out please. You cannot hide from me."

Jack heard a muffled cry and then a moment of silence before the door rattled again.

He bolted into the bedroom and turned on the light.

"Freeze!" he yelled. "Get down! Get down now!"

Rostov spun, his face contorted in sudden rage as pulled a knife from his sleeve and launched himself at Jack.

They went down in a tangle of arms and legs as Isabella burst from the bathroom. Jack caught a momentary flash of nightgown and knew she was trying to help.

"Get out!" he shouted. "Get out of the room!"

Isabella ran out of the room and into the hall, screaming as she went.

Rostov grabbed Jack by the wrist, trying to wrestle the gun from his hand. It went off beside Rostov's ear, deafening as the bullet sailed past his head and into the wall behind him. Jack brought his knee up between Rostov's legs and sent him rolling. Rostov bolted to his feet, pain searing his testicles, as he kicked Jack once in the stomach and then ran from the room. The moment he made it into the hallway, he'd knew he had missed his chance. Isabella Abbott was nowhere in sight. With no time to search for her, he headed for the kitchen, sidestepping small tables and knocking down chairs as he went.

The night air was cool on his face as he burst from the hotel. He ran with his head down and without looking back. Only after he'd reached the safety of the forest did he stop and turn. Every light in the place was on, and the same man who'd caught him was standing on the terrace looking out into the dark—still holding the gun.

Rostov's heart was pounding, his hands shaking with rage, as he leaned over and puked from the pain between his legs. He'd been so close. Cupping himself as he groaned, he saw the man slip back inside.

It was the writer. He had recognized him on sight. But what need did a writer have for a Glock? Cursing the fates, he hurried away, desperate to take shelter in the old mine he'd found before they began to hunt for him. He'd underestimated the opposition, and it had almost gotten him killed. He couldn't afford to let it happen again.

He ran and didn't stop again until he'd gained the safety of his hiding place. Slipping past the deadfall of timber blocking the entrance to the mine, he crawled on his hands and knees to the place where he'd made his bed. It was far enough away from the opening that he could safely build a fire—something that had become increasingly necessary as the nights continued to grow colder.

He tossed some tinder on the embers and then rocked back on his heels, watching them as they caught. Only after the flames were glowing did he lay a small log on the fire. Then he dug through his backpack and pulled out a stick of dried beef. After the fine food and hearty meals he'd been eating for the past week at the hotel, it was a sorry way to fend off his hunger.

The hotel was in an uproar. After the gunshot, the Silvias had been in the group of guests who'd rushed to the top of the stairs in concern. Leonardo was ready to pack their things and take Maria back to New York, but she was firm.

"No, Leonardo. I will not go until I take back a baby in my belly."

"If we wanted to be shot in our beds, we could have stayed home and saved ourselves a trip to Montana," he muttered, as he hurried her back to their room.

"No one is hurt and the bad man is gone," Maria said, and locked them in their room.

\* \* \*

Isabella was trying not to get hysterical. Only her Uncle John and Uncle Rufus were on the premises. The others had stayed at the hospital with Thomas. Once she'd assured them that she was okay, she hustled them back to their rooms. She wasn't convinced that the chaos was over, and the last thing she wanted was for another uncle to succumb to the shock of what was going on as Uncle Thomas had done.

Just as the last of the guests were going back to their rooms, Jack ran back into the lobby. She took one look at him and walked into his arms.

His newly healing ribs were aching from the kick he'd received, but pain was nothing compared to having this woman in his arms. He held her there at the foot of the stairs with the portrait hanging above them, a silent witness to their embrace.

"You saved my life."

Jack masked a shudder. He'd come damn close to being too late to brag about it.

"It's a good thing you woke up," he said. "Or I wouldn't have had the chance."

"It was Daddy," she said.

"What?"

"I was dreaming, and suddenly Daddy was in the dream, telling me to forget about secrets and wake up, because someone was at the door."

"Hell," Jack muttered. "That's quite an alarm system you've got going."

Isabella chose not to tell him it wasn't the first time that her father had come to her in her dreams. There were some things better left unsaid.

"I thought he'd killed you," she said. "I heard the gunshot, and then he came running out and you—"

"Did you call the police?"

"Yes."

He sighed. "It was Victor Ross."

"I know. I saw him. Did you hear him taunting me?"

He smoothed the tangle of hair from her eyes and then rocked her where they stood.

"Yes, baby, I heard."

"Why, Jack? Why is this happening?"

"I don't know," he said.

She pulled out of his arms.

"Don't lie to me."

"I'm not. I swear. I don't know why the man is still here, but I suspect it has something to do with your uncles."

"Then why come after me?" she asked.

"Who do your uncles love most?" he asked.

Her eyes widened. "Me...I think. Are you saying that Ross was going to use me to get to them?"

"Again, I don't know. But it makes more sense than anything else I can think of. He wants something. I just don't know what."

"Dear God...if only Daddy were still alive."

Jack thought of the photo lying back in his room.

He wasn't so sure that Samuel Abbott would have been any more cooperative than the other old men had been. Obviously they had all faked their own deaths and taken up bogus identities. He was just waiting for confirmation of it from Steven Randolph. It was the why of it all that held the key.

"I hear sirens," Jack said. "You sit here where I can see you. I'm going to unlock the front door."

It took the better part of two hours for the local sheriff's office to secure the crime scene. The crime scene investigator had left Isabella's room in a mess. Fingerprint powder was everywhere. There were hundreds of prints, but Jack knew none of them would belong to Victor Ross, because when they'd been fighting, Jack had seen he was wearing gloves.

Also, identifying himself as a Federal agent had caused quite a stir. He'd told them as little as possible as to why he was here, only that he was following the man who'd killed Frank Walton. They hadn't asked him why an agent with the FBI would be working a botched Brighton Beach mugging, but he'd seen the look the sheriff gave him and knew they suspected more was going on. At least they hadn't asked, which had saved him the trouble of refusing to answer.

Isabella had been questioned repeatedly about Victor Ross, from the time she'd hired him up to yesterday, when she'd paid him for the week's work. Her confusion was obvious, and her patience was growing thin. Finally she got to her feet and moved to the front door.

"Gentlemen, it's late. I've told you everything I know at least four times. If I remember anything else I will call. Otherwise...good night."

Knowing when to retreat had always been one of the sheriff's strong points. He tipped his hat to Isabella, gave Jack a long, considering stare and then left.

Isabella turned the lock, then dropped her head and leaned forward, bracing herself against the door with the flats of her hands.

"Oh God."

Suddenly her whole body was shaking. Jack caught her before she slid to the floor.

"Come with me," he said gently, then led her toward the stairs.

"Where are you taking me?"

"To my room. At least there I know you'll be safe."

Her chin quivered as they reached the landing.

"I don't think I'll ever feel safe again."

"Yes, you will. I promise." He opened the door to his room. "See that bed?"

She nodded.

"Get in it."

"Where will you sleep?"

"Beside you...and it will be okay."

She only looked at him once, just to assure herself that he meant what he said. He'd said it would be okay, and it had to be, because she couldn't take any more surprises.

"Jack?"

"What, honey?"

"I'm glad you're here."

"Yes, baby, so am I. Now go to bed."

Jack pulled back the covers, then turned her around to face him.

"Here, honey, let's take off your robe. Now your shoes."

She sat on the edge of the bed, letting him tend to her as if she were a child. Unable to argue, unwilling to fight, she rolled over on her side and curled up, her knees against her chest.

Jack locked the door, pulled off his socks and shirt, and laid his gun on the table beside the bed. He didn't think he would need it again tonight, but better safe than sorry.

He looked at her then, wondering, as he got in beside her, why this didn't seem strange. He had women from time to time, but he never spent the night. It always seemed a step toward something final that he wasn't ready to make.

He saw her shudder as he reached for the covers.

"Are you cold?"

"All the way to my bones."

"Then come here to me," he said softly, and pulled her back against the curve of his body.

She stiffened, but when the only thing he did was cradle her, she began to relax.

"I've never slept with a man before. I mean, I've had sex…but not in a bed."

Jack grinned, glad she couldn't see his face.

"Back seat of a car?"

"Barn loft."

His grin widened.

"Damn, Tink, you never fail to surprise me."

Her eyes closed as a small sigh slid out from between her lips.

"It's what being a woman is all about," she mumbled.

"What? Having sex in a barn loft?"

"No."

"Then what?"

"Surprises. It's all about surprises."

It was the last thing she said before falling asleep.

Jack didn't think he was going to be able to relax. Her bottom was soft and tempting and pressed up against his groin, and the steady rise and fall of her breasts beneath his hand was more than he thought he could take.

He closed his eyes for a moment, just planning to rest, but having Isabella in his arms was too comfortable and so familiar. He relaxed within seconds and soon fell asleep.

While Jack and Isabella were sound asleep, John and Rufus had yet to close their eyes. Ever since they'd gone back upstairs, they'd been in urgent conversation, trying to find a way out of the mess they were in.

"It's not as though we never thought it would happen," John said.

Unable to sit still for long, Rufus was pacing from window to couch and back again.

"But not now," he moaned. "For the first five years, I lived every day in fear, certain we'd be found out. Then the years began to pass without incident, and before we knew it, we'd grown old." He threw up his hands in frustration as he looked at his friend. "It isn't fair, you know...happening now."

"You know what Samuel would say if he were still alive."

Rufus nodded. "Yes, that life isn't fair, but it's life, and the alternative is not acceptable."

John sighed. "I don't know if he was right about that. Right now, I'm thinking he and Frank are the lucky ones. They got out before the proverbial shit hit the fan."

"They didn't 'get out.' They died," Rufus muttered.

The solemn expression on John's long, thin face made it appear even longer.

"Same thing," he said, then pointed to the phone. "Someone's got to call David and Jasper. They've got to know about Isabella before they hear the gossip in town."

"I hate to call the room this late," Rufus said.

"What if Thomas is sleeping? We shouldn't disturb his rest."

"Listen to what you're saying," John said. "So what if Thomas's rest is disturbed? We almost lost our girl tonight. If it hadn't been for that Dolan fellow, it would have happened."

Rufus's ruddy face turned pale. "He's FBI, John. It's only a matter of time before this comes down around our ears."

"So what? We accepted that possibility long ago. Right now our concern should be making certain Isabella doesn't go down with us."

Rufus's shoulders slumped. "You're right. Of course you're right. Our poor little girl. Dear God, she can't know what we've done. It would destroy her."

"Then I say we call David."

"You do it," Rufus said. "I'm too shaken."

John sighed as he went for the phone. It was true. When things went wrong, Rufus was always the first one to fade.

He dialed the phone. Since it was after hours, the switchboard was closed and the phone was answered in the ER.

"This is John Michaels," he said. "I need to speak to Dr. Schultz. It's an emergency."

The nurse recognized the name and the voice, and since everyone in the small hospital was well aware that Thomas Mowry had been admitted only hours earlier, she knew David Schultz was still on the premises.

"Just a moment, Mr. Michaels. I'll ring the nurses' station. They'll know where he is."

"Thank you," John said, and waited for the call to be transferred.

"Second floor nurses' station."

"This is John Michaels. I need to speak with Dr. Schultz. It's an emergency."

"He's in Mr. Mowry's room. I'll transfer the call for you."

Moments later, the phone rang and John heard David answer.

"David...it's John. How is Thomas?"

"He's fine. Sedated and sleeping easily. He showed no signs of having had an attack, nor of any damage to the heart muscle, so I think we're okay here."

"That's good, because we're not okay here."

"What's wrong?"

"Someone broke into Isabella's room tonight. She woke up before he got inside and locked herself in her bathroom, then called Jack Dolan. He saved her from God only knows what, but the man got away."

"Good Lord!" David gasped. "Do they know who it was?"

"Yes. Victor Ross."

There was a moment of silence. John knew that

David was absorbing the shock, just as they'd had to do.

"What are we going to do?" John finally asked. "This is falling down around our ears, but we've got to protect her. You know how Samuel felt about this. We swore an oath to him, David. We promised on everything we held dear that we would never tell her. But if this goes on much longer, we won't have to. She's going to find out from someone else, and when she does, it will destroy her."

"Dear God...I never meant—"

"None of us did," John said. "But we've known for years that every project was failing. We should have stopped then, when the first ones started to self-destruct."

Weary and suddenly heartsick, David rubbed the bridge of his nose.

"Self-destruct? Why don't we just come out and say what's what instead of using such a clean, clinical expression? They committed suicide. Ugly, but plain and simple."

John's voice started to shake. "It was because of the voices...but if that had been the case, then the medications for schizophrenia should have worked."

"I know, I know, but remember what Samuel said about that."

John sighed. "Yes, he said it was because the voices they heard weren't because they were crazy. They were just caught up in their old memories."

"Yes, exactly, and they didn't know how to process them."

"And that's because they didn't know what we'd done," John said. "God help them...God help them all," he muttered.

"There's no one left for Him to help," David said.

"Yes, there is, and we've got to do our part."

Knowing that his old friend was right, David made a quick decision.

"Can you and Rufus get to the lab without being missed?"

"Yes, the police are gone and everyone is in bed."

"Then go pick up where we left off. I'll leave Jasper with Thomas and get there as soon as I can. We've come too far on this last project to pull back now, but we're going to have to hurry to get it done. After that, it won't matter who knows what."

"It's going to matter to Isabella."

"She'll know only what we choose to tell her," David said sharply. "Now get Rufus and get to work."

"He's here with me now. You know where we'll be."

They disconnected, then John turned to his old friend.

"Are you up to a bout of midnight madness?"

Rufus shrugged. "I thought we'd already had some of that."

"David will be joining us as soon as he can. He thinks, if we hurry, we can finalize the last implant before everything comes undone."

Rufus snorted. "It's already unwinding, for God's sake. However, I'm game if you are. I'll get dressed and be with you shortly."

"I'll wait for you in David's room," John said.

Rufus nodded. "I won't be long."

Maria Silvia lay curled up against her husband's back, her arm flung across his belly, taking comfort in the steady rise and fall of his chest, as well as the occasional soft snore.

The incident downstairs had been more unsettling to her than she was willing to admit. She was a big believer in omens, and what had happened downstairs earlier left her shaken. Was this God's way of telling her that what they were trying to do was all wrong? Was it truly her fate to go through life childless?

She drew a deep, shuddering breath and then crawled out of bed. Careful not to wake Leonardo, she dropped to her knees by the side of the bed and started to pray.

It was the soft breath on the side of his face that brought Jack from a deep and dreamless sleep to an abrupt awakening. Dawn was imminent. Light was returning, changing the night into shades of gray.

He looked down at Isabella, but he was unprepared for the emotions that hit him gut first.

She was wrapped in his embrace—one arm thrown across his chest, her head pillowed on his shoulder. Layers of dark lashes rimmed her eyelids. Long and black, they lay against her cheeks like thick, tiny feathers. Her face in repose was stunningly beautiful, like the portrait of the woman that hung over the stairs. He remembered the first time he'd seen her, standing in the lobby in the dark, and imagined he was seeing a ghost.

But the woman in his arms was no ghost. She was warm flesh and blood, and last night he'd come close to losing her before he'd had a chance to explore the passion that was between them. Unable to resist, he leaned down and brushed a kiss across her mouth. Thinking of all that had to be done this day, he tried to scoot his arm out from beneath her head without waking her up. But the moment he moved, she woke.

She opened her eyes without speaking. Her hair was in tangles, her thoughts still in the half light between night and day.

Breath caught in the back of Jack's throat. The look in her eyes said it all. When she slid her arms around his neck, he didn't hesitate to follow where she wanted him to go.

Lying stretched out atop her with a hand on either side of her shoulders to keep from crushing her with his weight, his body began to come alive. Muscles hardened. Need pushed at him. He knew where he wanted to be, but it would be insane to let it all go.

"John Jacob Dolan."

The way she said his name made him weak. Then she lowered her eyes, letting her gaze slide past his face to his bare chest. Splaying her fingers across the band of muscles beneath her palms, she traced the shape of his body.

"Isabella..."

Ignoring the warning, she ran her fingers around his lips, as if committing the feel and shape to her memory.

"You're playing with—"

"I'm not playing. I'm serious. Make love to me, Jack. Now. Before I lose what's left of my mind."

He smiled wryly. "Don't be shy, Tinkerbell. Tell me what you're really thinking."

Her eyelids fluttered as she arched her body toward him.

"Jack..."

"My God," he muttered, and threw back the covers.

Her fingers curled around his arms, her voice low and anxious.

"Don't make me beg."

"Honey...it was the last thing on my mind," he said.

"Then what—"

"We've got on too many clothes."

She lowered her eyes, watching hungrily as he

stripped. His body was lean and hard, and his erection made the ache in her belly that much worse. But when she started to take off her nightgown, he stopped her.

"No. Let me."

She lay back on the bed, giving herself up to whatever he needed, all the while knowing that she would get even more in return.

The air in the room felt cool against her bare skin, but when she inhaled slowly and closed her eyes, the heat from his mouth warmed her inside and out.

"This isn't about sex," she said softly.

Jack circled her navel with his tongue as he scooted his hands beneath her backside.

"The hell you say," he groaned, as he shoved his knee between her legs.

There was a moment when he looked down at her face—a fraction of a second when all she had to do was say stop. But she didn't. Instead, she reached for him gently and guided him in.

Warmth flooded—both through him and around him—rendering him momentarily mute. He wanted to tell her how beautiful she was in the early morning sunlight, and how perfectly the size of her breasts fit the palms of his hands. He wanted her to know that he understood what she'd meant, but he couldn't think past the gut-wrenching need to start moving.

So he did what he needed and took her on a fast ride. When it ended, Isabella laughed through her tears, while he collapsed in her arms, certain he would never walk again.

They lay within the quiet of the old house, feeling the ricocheting rhythm of each other's heart and knowing that nothing between them could ever be the same.

But even more worrisome was the knowledge that Isabella had been right.

It hadn't been about sex.

This was love.

# 14

"I have to get up," Isabella said.

Jack buried his face in the curve of her neck, reluctant to let her go. Once they left his room, reality would set in. He would still be investigating her uncles, and she would still be in danger.

"I don't want to let you go."

Isabella shivered suddenly. Jack felt her tremble and raised himself up on one elbow to look down at her face.

"What's wrong?"

"I don't know. A premonition?"

He frowned. "About what?"

"Me. You. Us."

He kissed her then, gently grazing her mouth, then harder when she threaded her fingers at the back of his neck and kissed him back. When they stopped, they were both breathless.

"I'm out of control, aren't I?" she asked.

Jack smiled. "Love doesn't have control buttons, sweetheart. Just on and off switches."

She sighed. "Then are we on?"

"What do you think?"

"My heart is racing."

One corner of his mouth tilted upward as he laid a hand on her breast.

"Yeah, I can feel it."

"What else can you feel?" she asked.

"Your skin…it's like smooth, white silk."

She arched an eyebrow.

"Your heart is racing, too."

He nodded. "Yeah, I know."

"Are you afraid?"

"Yes."

"Of what just happened? Of me?" she asked.

"Neither."

"Then what?"

Jack sat up in bed and then took her in his arms, cradling her against him as he would a child.

"Ever since the moment I walked into the lobby and saw that painting on the wall, somehow I knew my life would never be the same. I don't know how. I just knew it. Then I saw you, and yes, I'll admit it, I thought you were a ghost."

"I knew it," she crowed. "I saw the shock in your eyes."

"Yes, but there was more than shock. There was guilt. I had a duty to perform, and I was fantasizing about a woman who was part of the investigation."

A slight frown creased her forehead as her mood shifted.

"You never have told me why the United States government is interested in Uncle Frank's death...other than the fact that he was killed by a Russian citizen. I'm not up on government protocol, but I know something more is going on.''

"I can't. Not yet.''

She sighed. "Fine.''

He cursed beneath his breath. "No, it's not fine, but for now it's the best I can do.''

Jack felt her pulling away, both emotionally and physically. It hurt, but it was no more than he'd expected.

She got out of bed and began looking for her nightgown in the tangle of bedclothes. He put on a pair of sweats and then pushed back the blanket, dug out the nightgown and handed it to her without saying a word.

"Thank you,'' she muttered, and slipped it over her head.

"Here's your robe...and your slippers.''

She let him dress her, then steadied herself by holding on to his shoulder as she stepped into her shoes.

"If Uncle Thomas is still in the hospital, I'll be going into Braden later to see him.''

"You don't go alone.''

"Then I'll take one of my uncles.''

Jack braced himself for the moment when she would walk out the door, and yet when she reached for the knob, he felt physical pain.

"You wanted to know what scares me,'' he said.

She hesitated, then turned around.

"Yes, I do."

"It's this...the angry distance that's between us now. Last night you slept in my arms. This morning we made love. I did not take that lightly. There is no off switch on what I feel for you, Isabella, and my biggest fear is that you will hate me when this is over."

She looked at him there, standing by the foot of the bed. His physical strength was a given, but in admitting that he cared for her without knowing how she felt, he'd just done something that took far more strength.

"No, Jack. I can't hate you...even if I tried. But I hate what's happening. Losing my father left me without an anchor. Losing Uncle Frank has somehow left me in jeopardy. If you had not come to White Mountain, there's no telling what would have happened to me."

"Just give me time," he begged. "I'll tell you everything when I'm certain that it won't cause more harm."

She sighed, then nodded. "Fair enough."

"I'm going down to breakfast as soon as I make a couple of calls."

"Want some company?"

"Honey, I think we've gone past the *company* stage, and yes, I want you to eat breakfast with me."

"I'll be there as soon as I can shower and change, but I'm going to have to wade through the mess the police made to do it."

"I'll wait."

"You don't have—"

Jack crossed the floor and cupped her face in his hands.

"I said I'll wait. For as long as it takes."

The tenderness in his voice was almost her undoing, as was what he had just said. He'd been referring to more than a simple date for breakfast.

"And then what?" she asked, her voice trembling.

An urgency gnawed in the pit of Jack's belly. He couldn't look at her without wanting to take her to bed. He wanted to give her the world, and except for this morning, when they'd made love, all he'd given her was grief.

"What do you want?" he asked.

She hesitated, embarrassed to admit what was in her heart, then thought of how swiftly life could end. She was already twenty-eight years old. Most of her school friends had been married for years, and some had children already in school. She knew what she wanted, but not whether she had the guts to admit it.

"Isabella."

She looked up.

"You. I want you."

"But, honey…you've already got me," he said gently.

"But for how long?" she asked, and then, afraid of his answer, she hurried away.

Jack groaned beneath his breath and then closed the door. Before he got in the shower, he reached for the laptop, anxious to check his messages.

As he hoped, there was another one from Dubloh7. He opened it. Within seconds of reading the first paragraph, his suspicions had been confirmed. The name Samuel Abbott belonged to a man who'd died in 1946. David Schultz had died in 1955, at the age of 20. Thomas Mowry had died in 1958, at the age of ten. John Michaels was a name belonging to a man who'd died in 1939. Rufus Toombs was the name of a man who'd died in prison in 1964, while the real Jasper Arnold had passed away in 1960.

Now he knew, but what he was going to do with the information remained to be seen.

David shoved the microscope aside and stood, stretching wearily as he stared at a small spot on the ceiling.

"It didn't divide, did it?" Rufus asked.

David shook his head.

"The sample was too old. We don't have enough viable DNA to make it work. It's time to quit now, before it's too late."

David shook his head. "Not just yet," he muttered. "I wish Samuel were still alive. He'd know what to do."

John slapped a lab table with the flat of his hand.

"Damn it all to hell…Samuel was no better than

the rest of us. If he had been, we wouldn't be looking at a one-hundred percent failure rate.''

''Ninety-nine point nine,'' David corrected. ''Everything didn't fail, and you know it.''

''I've said it before—that one doesn't count,'' John muttered.

David spun, suddenly loud and angry.

''Why the hell not? We implanted that mother the same way we've done every other woman who wanted a child. The mother conceived. She carried her baby the full nine months without a hitch. The child is the only healthy adult we have.''

David snorted angrily. ''And why you've chosen to rehash old history is beyond me. We've got the world coming at us from all sides. Let's try and finish what we've started before we're crushed. What do you say?''

''Fine,'' John said. ''But there's only enough DNA nucleus for one more try. After that, the writing is on the wall, my friends.''

Shock spread across David's face.

''Only one?'' he asked.

''And considering what we had to work with, lucky to have that many,'' Rufus muttered. ''You try getting DNA out of three-hundred-year-old bones and see what you come up with.''

David's shoulders slumped. ''I'm sorry. You're right. I know you're right. And were it not for your breakthrough research last year, we wouldn't be able to do even that.''

Rufus was mollified enough by the praise to stop arguing.

"Where are Samuel's notes on his last tests? Maybe there's something we're missing."

"They're right here," David said. "I'm not missing anything but some luck."

"Then here's to luck," John said. "And a big hearty breakfast. I'm starving."

"There's a woman upstairs who's come a long way for a child. Let's just remember the promise she made to God and make this work."

Rufus chuckled as he picked up the last piece of bone.

"Irony...that's what this is.... Irony."

"How so?" John asked.

Rufus held up the bone. "Saint Bartholomew here gave his life to God and died for his troubles."

David shook his head. "He was just in the wrong place at the wrong time in history. Europe in the seventeen hundreds was a hotbed of hypocrisy and mysticism. They branded him a heretic and hanged him. Then, ten years later, they were praying to his remains and expecting miracles. Go figure."

"But the miracles did happen. Remember that," John said. "They've been happening for centuries. He did not die a saint. It was the Catholic church that gave him the title, and you know they don't give it lightly."

Rufus smiled. "So we give a man of God to a

woman who's promised to give him back to God. There's the irony.''

David tuned out their abstract chatter as he chose a new egg and began to remove the nucleus. A short while later, he looked up.

"I'm ready when you are," he said.

Rufus nodded. "This is it, my friend, and if this doesn't work, then we move to plan B."

David snorted. "There is no plan B."

Rufus waddled over to David's lab table, deftly moving his cumbersome bulk between the equipment.

"Here…and be gentle. The fellow was supposed to be celibate, although back in those days, it was iffy.''

It was the unexpected bawdiness of Rufus's comment that settled their nerves. Laughter was brief as David began the process.

"Step one," David said, then took the adult nucleus Rufus handed him and injected it into the dish beside the one he'd harvested from Maria Silvia.

"Step two," he said, and shot the adult nucleus with an electrical impulse, trying to shock it to life in lieu of human sperm.

"Step three," he said, checking settings as they crowded around the computer monitor.

The image on screen was exactly what they would see under a microscope, only magnified for easier viewing—one empty egg from Maria and the adult DNA from a long-dead monk. Theoretically the electrical impulse would charge the adult nucleus to behave as human sperm—piercing the outer membrane and cytoplasm of Maria's egg and becoming one with it. Cell division wouldn't happen without that.

They watched the monitor with their hearts in their throats, thinking of Samuel, who'd died before his dream had been realized, remembering Frank who'd been martyred because of it, and praying for Thomas, who had been beaten down by it. If they failed now, it was over.

One long second followed another until Rufus slapped the arms of his chair in disgust. "That's that, then," he said. "It isn't going to work." He got up from his seat and began removing his lab coat.

John nodded in agreement and had started to walk away when David suddenly shouted.

"Wait!"

They rushed back, their gazes riveted to the screen.

"See! There!" David cried. "It's working! By God...it's working."

They stared in disbelief, watching as the adult nucleus began to move. Melding itself to Maria's egg, it began to pierce the outer shell.

Division had started.

They stood in humble silence, enraptured by the creation of life. Maria Silvia didn't know it yet, but her child was on the way.

\* \* \*

Isabella arrived at her door, only to realize that her keys were inside. If it was locked, she was going to have to go to the registration desk in her night clothes. Just as she reached for the doorknob, two of her household staff opened the door and came out. When they saw her, they both smiled, but it was Mavis who started talking.

"Oh, Miss Abbott, thank goodness you're all right. We heard all about what happened to you last night, so Shirley and I came in early to clean up. Everything is back in order except for the bullet hole in the wall and that little green lamp that sat by your father's chair. I'm afraid it's broken beyond repair."

"It doesn't take long for news to travel, does it? As for the damages, considering what might have happened, they're nothing. I was really dreading coming back to the mess the police had made, so thank you for coming in early. My gratitude will be reflected in your paychecks."

"It's not necessary. Really," Mavis said.

"It is for me. Thanks again," Isabella said, and opened the door as they left to begin their regular shift.

She paused in the doorway, remembering the abject terror with which she'd left last night. This was the only home she'd ever known. She'd learned to roller skate in the hallways and had sat in her father's lap before this very fireplace as he read her to sleep each night. She wasn't going to let evil destroy every good memory she had.

Her eyes narrowed angrily. Lifting her chin, she strode inside, firmly shutting and locking the door behind her. Then, to be on the safe side, she turned the dead bolt in place. Not because she thought Victor Ross would come back in broad daylight, but because until she got the locks changed, she would take no further chances.

Hurrying into her bedroom, she stripped off her clothes as she headed for the shower. Half an hour later, she was dressed. Two phone calls and she would be ready to meet Jack for breakfast. She glanced at the clock. It was almost eight. Maybe the locksmith would be in his office by now.

She called, and to her relief she got him instead of an answering machine. When she explained her problem, he promised to be out before noon. When she hung up the phone, she sat for a moment, thinking about the next call to be made. If it was as simple as the first, her day would be off to a fine start.

She dialed the hospital and asked for Thomas Mowry's room. It was Jasper who answered.

"Hello?"

"Uncle Jasper, it's me. How is Thomas?"

"He's fine, just fine. In fact, he's going home as soon as he has some breakfast. But it's you who we're concerned with. John called us last night and told us what happened. David wanted to rush right home to you then, but John assured us you were all right and under Mr. Dolan's protection for the night.''

She thought of sleeping with Jack and waking up in his arms. She hadn't just been protected. She'd been loved.

"It was very frightening, but yes, I'm fine. Jack saved my life, Uncle Jasper.''

"Then we owe him a great deal. You are so very precious to us all, my dear.''

A lump came in Isabella's throat, but she wouldn't give in to her emotions. The uncles loved her, she knew. But the time had come for some explanations, and she wasn't going to quit until she got some.

"So, you'll be home before noon?''

"Someone will have to come get us.''

"What happened to the car you drove last night?''

"Oh! I forgot to tell you. You know how I nod off at night. Well, David stayed up with Thomas until almost daylight. When I woke up and saw how exhausted he was, I sent him home. He's probably sound asleep right now, so I wouldn't disturb him. He'll come down when he's rested.''

"Okay, and I'll make sure that none of the household staff clean up there today.''

"Good idea, darling. Well, here they come now with Thomas's breakfast. I'd better go and see if I can talk them into bringing one more for me.''

"I'll pick you up around eleven. If you're ready earlier, give me a call."

"All right, sweetheart, and drive safely." Then he thought about what had happened last night and added. "Do you think you should come alone?"

"I won't be alone," she said. "I'll ask Jack to come with me."

A brief silence followed her announcement; then she heard Thomas talking in the background and realized Jasper's attention had been momentarily diverted.

"Uncle Jasper...did you hear what I said?"

"Yes, yes. I'm sorry. Thomas was talking to me at the same time, and I can't hear thunder out of my right ear, so I had to lower the phone to hear what he was saying."

"Is he really okay?"

Jasper laughed. "I'd say so. He was asking me to tell the nurses that he likes butter on his toast, not margarine."

Isabella laughed, and she was still smiling when she left to meet Jack for breakfast.

Jack was wiping the last of the shaving cream from his neck when his cell phone began to ring. There was only one person who would be calling him on that phone. He raced to answer.

"Dolan here."

It was the director.

"Good morning, Jack. I hope I'm not calling too early."

"No, sir. I was up. In fact, I was up most of the night."

"Burning the candle at both ends?"

"Ross broke into Isabella Abbott's room last night."

"Was she harmed?"

"No, and he got away."

"I think it's time we got a team in there. Did some serious searching in the mountains."

"Yes, sir. I concur."

"I'll have them there before the day is over. You're in charge. Tell them everything you know, but stay on-site at the hotel. Until we know why Miss Abbott is the target, I doubt it will be safe to leave her alone."

"Yes, sir. I already told her as much this morning."

"You've already talked to her?"

Jack hesitated briefly, then spoke.

"She spent the remainder of the night in my room, sir. I felt it was safer guarding her here, since Ross gained entry into her room with a key."

"Remember what you're about, Dolan. Don't get business mixed up with anything personal."

"Well, it's too damned late for that, sir, but I'm handling it. That's all I can say."

"Damn it, Dolan, that's against policy and you

know it. It taints the investigation. If this goes to court..."

"So far, sir, the only crime that I even suspect these men of is faking their own deaths. Yes, they assumed false identities, but they're well thought of in the community, and a couple of them founded a fertility clinic here that seems to be thriving. There was no record of anything of value going down in the plane but the men themselves. No missing money. No government secrets. And, according to the latest info I got from Quantico, they have not profited in any way from living under their assumed names. They don't draw social security or Medicare or anything one would normally expect from men of their ages. As far as I can tell, they were seven men who quit who they were to become someone else. I don't know why our Soviet friends were so interested in Frank Walton, or why Ross tried to get Isabella, but unless the old men start talking, we aren't going to find out."

"Why do you say that?"

"Because they've reached the age where the threat of death is no help in making them talk."

"Hmm...then maybe you've just answered your own question as to why Ross tried to get to Isabella Abbott."

"What do you mean, sir?"

"Maybe our Soviet friend wants some answers, too, and figures the best way to get to the men is through her."

Jack shoved his fingers through his hair in frustration.

"Yes, I've already thought of that."

"Well fine, but you're too close to the situation. Now put some distance between you and the woman so your brain has something to think about besides her, okay?"

"Okay."

"I want this man alive."

"I'll do my best. Oh…I almost forgot. I got some interesting info from Quantico."

"Like what?"

"Every one of the doctors who supposedly went down in that plane was working on similar medical research."

"What was it? Chemical warfare?"

"No. Oddly enough, they were all researching DNA…you know, gene manipulation geared toward curing disease. From what I learned, they were pretty far ahead of the times for the sixties and seventies. And that's not all. Right before they all disappeared, there were reports that their grants were being pulled and their studies were going to be over."

"So what are you saying? That you think they faked their own deaths out of something like spite?"

"I'm not drawing any conclusions. I'm just telling you what I know."

Jack heard the director's frustrated sigh and knew just how he felt.

"Sir...short of arresting everyone, with no evidence to back up the arrests, we're doing all we can."

"All right, but remember why you're there."

It was an indirect order for Jack to back off from Isabella. He heard, but he was pretty sure he wasn't going to obey.

He hung up and clipped the cell phone to his slacks as he headed out the door. It had been almost an hour since he'd seen Isabella, and it felt like forever. He took the stairs at a jog.

Isabella saw him coming down the stairs. When the mere sight of him made her heart skip a beat, she knew she was lost. He wasn't at all like the men she'd grown up around. No blue jeans, no Stetson, no cowboy boots. He didn't chew tobacco or drive a pickup, and she was assuming he didn't own cattle or several thousand acres of ranch land. But his soft, southern drawl made her weak with longing, and his mouth made her think shameless thoughts. His body was long and lean and hard as a rock, and he made love to her like a thief, stealing her sanity and, finally, her heart.

"Jack...I'm here," she called.

He turned toward the sound of her voice, and when he reached her, he picked her up off her feet and swung her around where they stood.

Isabella gasped and then laughed aloud, causing several diners' heads to turn.

"You crazy man. Put me down. People are looking."

"Let them watch," he growled, and then centered a swift kiss on her lips.

"What happened to you?" she asked, when he finally put her down.

"Nothing. I just missed you."

"I have to go to the hospital at eleven and bring Uncle Thomas home."

Jack thought of the impending arrival of the search team and figured he still had some time to spare.

"I'm coming with you."

"Thank you. I would appreciate it."

He grabbed her by the hand. "Come on, honey. One thing at a time. First we eat, and I'm starved."

Isabella went where he led her—because she wanted to go, and because it was a good reason to put off the inevitable confrontation with her uncles.

As they passed under the painting, Jack glanced up. The Mona Lisa smile on the first Isabella Abbott's face was haunting. She knew all the answers, but she was in no shape to tell.

As they walked on past, he wondered whether even if she was still living, she would be any more cooperative than the uncles had been. He doubted it. She had to be the lone woman from the photograph taken at the plane. Whatever was going on, she'd known about it, and she'd taken the knowledge to her grave.

* * *

Maria Silvia's heart was pounding as an orderly wheeled her into surgery.

"There's our girl!"

She turned her head and saw her doctor's eyes smiling at her over his surgical mask.

"Are you ready for this?" he asked.

Tears rolled from the corners of her eyes.

"I have been waiting for it all my life."

"Great. We're ready to go, too, so I want you to relax. This team is the best, and what we're going to do has been done here thousands of times before. Now, I want you to relax and let us do the work."

"Okay," she said.

"And no more tears," David said.

She closed her eyes, willing herself not to cry.

"No more tears," she promised.

She felt a prick in her arm, and then everything went gray.

It was three o'clock in the afternoon when the front doors of Abbott House opened with a bang. Delia looked up just as a half-dozen men swarmed toward her. They were backpacked and booted and dressed in camouflage gear. And they were all packing guns.

She hadn't been on the premises when the break-in had occurred, but she'd heard all about it. Fearing more of the same, she ran toward the office, calling Isabella's name as she went.

Isabella was up to her eyeballs in monthly reports when she heard the panic in Delia's voice. She bolted from her desk, meeting the little desk clerk at the door.

"What's wrong?" she asked.

Delia pointed.

Isabella looked over Delia's shoulder. More than a dozen men were standing in the lobby, and she knew who they were looking for.

"You finish the workman's comp report and I'll handle this."

"It's a deal," Delia said, and shut herself in the office.

"Gentlemen. Welcome to Abbott House. I'm Isabella Abbott, and I'm guessing you would be looking for Jack Dolan."

"Yes, ma'am. Agent Travis at your service."

"Will you be needing rooms?" she asked.

"No, ma'am. We'll be on the mountain."

"It gets pretty cold up there this time of year," Isabella warned.

"Yes, ma'am. A sure sign the snakes won't be out. I hate snakes."

Isabella grinned. "Make yourselves comfortable, and I'll tell Jack you're here."

She called his room, but he didn't answer. Frowning, she hung up the phone and then headed for the stairs. Even after she knocked twice, there was still no response. She turned the knob out of habit, assuming that it would be locked. Surprised when it turned in her hand, she pushed the door open a few inches and called out.

"Jack! It's me! Are you decent?"

When there was still no answer, she opened the door a little wider, and as she did, heard the shower running in the bathroom. Hesitating, she started to go back out and then thought of the men waiting downstairs. Jack would want to know they were here. He'd been waiting for them most of the day. She stepped inside, closing the door behind her.

"Jack! Hello!"

No response was forthcoming.

Rolling her eyes at her own audacity, Isabella started toward the bathroom, calling his name as she went.

Jack was rinsing the shampoo out of his hair when he thought he heard someone call out his name. Stepping back from the spray, he listened for a few seconds, but heard nothing. Shrugging, he finished rinsing out the suds and then turned a couple of times beneath the jets to wash the shampoo off his body, too. He turned off the water and then shoved back the shower curtain. Isabella handed him a bath towel.

"You didn't lock your door," she said.

He took one look at the blush on her face and grinned.

"Subliminal messaging," he said, as he wrapped

the towel around his waist and stepped out of the shower.

"The search team is downstairs," she said.

He started unbuttoning her blouse.

"We don't want to get this pretty blue shirt wet."

Isabella's eyes widened.

"Jack...we can't do this now. They're downstairs and they're armed, for God's sake. Delia nearly came undone."

"The only thing that's coming undone are your clothes," he whispered, and slid a still wet hand down the front of her breast.

The fluid warmth of his touch was as erotic as anything Isabella had ever felt in her life. She sighed, unwilling to argue with him anymore. All she wanted was Jack. On her. Inside her. Now.

When he backed her toward the bed, she picked up the phone. Without looking, she dialed the office.

Delia answered.

"Delia, tell the men that Agent Dolan has been detained. Send them to the dining room. Feed them anything they want, on the house."

"All right, but don't you—"

Isabella hung up.

Jack locked the door, then turned toward the bed.

She took a deep breath and then stepped out of her slacks.

Jack dropped his towel.

## 15

Jack's hair was still damp when he descended the stairs, and the bemused smile he was wearing said a lot for his state of mind. He found Travis and his men in the dining room, polishing off pie and coffee.

When Travis saw Jack enter the dining room, he stood, eyeing Dolan's casual saunter as he came toward them.

They shook hands, then Jack nodded to the other men nearby.

"Dolan...it's been a while."

"A couple of years, at least. Where was it? Chicago?"

"Boston. The Berringer kidnapping."

"Oh yes. Tough case. Let's hope this one has a better ending."

"You're in charge," Travis said. "Just fill us in."

"Let's move this outside, where we'll have a little more privacy."

Travis grinned. "Yeah, there's a whole hell of a

lot of privacy out there. Except for deer and raccoons, you've pretty much got the place to yourselves.''

"Except for the recent appearance of the red skunk you're going to help me find."

"My men are the best there is. If he's still on the mountain, we'll get him," Travis said.

"I need you to make that happen," Jack said. "He's killed once and, for reasons we don't understand, is targeting Miss Abbott, whom you already met."

Travis looked at Jack.

"She's stunning."

"Yeah."

"Her portrait is a real eye catcher, too."

"That's not her. It's her mother."

Travis frowned. "Wow! How do you tell them apart."

"Her mother is dead," Jack said. "I'd like to make sure the same thing doesn't happen to Isabella."

"Something personal?"

Jack ignored the question.

Travis grinned.

"The office frowns on fraternization with suspects, you know."

"She's not a suspect, she's a victim, and it's also none of your business," Jack muttered.

Travis laughed and slapped Jack on the shoulder.

"So tell us about who we're looking for and we'll be out of your very damp hair."

Jack grinned. "Go to hell."

"Headin' that way," Travis said. "Just point us in the right direction."


A short while later, Isabella came out of her room and headed down the hall. Her expression was drawn, her eyes welling with tears.

Jack, back inside the hotel, saw her coming and smiled, but the moment he saw her face, his smile slipped away.

"Sweetheart…what's wrong?"

"I just got a call from a friend in town."

"And?"

"Oh…it's about someone you don't know. His name was John Running Horse and—"

"But I do know him," Jack said. "I talked to him only a couple of days ago. He was saying something about getting a guitar and going to Nashville…or Memphis. And he was talking about his mother."

"Yes, that's him," she said. "He's dead."

"What happened?" Jack asked.

"He was hitchhiking…at least, they think he was…and he got hit by a car." She sighed. "I guess he was finally on his way to Memphis."

"That's too bad," Jack said. "At least now he'll

be with his mother. A lady at the drugstore told me she'd been dead for years.''

Isabella nodded. ''It's so sad. Makes you wonder why some people are born whole, while others are missing tiny bits.''

''Was he your friend?'' Jack asked.

She shrugged. ''He didn't know how to have friends,'' she said softly. ''But I knew him, and I'm so sorry he's dead.''

Jack hugged her, because there was nothing else he could do. As he walked her into the lobby, he couldn't help wondering about her state of mind. There had been far too much death in her life as it was, and he feared the worst wasn't over yet.

David saw them together and started to turn away, but Isabella waved him over.

''Uncle David...I've just received the saddest news,'' she said.

''What is it?'' he asked.

''You know John Running Horse?''

David's expression stilled.

''Yes, of course. What happened?''

''He's dead.''

David's shoulders slumped, and Jack would have sworn he heard the old man grunt.

''How?'' David asked.

''He was hitchhiking and got hit by a car. They think he was finally on his way to Memphis. The woman who called me said he was halfway to Butte when it happened.''

"Oh Lord," David mumbled. "What a waste… what a waste."

Isabella hugged him, then patted his face.

"We're going out onto the terrace for a while. Would you like to join us?"

"No. You don't need a chaperone. Go enjoy yourselves. Life is far too short."

Isabella nodded, then glanced at Jack. He slipped his hand beneath her elbow and led her through the dining room.

David watched them for a moment and then turned away. He needed to find the others and give them the news.

Vasili Rostov was standing on the edge of a ravine with his binoculars, scanning the valley below. Something was happening at the hotel, and he didn't think it had anything to do with the arrival of new guests.

Four all-terrain vehicles and two large gray vans were parked in the lot, and there were at least a dozen men milling about, wearing what appeared to be army gear. Even from this distance, he could tell they were armed. Cursing himself for ever getting mixed up in this mess, he watched as they loaded up and headed toward the foot of White Mountain. A short while later they disappeared from view, but he knew what would come next. They would disperse into search teams. When that happened, he had better be gone.

Wasting no time making his decision, he picked up his gear and started moving downward, veering left as he walked, constantly moving away from the last place he'd seen the men. As he walked, he kept pondering his options. He could get out now, go back to Russia and suffer the consequences. But the thought of spending his last years in disgraced exile disgusted him. He'd spent his life in service to his country and even given up a hard-won retirement to carry out this mission for Mother Russia. He wasn't going to give her the rest of his life just because of one old man's untimely death.

There was also Brighton Beach. It was a place where a man like him could get lost. It wouldn't take much to change his appearance. If he shaved his head and kept growing his beard, he would be completely unrecognizable. But there was the question of money. What he'd come with was almost gone.

He'd made a mistake going after the woman. He knew that now. She was obviously valuable enough to the men, but she was also too visible. Getting a hostage out of a hotel full of guests and remaining undetected wasn't going to happen up here. There was no city to get lost in, no traffic to slow everyone down. The wide-open spaces that housed few inhabitants also afforded little cover in which to hide. There were only the trees and the mountains, and in a situation like that, two men with some good tracking dogs could find them within hours.

But he still had the diary. There had to be something to be gained from it. As he walked, it slowly came to him, and by the time he reached the foothills, he knew exactly what he was going to do.

It was sundown when Rostov reached the valley. Staying well within the trees, he circled the rear of the hotel grounds until he came to the old gardener's shed. Confident it would be the last place where they would look for him, he slipped inside and tossed his things beneath a work bench. With one last look toward the hotel to make sure he'd gotten in unobserved, he went to his old room, then shoved a chair beneath the knob and crawled onto the bed. There was just enough time to rest before he put his plan into motion.

Isabella entered the dining room just as the waitress who'd taken her uncles' orders was leaving. When they saw her, they smiled and waved her over.

"Darling...won't you join us?" David asked.

"I'd love to," she said, and then let her gaze rest on Thomas, who'd been released from the hospital earlier that day.

"Uncle Thomas, are you sure you're up to this? I could bring a tray to your room if you'd rather."

"No, dear, I'm fine, and I'm sorry I gave everyone such a scare. Nothing's wrong with me except old age."

She smiled, but looking around the table at their dear, familiar faces made her heart ache. She'd thought she knew these men as well as she knew herself, and now, for the first time in her life, she felt as if she were looking at strangers.

"I'll just catch the waitress and give her my order. Be back in a few," she said.

As soon as she was gone, they huddled.

"She's upset with us," Jasper said. "I could tell it when she and that Dolan man came to pick us up at the hospital."

John frowned. "I don't think so. She's just upset at the whole situation. She has no reason to be upset with us."

David shook his head. "Oh, but she does," he muttered. "She's not stupid, and that Federal agent is bound to have said some things to her that she doesn't understand. God only knows what he found out, but one thing's for sure, he knows about Frank."

"Why do you say that?" Rufus asked.

"He was looking right at me when he announced that the man who killed Frank was Russian. He was watching for my reaction. That tells me he suspects a lot more than he can prove.''

''Then what are we going to do?'' Thomas asked.

''I don't know,'' David said. ''If you come up with any ideas, let me know.''

''We could always disappear again,'' Jasper said.

The other four moaned in unison.

''We're too old,'' Thomas said.

''And there's Isabella,'' David added. ''We are not going to abandon her.''

''I don't think she would be alone,'' John said. ''She's getting involved with Dolan.''

''How do you know that?'' Thomas asked.

''She spent the night in his room after the attack.''

''Yes, but did you ever think it could be because he felt she needed to be guarded?'' Rufus asked.

''She likes him,'' David said. ''I've known that for days.''

Rufus leaned closer, lowering his voice even more.

''Do you think it's mutual?''

David watched Isabella from across the room. Her elegance was inherent with her beauty. Just like her mother's had been.

''If it's not, he's crazy,'' David said. ''And by the way, where *is* Dolan?''

''He went with the search team to get them started. Said he was going to show them where he found that Russian knife. But he said he'd be back. Didn't want to leave Isabella unguarded at night.''

Before they could say anything more on the subject, Isabella returned. She sat down in her chair, groaning softly as she stretched, then leaned back.

''My feet are killing me,'' she muttered. ''What a day this has been.'' Then she looked up, aware that the uncles were staring at her. ''What?''

''Nothing,'' David said quickly, and gave her smile. ''What are you having for dinner?''

''Trout with steamed asparagus tips.''

''So am I,'' Thomas said.

She leaned over and patted his hand, then brushed a wayward strand of white hair away from his forehead.

''We always did like the same things, didn't we, Uncle Thomas?''

He beamed, pleased by her attention and the fact that they shared something so common as their taste in food.

''Yes, we did. Remember how you used to crawl up in my lap and dig through my coat pockets for my M&M's?''

Isabella chuckled. ''Those were mine all along. You just pretended they were yours to hear me squeal.''

They laughed aloud, and the moment passed. A few minutes later their food began to arrive and the banter between the men increased. A lump came up in Isabella's throat as she watched them. They were so dear to her heart. How could she confront them without hurting their feelings?

"Isabella?"

"Hmm? What? I'm sorry, Uncle John, what did you say?"

He pointed. "The pepper. Would you please pass the pepper?"

"Oh. Sure."

She handed it over, then looked past the diners to the French doors that led to the terrace. It was almost dark. Jack had gone with the search team earlier. She wondered when he would come back.

"Isabella, isn't your trout to your liking?" David asked.

She looked down at her plate in dismay. She had no idea how long it had been sitting there, and she had yet to take a bite.

"Oh! I'm sure it is," she said. "I was just wondering if Jack was all right."

The five men arched their eyebrows and nodded silently to each other as they continued to eat. So David had been right all along. She did care for him.

"Do you love him?" David asked.

Startled by the question, she dropped the bite of trout on her fork back onto the plate.

"If I answer your question, will you answer one of mine?" she fired back.

David felt himself pale but managed to smile.

"Why, darling…if I didn't know you better, I'd think you were angry with us."

She took a deep breath. *Just say it.* "I don't think 'angry' is the right word," she said. "But I *am* upset."

"Why?" Thomas asked. "What have we done?"

David glared at his old friend. His wording left them open to all kinds of questions, none of which he wanted to address.

"I don't know," she said. "And that's the trouble. I think you're keeping something from me, and you know it's not fair."

"What on earth makes you say that?" Jasper asked. "You know you mean the world to us all."

"Jack Dolan has a picture."

David's heart skipped a beat.

"What kind of a picture, darling?"

"It's an old picture, taken in the early seventies, I believe. It's of seven men in business suits in the act of boarding a plane. There's also a woman, but you can't see her face, and two pilots. They're just going up the ramp."

She heard a quick intake of breath from one of the men to her right, but she wouldn't take her gaze from David.

"I didn't recognize all of them, but one of the men is Daddy, so I'm guessing the woman is my mother. I also recognized Uncle Frank. And, Uncle David, I think you're in the picture, too."

David frowned, pretending to test his memory, although it wasn't necessary. He knew damn well what picture she was referring to. It was the last time he'd been called Anton Spicer.

"My problem is, Jack has a picture of my family and he won't tell me why. I know it has something to do with Uncle Frank's murder and with what's happening now. That's why I'm upset. Now finish your food before it gets cold. The cook made peach cobbler for dessert, and I know it's your favorite."

David nodded. "That it is," he said. "That it is."

They resumed their meal, but the atmosphere at the table was no longer light and cheery.

Isabella wanted to cry. Instead, she took another piece of fish and popped it into her mouth, forcing herself to chew and swallow, although it was suddenly tasteless. She made herself find a topic of discussion that wouldn't cause them any more pain.

"So, Uncle David...I understand the Silvia family will be leaving tomorrow. How did her procedure go?"

Glad to have something else to talk about, David nodded and smiled.

"It went well, I think, although you know how risky these things are. Only time and God will tell. And I think they've already checked out."

"Really? Well, I hope for her sake it's successful," Isabella said. "I've never seen a woman so desperate for a child."

David nodded, then pointed at Jasper. "Would you please pass the bread?" he asked.

Jasper passed the basket of rolls and their meal progressed. It wasn't until they were finishing dessert and Isabella started to get up that David took her by the hand.

"I'm sorry you feel hurt," he said softly.

"So am I, Uncle David."

He looked at her closely, searching her face for signs of anger, but he saw nothing other than anxiety.

"Before you go to bed tonight, come to my room. We'll talk."

Her eyes lit from within, and her mouth curved in a smile.

"Really?"

"Yes, really."

"I'll be there." Then she bent down and kissed his forehead. "Thank you, Uncle David. Thank you so much."

The moment she was out of hearing distance, the table erupted in a series of gasps and hisses.

"Have you lost your mind?" Rufus asked.

"What are you going to say?" John countered.

"You can't tell," Thomas argued. "We promised Samuel."

"Shut up, all of you," Jasper said. "David knows what he's doing."

David shook his head. "I don't know what I'm

going to say, but she deserves some kind of an answer.''

"Are you going to lie to her?" Thomas asked.

David's shoulders slumped. "I'll do what's necessary to keep her safe. We all will. Is that understood?"

They nodded in agreement as the table went suddenly silent.

"This isn't good, is it?" Rufus finally asked.

"No," David said. "And it hasn't been for a long, long time."

Rostov rolled to the side of the bed and sat up. It was 10:15. The old men would be in their rooms by now, although the dining room would still be open. Plenty of time to do what he had to do and still get out undetected.

He crept through the shed and then peered through the window. There was no moon, and except for the security lights at the edges of the grounds, the night was dark—perfect for what he had in mind. He moved to the opposite side of the shed and looked toward White Mountain. Somewhere up there, the search team had bedded down for the night. A small grin tilted one corner of his mouth as he thought of them looking for him in that wilderness. They could look for days for all he cared. They wouldn't find him. No one found the Hawk unless he wanted to be found.

He didn't think any guards had been left at the hotel, but it wouldn't take him long to find out. Fingering the knife at his belt and the gun in his pocket, he slipped out of the shed and disappeared into the darkness.

Jack squatted down beside Travis as another agent sat nearby, running a ground check on some aerial surveillance equipment. Overhead, he could hear a circling helicopter.

"What's he doing?" Jack asked, pointing to the man behind Travis.

"Checking to see if we're online with the chopper above us.

They've got heat-seeking radar on board. It'll give us a picture of anything warm-blooded that's on the move."

Jack shook his head as he stood. "You better tell them I'm leaving camp so they won't think I'm the target," he said.

Travis frowned. "You aren't going back down this mountain in the dark?"

Jack nodded. "I'm not leaving Isabella alone and I'm already later than I'd planned. She's not safe until Ross is found."

"I'll send a couple of my men with you."

"No need. I'll travel faster alone. Besides, you've got your thing to do. I've got mine."

Travis grinned. "Damn it, Dolan, that's not fair. Yours is prettier."

Jack ignored the taunt and shouldered his rifle.

"Remember what I said. Tell the eye in the sky up there to cut me some slack."

"Got your radio?" Travis asked.

Jack patted the two-way hooked to his belt.

"Yep, and if I see any boogers, I'll give a yell."

"We've already swept the lower east quadrant. We're starting on the upper side now."

Jack said. "With no moon and the trees so thick you can hardly see through them, it's not safe to be moving around up here after dark. You're not familiar with this place. One wrong step and someone's going to fall off the mountain."

"This isn't the first time we've conducted a search in the dark," Travis said.

"Fine," Jack said. "You're the expert on tracking. Just keep me posted and let me know if you need anything."

"Will do," Travis said.

Jack looked back at the camp one last time, then turned on his flashlight and headed down the trail. Once he left the perimeter of the search camp, he was immediately swallowed up by the forest. If the path had not been so well defined, it would have been easy to get lost.

The farther he moved down the mountain, the more aware he became of the sounds above him.

Unless Victor Ross had suddenly gone deaf, he had to know what was happening, and if he *was* the Hawk, as they suspected, there was no way he was hiding in a hole somewhere. He would be on the move and getting as far away from White Mountain as possible.

But what if he wasn't? Jack thought. What if he was still willing to risk his life to get what he'd come for? Suddenly anxious to talk to Isabella, he unclipped his cell phone from his belt and dialed the number for the hotel.

"Abbott House."

"Delia, this is Jack Dolan. I need to speak to Isabella."

"She's not in the office, Mr. Dolan. I think she's in the dining room having dinner with her uncles."

"Would you please check? I'll hold."

"Certainly."

He heard her lay the phone down, then heard the sound of her footsteps as she crossed the lobby floor. A minute passed, and then another. Just when he thought Delia had forgotten him, she was back.

"I'm sorry, Mr. Dolan. She'd already left the dining room. Maybe she's in the family quarters. If you'll hold, I'll transfer your call."

Again Jack waited and counted the number of rings, but Isabella didn't answer. The hair rose on the back of his neck as the tenth ring came and went. He kept telling himself that she could be anywhere...even in the shower. Just because one woman couldn't find her and she didn't answer her phone, that didn't mean she was in danger.

But even as he clipped the phone back on his belt, he was increasing his stride. After what they'd been through with Ross, he wasn't going to assume anything was all right.

He reached for the radio and keyed it on.

"Travis...this is Dolan. Over."

"Travis here. What do you need?"

"I need a favor," he said. "Have that chopper fly over the hotel and do a thorough sweep of the grounds, especially the surrounding trees. When I left earlier there was only one couple staying in the hotel. The rest of them were staff or just diners who come and go for the food, so there shouldn't be any outside activity at this time of night."

"Will do," Travis said. "Hang tight. I'll let you know if anything shows."

"Thanks," Jack said, and wished he could see well enough to jog. He didn't like what his gut was telling him, and he was too far away from Isabella to be of any immediate help.

A few minutes later he saw the chopper fly over him and head down the mountain. It stayed high, so as not to alert anyone of the search, and then began to circle. Jack glanced at his watch. It was almost nine-thirty. He hadn't meant to stay out this long.

He reached for his cell phone again and rang the

hotel. Again Delia put him through to the family quarters, and again there was no answer. He clipped the phone back on his belt with a curse. Within minutes, he was off the mountain, but with at least a mile of valley between him and Abbott House. Just being able to see it in the distance made him easier. But the relief didn't last.

"Dolan...this is Travis. Do you read me?"

Jack grabbed the two-way. "I'm here."

"The chopper picked up something moving up the east end of the hotel."

"Up the hotel? What the hell do you mean?"

"I don't know. It's just what they said. Short of turning on a spotlight, it's the best they could do. Hold on a second."

Jack could hear Travis talking to the chopper pilot on another radio.

"He asks if there's a fire escape on that side of the building?" Travis said.

Jack's heart sank. "Yes, damn it, there is. Ask him if he can still see the target."

Travis repeated Jack's question to the pilot, then relayed the answer.

"He says whoever it was is no longer outside the building or on the grounds."

"Son of a bitch," Jack muttered. "I'll lay odds it's our man."

"What do you want us to do?" Travis asked.

Jack hesitated. If he pulled them off the search

only to find it was just one of the uncles or a staff member, it could give Victor Ross the time he needed to escape. But if Ross was already off the mountain...

"Is there any place the chopper can land near the hotel?" Jack asked.

"No. Too many trees," Travis said.

Jack's gut knotted. It was left up to him.

"Give me fifteen minutes to check it out first," he said. "If you don't hear from me, get down here fast."

"Will do," Travis said. "And be careful."

Jack slipped the two-way back into the case and started to run. It was no big deal for him to run a mile in five or six minutes, but it was dark, and he didn't know the terrain. Fifteen minutes was cutting it close, but anything more could be putting everyone, including Isabella, at risk.

# 16

It was almost a quarter to ten when Isabella started up to David's room. Ever since dinner, when he'd told her to come up, anticipation had spoiled her from concentrating on anything else. Instead of using the elevator, she took the stairs, too anxious to wait for the lumbering old car to descend. As she reached the third-floor landing, she noticed that two of the bulbs had burned out in the hall and made a mental note to tell housekeeping tomorrow. Her step was light, her heart even lighter, as she hurried to the room at the end. All evening she'd been chastizing herself, blaming her distrust of her uncles on everything from grief to Jack Dolan's arrival. She should have known the uncles wouldn't keep things from her—unless, of course, it was for her own protection. Now that they realized their secrets had been destructive rather than protective, they were ready to rectify the problem.

She knocked on David's door. When he called out to her that the door was unlocked, she turned the knob and went in. To her surprise, he was standing by the fireplace, still wearing the clothes he'd had on at dinner.

She crossed the room and kissed him on the cheek. He smelled of aftershave. And something else. Bourbon? She frowned. David Schultz wasn't much of a drinker, and if he'd had to fortify himself with a shot of whiskey to have this conversation, then maybe this wasn't going to be as easy as she had hoped.

"Uncle David...I would have thought that by now you'd be in your pajamas and robe."

"Later," he said, then added a small log to the fire. "Are you warm enough, dear? The nights are getting quite cold."

She sat in her favorite armchair beside the fireplace, then leaned forward, locking her hands on her knees.

"I'm fine, Uncle David. Sit down and quit fussing."

He smiled at her then and did as she asked, and Isabella thought what an elegant gentleman David Schultz was. Tall, well-read and dignified, he had always reminded her a bit of Gregory Peck.

"Uncle David?"

David braced himself. "Yes?"

"Can I ask you something rather personal?"

It wasn't quite what he'd expected, and yet he was hesitant to agree. Still, he'd promised her that they would talk, and if this was the way it was to begin, then so be it.

"Certainly, my dear. Ask away."

"Why didn't any of you marry?"

It was the absolute last thing he had expected her to say, and because it took him unawares, he told her the truth.

"I can't speak for the others, but the only woman I ever wanted to marry was already married to your father."

Horrified that she'd brought up something that was obviously painful for him, she couldn't do anything but stutter.

"Oh...Uncle David...I'm sorry...I shouldn't have—"

He laughed. "It's all right, dear. Everyone knew it...including your mother. You see, it wasn't as if your father and I had fought for her hand or anything quite so dramatic. It's just that when I met Isabella, she was already married to Samuel. I wasn't the only one who succumbed to her charms. I think Jasper was quite taken with her, too."

Isabella smiled.

"There! That smile!" David said, pointing at her face. "It's hers all over. And it's the first and last thing about her that I choose to remember."

"Were you there when she died?" Isabella asked.

David's expression changed. Isabella imagined she could see his mind sliding back through time.

"Yes. I delivered you."

Isabella's eyes widened in disbelief.

"I don't think I knew that."

He shrugged. "It was a long time ago, and death comes to all of us. Each in our own time."

"Do you really believe that?" she asked.

He stared into the fire for what seemed to Isabella like an eternity; then he nodded.

"Yes, I believe I do."

"Then you're telling me that when Uncle Frank was murdered in Brighton Beach, it was his time to die?"

David made himself look at her face before he answered. Everything hinged on the fact that she must believe what he said.

"I believe in fate, Isabella. Therefore, I believe that it was Frank's time to die, and in the manner in which it happened."

"Do you think the man who killed him was the Russian Jack is looking for?"

The closer he stayed to the truth, the better off he would be.

"Probably. I think your Mr. Dolan is a very capable man and knows what he's doing."

"Why would that man come here after me? What could he possibly hope to gain? It's not like I'm worth anything special."

David stood abruptly, suddenly towering over her chair.

"Don't ever say that," he said. "You are worth the world to all of us, and you always have been. We've loved you as if you were our own child since the moment you took your first breath." Then his voice gentled. "Maybe even before that."

"I'm sorry," she said. "I didn't mean that to come out quite as pitifully as it sounded. What I meant to say was that anyone hoping to gain money from my ransom would be out of luck."

He laid a hand on the top of her hair, as if settling himself by a mere touch.

"And I'm sorry, too. I shouldn't have raised my voice."

She stood, then laid her head against his chest, feeling the warmth of his body and the comfort of his embrace as he pulled her into his arms.

"Tell me about the picture, Uncle David."

She felt him take a deep breath, then exhale on a great sigh. As he did, she looked up.

"What is there to tell, dear? I haven't seen it, but I'm guessing it was simply a picture of us boarding a plane. We did travel some back in our earlier days."

She frowned. "Then why would that picture in particular be of any consequence to the FBI?"

"I couldn't really say. Didn't you ask Mr. Dolan?"

"You know I did. I told you he wouldn't tell me anything."

"Then maybe there's nothing to tell."

She stared, unable to believe he was doing it again.

"You're talking in circles, Uncle David. Just

once, can't you answer a question without asking another?''

Before he could speak, the door flew open and Vasili Rostov was in the room.

"How perfect," he said, then shut the door behind him.

Isabella screamed and started to run toward the phone when Rostov pulled a gun.

"Stop now or I shoot!" he yelled.

"Don't shoot, don't shoot! For God's sake, don't shoot!" David shouted, and threw himself in front of Isabella.

They went down in a tangle of arms and legs, but Rostov grabbed Isabella's arm and yanked her up from the floor.

"You keep quiet or I swear I will kill him," he said, pointing the gun at David.

Isabella was shaking so hard she could hardly stand.

"Don't hurt him," she whispered. "I won't say a word."

"Then sit," he said, pushing her into a chair. "And you! Sit beside her where I can see you both."

David crawled to his feet and then sat on the arm of Isabella's chair. He could feel her trembling and knew she was scared to death, but all he could think was that if he hadn't asked her to come to his room, she would have been safe.

"Who are you, and what do you want?" David asked.

Rostov smiled. "Why...I'm the gardener, aren't I, Miss Abbott?"

Isabella didn't answer. She was afraid if she opened her mouth, she would scream. *Oh God...oh God...keep us safe.*

Rostov waved the gun toward David.

"You...call the other men...the ones she calls the uncles. Tell them to come here now. And if you give me away, I'll shoot her where she sits."

"Yes, yes, I will," David said. "Just leave her alone."

Rostov's eyes narrowed in pleasure as the old man went to the phone. This was more than he could have hoped for. Surely it proved his luck was turning.

"I can see she is important to you. So Waller didn't overstate the obvious. She *is* the key, after all."

Isabella saw shock come and go on her uncle's face, and then he turned away to pick up the phone.

"What do you mean?" she whispered. "Why did you say I was the key?"

Rostov smiled. "As soon as the others arrive, we will talk."

David's hands were shaking as he dialed Jasper's room. When Jasper answered, David didn't waste words.

''Get the others and come to my room. Immediately.''

He hung up before Jasper could question him.

''There,'' he said. ''I've done what you asked. You don't need Isabella. I know you can't let her go yet, but just tie her up and take us instead. No one will find her until you're far, far away.''

Rostov laughed. ''I don't want you, old man. I don't want any of you.'' Then he pointed the gun at Isabella. ''I don't even *want* her…not that she wouldn't be special, I'm sure.''

Isabella's stomach churned as her mind was screaming Jack's name.

''Then what in hell do you hope to gain from all this?'' David asked.

''Shut up! You will all know soon enough,'' Rostov snapped.

Seconds later, they heard voices in the hall, then the sound of approaching footsteps.

''They're coming,'' Isabella moaned. ''Oh Lord, they're walking into a trap.''

''Open your mouth and he's dead,'' Rostov snapped, and jammed the gun against David's cheek.

She cast a frantic look at David's face. His eyes were closed, his face white as a sheet.

The door swung inward. Jasper was in front, with the others close behind.

''David, what on earth is—''

He gasped, then froze.

"Get inside," Rostov snapped. "Do it now, or he's a dead man."

The quartet slipped inside, then plastered themselves against the wall—four old men, horror-stricken and mute.

"What's happening?" Thomas finally asked, his voice shaky with fear.

"Please let him sit down," Isabella begged. "He just got out of the hospital."

Rostov frowned, then waved the old man to the other chair opposite the fire. John took Thomas by one arm, and Rufus took the other, as they helped Thomas to a seat. Jasper's gaze was fixed on David, as if trying to read his mind, but David wouldn't look at him. He wouldn't look anywhere but at the floor.

"Now...how would you say this? Oh yes...I know," Rostov said. "Is not this cozy?"

Suddenly David looked up, his face contorted in anger.

"They're here, as you asked. Now what do you want?"

Rostov took Frank's diary from his pocket and tossed it onto the floor by their feet.

"What's that?" Jasper asked.

"Vaclav Waller's diary," Rostov said.

"Jesus, Mary and Joseph," Rufus muttered, and cast a frantic look at the others.

"Who's Vaclav Waller?" Isabella asked.

Rostov smirked. "So…she doesn't know all the little secrets, eh?"

"Shut up," David said. "Just tell us what you want and be gone."

"Money!" Rostov said. "I need money to disappear."

"I have money in the safe," Isabella said as she jumped to her feet. "You can have it all. Just don't hurt us."

Rostov slapped her aside with the butt of his gun. She staggered and fell in front of where Thomas was sitting, and as she did, it brought five old men to their feet.

Rostov took a step back and aimed the gun at her head.

"One move and she's dead," he said. "Sit down, and don't get up unless I tell you." Then he looked at Isabella. "That goes for you, too."

Her ears were ringing from the blow as she crawled to her knees. Jasper glared at Rostov and then helped her back to her chair, as if daring the Russian to shoot.

Rostov sneered. This was better than he'd hoped for. It was obvious that they would do anything to keep her safe.

"I don't want your petty cash, Isabella Abbott. I want money enough to disappear. I have decided I do not want to return to Russia."

"Why did you come in the first place?" she asked.

Rostov looked at her, a little surprised by her attitude. Most women would be cowering from his threat. She was bruised and bleeding and still had the nerve to meet his gaze.

"Because I was sent," he said.

"To kill Uncle Frank?"

He snorted lightly. "Uncle Frank chose to kill himself."

"I don't believe you," Isabella said. "He wouldn't do that."

"Ah...but he did," Rostov said. "He chose to die rather than to come with me." He shrugged. "I can't say I blame him. Russia does not look favorably upon her defectors. Besides, he was already dying. My arrival only hastened his exit."

"Dying?" she gasped.

Rostov shrugged. "Some kind of cancer, I suppose. The medicine was in his room, along with the diary. All you had to do was look."

Isabella gasped again in disbelief, looking for her uncles to deny what he'd said. But when they kept silent, she realized that what Rostov had said was no secret to them.

She looked at David. "Is this it?" she asked. "Is this the secret? Was his name Vaclav Waller, and did you all help him defect?"

David's head was bowed, and the others wouldn't look at her.

Anger welled in Isabella, pushing past her fear. Her body was shaking, her face streaked with tears.

"Why won't somebody tell me what's going on?"

"Shut up!" Rostov yelled. "All you need to know is that I want one hundred thousand dollars in small bills or you die."

Jack slipped into the dining room through the terrace doors. The room was empty of guests. Only a few of the wait staff were in the area, straightening up chairs and sweeping up for the night. They were startled by his sudden appearance, as well as the rifle on his back.

"Have you seen Isabella?" he asked.

"Not since dinner," a waitress said.

He moved through the room into the lobby. Delia was not at the desk. He slipped past the stairs toward the family quarters and knocked on her door. No one answered, and the door was locked. Quietly, he picked the lock and slipped inside. The rooms were empty and quiet. Too quiet.

Exiting quickly, he made for the stairs, taking them two at a time. When he reached the third floor landing, he plastered himself against the wall, listening for sounds of trouble, but he heard nothing.

He started down the hall, pausing at every door to listen for sounds of life inside, but everything was quiet. Then, just as he was about to call out her name, he heard someone shout.

Grabbing his handgun, he started down the hall, moving quietly but with haste. Again he heard voices, this time all talking at once. He frowned. Then he heard Isabella shout and someone telling her to shut up, and he knew he'd found Victor Ross.

His heart sank. Ross had done the unthinkable. He'd come back to the scene of the crime—something none of them had expected. He glanced at his watch. It was past time to call in. Travis would already be heading down the mountain. But from the sounds inside the room, he couldn't afford to wait for the men to arrive. The only thing he could do was go in before someone got hurt. Maybe he could stall Ross long enough for the search team to arrive, but Travis needed to know where they would be.

Reluctantly, Jack ran all the way to the end of the hall, then ducked into an alcove and keyed up the mike.

"Travis, this is Jack, come in. Over."

A short burst of static sounded, and then Jack heard Travis's voice.

"This is Travis. What did you find?"

"He's here," Jack said. "On the third floor, last room on the right. He's taken hostages. I can't tell how many, but I know Isabella is there. I heard her voice."

"We're on our way," Travis said.

"I can't wait," Jack said. "I'm going in now. Maybe I can stall him before he does something we can't fix."

"You need to wait," Travis said. "There's no telling—"

"I'm not taking the radio," Jack said. "I don't want him to know you're on the way. Just get here as fast and as silently as you can."

"I'll radio the chopper to drop some men."

"No!" Jack said abruptly. "He'll hear it. If he starts shooting, I won't be able to control the damage, and I won't risk their lives."

"Damn it, Dolan, you and I both know that the last thing a good agent does is give himself up as another hostage. You're playing into his hands if you do."

"Just shut up and hurry," Jack said, then turned off the radio and laid it on the floor.

Then he took out his handgun, slipped it in the top of his boot, pulled his pants down over it and dropped the holster on the floor. Maybe Ross would think the only weapon he was carrying was the rifle, so when he was disarmed, he would still have a chance.

He moved toward the room again, this time taking no measures to disguise his footsteps. He didn't want Ross to know he'd already been made.

Stunned by Ross's demand, Isabella shook her head in disbelief.

"Why on earth do you think we could come up with an amount of money like that? Look around you. This is an old hotel. The only guests we have are the ones who come to the clinic. The restaurant barely pays for itself. We are not wealthy people. Your demands are ridiculous.''

Rostov glared at her. "You lie. You live like a queen in this place. Your father and these old men are doctors…. American doctors have money."

"Only two are doctors," Isabella argued. "And they've been retired for years."

Rostov laughed. "So much you still don't know," he said, then pointed the gun at David's face. "Why don't you tell her? Why keep the little girl in the dark any longer?"

She looked at the men, waiting for them to deny what Ross was saying. They only gave her long looks of pity.

Suddenly she burst out in anger. "I can't stand this! No, I *won't* stand this! Not any longer! You're talking in riddles. All of you." Then she got to her feet and pointed at Ross. "There is no money, so shoot us now and leave us to die in peace."

Before Rostov could answer, there was a knock at the door.

"Isabella? Honey? Are you in there?"

Hope sprang and then sank within the same seconds. Jack! And Rostov would kill him.

"Jack, run! Ross is holding us hostage! You—"

Rostov hit her with his fist. She went down in a heap just as Jack came through the door, his rifle aimed at Victor Ross. He took one look at the woman on the floor and the man standing above her.

His voice was low, completely devoid of emotion, but the look in his eyes gave away his rage.

"You son of a bitch."

Rostov grinned. "So, we meet again," he said. "Something told me you are not the writer you claimed to be. Now put down your gun before I kill your woman."

Jack hesitated.

"Do it!" Rostov snapped. "I'm losing my patience with all of you."

Jack laid the rifle against the wall.

"Let me tend to her," he asked, pointing to Isabella.

"You don't touch her," Rostov said. "Not until I say that you can. Now get over there with the rest of them. I have much to do before this night is over."

Jack cursed himself for waiting too long to come in. If he hadn't, Isabella wouldn't be lying unconscious and bleeding on the floor.

"Now, where were we?" Rostov asked, as Jack stopped beside the fireplace, only inches from Isabella's head. "Ah yes, the money. You were going to get me the money."

"Why should we?" David asked. "You're going to kill us anyway."

Rostov's eyes narrowed thoughtfully. The man had a point. Then he glanced at the diary still lying on the floor. Maybe there was still something to be gained. He pointed his gun at the diary.

''I think you will pay me a lot to make sure no one ever reads this book.''

Jack's gaze immediately slid to the old, leather-bound volume on the floor near Isabella's feet.

David shook his head. ''If we're dead, what does it matter?''

Rostov sneered. ''It matters to her, doesn't it?'' he asked.

The old men were caught, and they knew it. They looked at each other, then, one by one, silently nodded.

''So...do we have a deal?'' Rostov asked.

''You have a deal,'' David said. ''But on one condition.''

''And that is?''

''You let these two live,'' David said, pointing to Jack and Isabella. ''You let them live, or kill us all now and leave with nothing.''

''Of course,'' Rostov said. ''I promise.''

They all knew what his promises were worth, but nothing more was said.

Rostov's gaze swept the room, trying to guess where a wall safe might be. Behind that painting? Beside the fireplace?

''Now, the money, please.''

Isabella groaned and then slowly opened her eyes. Her head ached, and it hurt to swallow. When she started to speak, a pain shot up her jaw and into her temple. She grabbed her face and moaned.

Jack dropped to his knees and cradled her in his arms.

"I'm here, sweetheart. Just lie still."

"I told you not to touch her!" Rostov shouted.

David stepped between them.

"You promised," he said.

Rostov cursed. "Get the money now! My patience leaves me."

"It's not here," David said. "But it's close by."

Rostov aimed the gun at Isabella's head.

"You lie!" he shouted. "I will wait no longer."

"He's not lying," Jasper suddenly said.

"No, it's true," Thomas chimed in.

"We can get to it from my apartment," David said. "But you have to come with me."

Rostov frowned. "What are you trying to pull? There is nothing beyond this room but a fire escape."

David smiled. "Oh, but you're wrong," he said softly. "Do you think we conducted our experiments in public laboratories?"

Jack felt Isabella flinch, but he squeezed her arm, hoping she got the message to stay quiet. He suspected they were about to learn why Frank Walton had been killed.

"Where?" Rostov asked, looking around the room. "Where do we go?"

"Down," David said. "We go down. But we leave them behind or there will be no money."

"No deal," Rostov said. "I see the money first or they die."

David relented, but only because he had no choice. He knew Ross was serious. He'd been the one to identify Frank's body in the Brighton Beach morgue.

"Get up," Rostov ordered, and waved the gun at Jack. "Get her up, too. We all go, and if you're lucky, we all come back."

Jack stood, then helped Isabella to her feet. She staggered, and he put his arm around her.

"Lean on me," he said softly.

Isabella went limp against his chest, steadying herself until she could walk.

"I am leaning on you, Jack. I think I have been since the day you arrived."

"Move," Rostov ordered.

David nodded to the other men, who followed him toward the bedroom.

"Where are you going?" Rostov shouted.

"You want the money?" David said. "You follow me."

# 17

David opened the door to his closet and walked inside. The other uncles followed behind him.

"What the hell?" Rostov muttered.

Jack was wondering the same thing but refrained from saying so.

Isabella was still disoriented enough not to realize that they'd walked into a closet until she saw David shove aside a stack of clothes and press down on a shelf. When the wall in front of them suddenly slid out of sight, she gasped.

An elevator car was open and waiting.

"Get in," David said.

"After you," Rostov snarled, realizing, as they all got in, that he would be in very close contact with all of them and could easily be overpowered. To insure his safety, he grabbed Isabella out of Jack Dolan's arms and put his gun in her ear. "She's with me," he said. "If anyone makes a wrong move, her brains are going to be on your face."

Isabella moaned and swayed where she stood.

"Don't hurt her," Jack said. "We're doing this your way, I swear. Right, men?"

The uncles nodded anxiously.

Satisfied that he still had the upper hand, Rostov boarded the elevator, and down they went.

Jack marveled silently at the lengths to which these old men had gone to keep their secrets. But even he was surprised when the car stopped and the door opened. Instead of being in some kind of laboratory, they had exited into a lighted tunnel.

"What's this?" Rostov asked. "I thought we were going to your laboratory?"

"We are," David said, pointing to the array of electric carts parked against the wall. "Pick a ride. I'll lead the way."

The old men piled into the carts, leaving Rostov with no options but to follow.

He shoved Isabella toward the last cart.

"You drive," he told Jack. "We're behind you. And remember..."

"We got the message," Jack snapped. "Just take the goddamned gun out of her ear before you trip and fall. Because I warn you, anything happens to her and you'll have no need for money or anything else."

Rostov pushed Isabella into the back seat and then slid in beside her as Jack took off down the tunnel, following the other three carts, which were already some distance ahead.

David's mind was set on destruction. It was the only thing left that they could do. But getting Isabella and Jack out without harm was going to take finesse.

"Jasper...you know what we have to do," David said.

"Yes."

"Rufus...are you in agreement?"

Rufus sighed and rubbed his ample paunch.

"Yes, and had I known tonight was the end, I would have had that second helping of peach cobbler."

They laughed because, for a moment, it made everything seem normal and right. But then they heard Ross shout out behind them to shut up and slow down, and their moment of humor passed.

All too soon the mile had been traversed, and they were at the laboratory doors.

Jack got out, then turned toward Isabella, but Rostov wasn't ready to give up his hostage. Not when they'd come so far and so deep.

"Where are we?" he asked.

"Beneath White Mountain," David said.

"I'll be damned," Jack muttered. "No wonder you were never found."

"Oh, we didn't hide ourselves down here," David said. "We hid in plain sight by going about our business like anyone else. We just did our experiments down here."

Rostov was getting nervous. He had never liked tight places, and knowing there was an entire mountain sitting on top of them made his flesh crawl.

"Stop talking and get inside," he ordered.

David keyed in the code, and the door swung open.

As the lights in the ceiling of the massive room began to come on, they entered.

Isabella stared in disbelief, first at the uncles, who moved among the lab tables and computers with such familiarity, then at the room itself. It was all stainless steel and glass, spotless and gleaming, with lights so bright overhead that it seemed to be lit by pure sunlight.

"The money!" Rostov yelled. "Where is the money?"

"Jasper will get it," David said.

Jasper moved toward what appeared to be a large metal floor safe near the door. Instinctively, Ross's attention was diverted, and he moved with him, Isabella still under his gun. When Jack started to follow, David grabbed him by the arm instead.

"Wait," he whispered. "I don't have much time, and there are things you need to know."

"Some of it I already do," Jack said. "You were all working on similar projects when your respective governments pulled the plugs, right?"

David smiled. "I knew you were smart." Then his smiled shifted. "You love our Isabella, don't you?"

"Yes."

"In spite of us?"

"In spite of everything," Jack said. "Just help me get her out of this alive."

"It will be done," David said. "But listen to me now, because her life could still be in danger, and only you will know."

They glanced toward the wall, where Jasper was on his knees.

"Our research was stopped, yes," David said. "But we believed in what we were doing. It was John Rhodes...I should say Samuel Abbott, who first suggested that we fake our deaths. Some of us were hesitant, but given the prospects of what awaited us, we quickly agreed. Yes, we took other identities, but we hurt no one. We have not profited in any monetary way from the names we assumed. We have not drawn any money from your government, nor taken any outside donations for our clinic. We have done good for the women who wanted babies. We have given back to the world what was taken from us."

"What was the big secret?" Jack asked. "There are hundreds of fertility clinics. Why lie about who you were? Except for Walton, uh...Waller, any of you could have just quit your government work. Why not take up private practice under your own identities?"

David glanced at the others. Jasper was almost into the safe. He had to hurry.

"Because it wasn't just about infertility."

Jack frowned. "So what was it about? You were

researching DNA...the human genome...gene therapy. What are you saying?''

"We applied our research to a select few of the women at the clinic without their knowledge.''

"Jesus Christ!" Jack muttered. "Do you know what—''

David's shoulders slumped. "Oh, we know all too well,'' he said softly.

"How many?" Jack snapped.

David thought about the Silvia woman and decided not to reveal their most recent project.

"Over the past thirty odd years, twenty in all.''

"What did you do to them, old man? And don't tell me you created a bunch of monsters, because I was starting to like you.''

"They were perfect babies,'' David said. "Beautiful, whole, healthy babies.''

"Then why the long face?" Jack asked. "Why not tell the world that—''

"They're all dead now...except for one.''

All the air went out of Jack in one swoop.

"How?''

"Mostly self-destructs. I think one died of a heart attack, and another from anorexia and a couple from accidents.''

"By self-destruct, are you implying they killed themselves?''

"Yes, sad to say, that is true.''

"Good God! Why? How?''

"It isn't the how of it that mattered,'' David said.

"It was the why. Reports were that they claimed to hear voices. Most of them just went mad."

Jack grabbed David's arm. "What the hell did you do to those babies?"

"Nothing but give them life again."

Jack heard, but it took a moment for the significance of what David had said to sink in. Then it hit him.

"Say that again."

"I said…we did nothing but give them a second chance at life."

Jack stared at the state-of-the-art equipment, then at the faces of the five old men.

"I don't want to say what I'm thinking," he muttered.

"Then don't," David said. "I'll say it for you. We cloned twenty people. And not just any people, but people who had a lot to offer the world. Mathematicians, doctors, scientists, politicians, leaders of our country…even a couple of rather famous entertainers that the world truly loved." Then he took Jack's arm, pleading with him. "Don't you understand? They had given the world so much the first time around, it only stood to reason that they could do it again."

"But it didn't work. Why not?" Jack asked.

David glanced nervously at Jasper, who was in the act of turning the last tumbler on the lock.

He squinted his eyes as he gazed into space.

"Do you believe in God?"

"Yes, but what does that have to do with—"

David turned, fixing him with a hard, studied stare.

"Samuel had a theory. We took everything into account when we created the clones...except for the fact that they would not have the same soul. Don't you see? When someone dies...and if you believe in God...then you believe the soul, or the spirit, or whatever you call it...ascends into heaven or descends into hell, as the case may be. Right?"

"Right," Jack said.

"So almost every time we began a new project, we were cloning DNA from someone who had already passed on. In effect, their spirit was already gone. The babies were perfect replicas—except for the one thing that had made them great."

Jack's breath slid out of his lungs in a whoosh, as if he'd been gut punched. Trying to explain this to the director—if, of course, he lived to tell the tale—would be impossible. Again something clicked.

"You said 'almost.' That isn't the same as always."

David nodded. "I said you were a smart man. Yes, you're right. We had twenty projects, and nineteen failures, the last of which we just learned of today."

Jack frowned. "Today? Who...?" Then it hit him. "John Running Horse?" When David didn't deny it, Jack fired another question. "Who the hell did you clone?"

"We had no idea that old memories would recur in some of the implants," David said. "They didn't in all of them, but John was an exception. It was good that people outside the reservation rarely saw his face. It would have started a riot, I think."

Jack frowned, his mind skimming back over everything he'd heard John Running Horse say. Memphis. Guitar. Singing. Suddenly his mouth dropped.

"God almighty, you didn't!"

David shrugged.

"How did you get his DNA?"

David shrugged. "Samuel always handled that part. He paid someone at the funeral home, I think. It was usually fairly simple."

Jack shoved a hand through his hair in disbelief.

"What in hell were you people thinking? That he would just up and reappear, the same old king of rock and roll? Didn't you take his family's feelings into consideration?"

"It was all about science."

Jack felt himself coming unglued. The ramifications of what they'd been doing were like something out of a horror film.

"Didn't you see him? Couldn't you tell how tormented he was? My God, man! I only saw him once, but I could feel his pain."

David's chin trembled. It wasn't anything he hadn't thought before. If only he'd had the guts to call a halt years ago, before they'd destroyed so many lives.

"One survived perfectly," he mumbled, saying it more to assuage his own guilt than to explain himself to Jack.

"One success out of twenty is damned poor odds," Jack said. "Do you know where the baby is?"

"Oh yes," David said. "I know. I helped raise her."

Suddenly the skin crawled on Jack's neck as he followed the path of David's gaze to Isabella.

"Sweet Jesus...not—"

"Samuel couldn't father children. It was his wife's greatest sorrow and his cross to bear. She wanted to be the first test subject, but Samuel wouldn't let her. Then she begged, and she cried, and he relented."

David's shoulders slumped, and for the first time since Jack had met him, David Schultz looked every one of his seventy-eight years.

"The pregnancy was perfect, and then she went into labor. She hemorrhaged and bled to death before we could stop it. We lifted the baby out of her belly as she took her last breath."

"I don't understand," Jack said. "If the others disintegrated mentally, then why hasn't Isabella shown the same signs? What's so different about her?"

"Samuel believed that Isabella wanted the child

so much that she somehow refused her place in heaven and sent her soul to the baby instead.''

The look on Jack's face was incredulous. David sighed.

''I know. I know. It's a lot to grasp, and frankly, as scientists, we rejected it soundly for years. However, there is no other explanation that we could fathom and have it make sense.'' He gave Jack a nervous glance. ''Does this change your feelings for her?''

''No,'' Jack muttered. ''Hell no.''

''Then know this, too,'' David said. ''She must never know what we've been doing, or she will guess the rest about herself.''

Jack nodded, knowing that he would lie to his death to protect her from the hell of what he'd learned.

''And there's something else you must remember. She *is* her mother, and her mother died from an aneurysm in the uterus. If she bears children, the same weakness will be hers, as well.''

Jack looked at her in horror, wondering how he was going to live with this knowledge and not give himself away.

''Are you saying she should never have children?''

''No. Only that you must somehow get the doctor to examine her closely enough to discover it on his own. It can be corrected, and had we known earlier, we could have saved Isabella's life.''

"But if she had lived, what would have happened to the child?" Jack asked.

David sighed. "Ah yes...ever the conundrum we have asked ourselves. At any rate, I have given you a great secret, and I'm trusting you with our beloved Isabella." Then he glanced at Jasper, who was in the act of opening the safe door. "Whatever happens in the next few minutes, you have to promise me that you will get Isabella out alive."

Startled, Jack's gaze moved toward the wall where the others were standing.

"What have you done?" he asked.

"You will see."

Suddenly Jasper slammed the door to the safe shut and turned a knob.

"It's done!" he shouted, and dived straight into Rostov's gun. The gun went off, and the bullet tore through Jasper's heart, but it didn't matter. Rufus and Thomas had already ripped Isabella from Rostov's grasp and shoved her away.

"Take her and run," David said.

Jack pulled the gun from his boot and started toward the melee, only to be yanked back.

"Get Isabella and run, I say!" David shouted. "You don't have much time."

Isabella bolted as Rostov spun, his gun aimed at her back.

Jack fired instinctively as he ran, then fired again, watching as both bullets hit Rostov square in the chest, while Isabella ran screaming into his arms.

"It's over," he said, holding her close against his chest. "It's finally over."

David shoved them toward the door. Thinking the old men were following, Jack and Isabella were outside the lab before they realized the others were still inside.

"We have started the countdown to demolition. The bomb will go off in fifteen minutes, and it takes eight to get from here to the elevator," David said. "Remember your promise."

Then he slammed the door before Jack could react.

Isabella screamed in disbelief and started pounding on the door, but to no avail. It was ten inches of solid steel, and the sound of her hands against the metal could not even be heard inside the lab.

"No! Uncle David! No! Please don't do this!" she begged, then frantically turned to Jack. "Make them open the door," she screamed. "Don't let them do this to me!"

Jack picked her up in his arms and carried her to the nearest cart, dropped her on the seat, then vaulted the hood. When she tried to climb out, he grabbed her by the arm.

"They aren't doing this *to* you, Isabella. They're doing it *for* you. Now stay where you are or their deaths will be in vain."

"Oh my God," she moaned, and covered her face with her hands as Jack turned the cart around and headed back up the tunnel.

His heart was pounding as he pressed the accelerator all the way to the floor, but it didn't go any faster on the return than it had on arrival. He kept glancing at his watch with every passing second, imagining a blast at their backs that would destroy them all.

Isabella was silent beside him, her head bowed, her hands covering her face. Every so often Jack saw her shoulders shake as she swallowed a sob. He feared for her sanity even more than her safety. She'd gone through hell and still didn't know the half of it. All he could do was pray to get them out alive and deal with her emotions later.

By his best guess, they were about halfway there when the car suddenly stopped. One minute it was moving, and the next it had rolled to a halt.

"Shit," he muttered, and tried to restart it. He heard nothing but a click.

"What's wrong?" Isabella asked.

"Batteries are dead," he said, and grabbed her by the hand. "Can you run?"

"I think so," she said, and then glanced back behind them as Jack pulled her out.

He grabbed her by the shoulders, making her look him in the eye.

"You can't think so. You have to do it."

She moaned with fright.

"Do you love me?" he yelled.

Her eyes welled. "Yes."

"Well that's damned good, because I love you

more than life, and if you don't run, we're both going to die."

He pulled as he ran, almost yanking her off her feet, and then the reality of what he'd just said sank in. He loved her! Dear God, he loved her! And there was a time bomb ticking at their heels.

Ignoring the pain in her head and the fear in her heart, she lengthened her stride to match his and ran with everything she had.

One minute passed, and then another. No matter how hard or how far they ran, all she could see was more lights and more tunnel.

"Jack?"

He heard the fear in her voice, but there was no time to reassure her.

"Don't talk," he said, as her shoes pounded the floor. "Run."

Once she stumbled and fell flat, momentarily knocking the breath from her body. Jack jerked her up and slid his arm around her waist, all but dragging her until she could maneuver on her own.

One precious minute passed, and then another and another, until Isabella's muscles were burning and her lungs tortured and heaving from lack of air. She had no sense of anything but the pain.

Suddenly they turned a corner and saw the end in sight.

"We're almost there," Jack yelled. "Just a few more yards."

Isabella choked back a sob as her legs gave way.

Jack picked her up again and slid an arm beneath her shoulders, carrying her the rest of the way.

Within seconds they had reached the elevator car. Jack shoved her inside, then closed the door and punched the button. Immediately, the car began to rise. He glanced at his watch. Thirteen minutes had passed. They were almost home.

The car shuddered, then stopped. But the door didn't open.

"What?" Isabella cried. "What's wrong?"

"I don't know," Jack said, as he frantically punched the emergency button.

As suddenly as it had stopped, the car began to move, only it wasn't going up, it was going back down.

"No!" Isabella screamed. "What's happening?"

Jack drew his gun, expecting the worst.

Seconds later the car stopped and the door opened. There was no one in sight.

Jack punched the up button again. Once again the door closed and the car started up.

Isabella grabbed Jack by the shoulders. Her cheekbone was bloody and swollen, her face streaked with dust. Her clothes were bloodstained and filthy, and Jack thought she'd never been more beautiful.

"I love you madly, Jack Dolan. Make this damn thing work."

He wanted to cry at the waste of it all and made himself laugh instead.

"Tinkerbell, I've done everything I know how to do. The rest is up to God." Then he kissed her hard and fast.

Just as suddenly as it had stopped before, they were at the top. The door slid open, and they found themselves staring at the inside of David's closet.

Jack grabbed her by the hand and out they went. As he passed the shelf, he pressed down hard. The wall of the closet slid back into place.

Isabella shook her head in disbelief.

"I can't believe I lived in this house all this time and never knew this was here."

But Jack wasn't convinced that they'd gotten far enough away. Something told him that the bomb the old men had set off wasn't going to just cave in a lab. They must have had the failsafe in place from the start. They'd been willing to die for what they'd believed in once and were not the type to leave anything to chance.

"We've got to get out of here," he said.

"But I thought—"

"Are there any guests in the hotel?"

"My God! Are you saying that this might—"

"I don't know what to expect," Jack said. "But I promised your Uncle David I would make sure you lived, and I intend to keep my word."

"I don't think so," she said. "We'll have to check the register."

Seconds later they were out of the room and running down the stairs, then across the lobby to the registration desk.

"Everyone's gone," she said. "Including the Silvias. They checked out at six."

Jack grabbed her again, this time pulling her through the dining room to the terrace beyond.

"Look!" Jack said, pointing in the distance at the row of bobbing lights moving their way. "It's the search team. They're off the mountain, and none too soon."

Before Isabella could answer, the earth beneath her feet began to shake.

"Jack! What—"

Then they heard it coming, ripping through rock and metal, tearing through the earth.

"No," Isabella moaned. "Oh no."

"I'm sorry, sweetheart. As sorry as I can be."

She lifted her face to the mountain, as if by watching she could somehow pay homage to five passing souls.

And then Isabella suddenly gasped and pointed.

"Jack! Look!"

He turned just as the top of the mountain split apart at the seams. Fire blew up and out, spitting rock and smoke into the air and spilling it out onto the snow.

"That wasn't a bomb," he muttered. "It was a holocaust."

"Are we all right?" she asked, thinking of radioactive fallout.

Jack frowned for a moment, considering what she'd asked, and then finally nodded.

"If I were a betting man, I would say yes. Despite everything, they cared too much about life to set off anything that would harm it."

Her eyes were welling, her mind shuttered against everything but the flames on White Mountain.

"We'll never know the whole truth, will we, Jack?"

He looked down, marking the reflection of the fire in her eyes and the silhouette of her face against the night. He inhaled slowly, thinking as he touched her that now he knew what it meant to be willing to die for love.

"No, baby, I guess we won't. Does it matter to you?"

She sighed and leaned against him.

"As long as I have you, nothing matters anymore."

# ———Epilogue———

Isabella laid the keys on the desk and looked back one last time across the lobby. Everything was polished and ready for the new owners of Abbott House.

Jack watched without speaking as she walked to the middle of the lobby and then looked up at the painting on the wall. She looked so lost, he couldn't bear for her to be there alone. He walked up behind her and then took her by the hand.

"We can still take it if you want to."

She looked at it for a moment, then shook her head.

"No. It belongs here, I think."

"The new owners agree," Jack said. "They seemed quite taken with it."

Isabella looked at him then and smiled.

"Maybe they'll see ghosts, too."

Jack put his hand against her face, loving the feel of her skin against his palm.

"No, I don't think her spirit wanders restlessly. I think she's all right."

"Yes, of course. Now she's with Daddy again."

Jack searched the features of her face, looking for someone who felt out of place. But all he could see was the peace in her eyes and the joy on her face.

"Yes, I'm sure she's with the man she loves."

She turned to him and smiled.

"Just like me."

"Yes, sweetheart, just like you."

*Queens, New York—Eleven Months Later*

Maria Silvia stood at the altar, wearing a soft gray dress and a Madonna-like smile as Leonardo held their son in his arms. The priest was talking to the godparents, admonishing them about their duties, but she already knew all that by heart. Her focus was on the baby...on the perfect, angelic expression on his face.

*You heard my prayer, Oh Lord...and now I hear You.*

"And what is the name to be given this child?" the priest asked.

Leonardo's heart was in his throat as he looked down at his son.

"David Bartholomew Silvia," he said. "For the doctor who helped us have him, and for my grandfather who never knew the joy of living in a country that was free."

Maria slipped her hand beneath Leonardo's arm as the priest dipped his hand in holy water and then made the sign of the cross on David's forehead.

"I christen thee David Bartholomew Silvia, in the name of the Father, and of the Son, and of the Holy Ghost."

Maria's pulse leaped, drowning out the sounds of everything except the small squeak her son made as the water touched his face.

"Shh," she whispered, and kissed the place where the holy water had been.

The baby smiled at the sound of his mother's voice and quickly settled.

All too soon the ceremony was over and the guests were moving toward the exit to attend the celebration of food and wine Maria had prepared at their home.

Leonardo suddenly stopped, then handed Maria the baby.

"I forgot to give Father Joseph his money," he said, and headed back to the altar before the priest left.

Maria cradled the baby as she waited. A friend came up and they began to talk.

The baby's gaze was focused on the sound of his mother's voice when, outside, a cloud that had been covering the sun began to pass. As it did, bright light spilled through the stained glass windows—rolling through the colors and painting them on the columns and the walls and even in Maria's hair.

When it happened, the baby's focus shifted from his mother's mouth to the window. He looked and blinked, then stilled. His pupils dilated; his tiny mouth went slack. The light grew, firing the colors until they appeared to be burning. And it was as if he was listening to something that only he could hear.

Suddenly the woman beside Maria cried. "Look! Look at little David. See how he stares at God's windows?"

Maria looked down at her son and the rapt expression on his face.

"It is as it should be," she said softly.

"What do you mean?" the woman said.

"See his face? He sees the angels."

"What angels?" her friend asked.

"The ones who will watch over him as he becomes a man of God."

"What?"

"I promised, you see," Maria said.

"Promised what?"

"The baby. God gave me a child to raise, and when it's time, I will give the man to God."

The woman laughed, a little shocked by what Maria had said.

"Well, sure, every mother would be proud to have a priest in the family, but what if David has other plans?"

Maria looked at her son, so tiny and helpless, then at the rapt expression in his eyes.

"Don't you see?" she said softly. "He already knows."

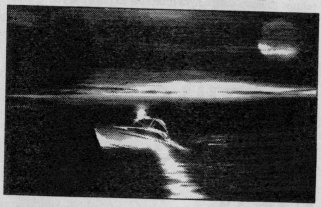

# BARBARA

NEW YORK TIMES BESTSELLING AUTHOR

# DELINSKY

Diandra Casey and Gregory York, childhood rivals and long-term adversaries, are vying for the same powerful position at the posh Casey and York department store. Intensely competitive, they are shocked to find themselves confined—together!—for one week in an elegant Boston town house. Away from the pressures of corporate life and alone with each other, they discover their feelings are suddenly taking unexpected twists and turns. Does the old house hold a surprising fate that they cannot resist? Dare they surrender to the pull of its mystery and the lure of a legend that binds their two families together, a legend too powerful and magnificent to understand…or deny?

## Fulfillment

"Barbara Delinsky knows
the human heart and its
immense capacity to
love and to believe."
—*Washington (PA)
Observer-Reporter*

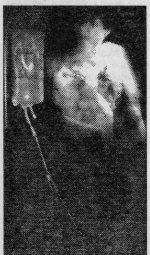

# DINAH McCALL

| | | | |
|---|---|---|---|
| 66808 | STORM WARNING | ___ $6.50 U.S. | ___ $7.99 CAN. |
| 66584 | THE RETURN | ___ $6.50 U.S. | ___ $7.99 CAN. |

*(limited quantities available)*

| | |
|---|---|
| TOTAL AMOUNT | $_____ |
| POSTAGE & HANDLING | $_____ |
| ($1.00 for one book; 50¢ for each additional) | |
| APPLICABLE TAXES* | $_____ |
| <u>TOTAL PAYABLE</u> | $_____ |

(check or money order—please do not send cash)

To order, complete this form and send it, along with a check or money order for the total above, payable to MIRA® Books, to: **In the U.S.:** 3010 Walden Avenue, P.O. Box 9077, Buffalo, NY 14269-9077; **In Canada:** P.O. Box 636, Fort Erie, Ontario, L2A 5X3.

Name:_____
Address:_____ City:_____
State/Prov.:_____ Zip/Postal Code:_____
Account Number (if applicable):_____
075 CSAS

*New York residents remit applicable sales taxes.
 Canadian residents remit applicable
 GST and provincial taxes.

**MIRA®**